THE FAVORED WIFE

AMY PENNZA

A NOTE ABOUT THE FAVORED WIFE

The Favored Wife is not my usual genre. Typically, I write paranormal romance. There is a reason for that. While I didn't grow up in precisely the same religion as Elizabeth does in the story, I was raised in a fundamentalist sect. The religious trauma stays with you—forever, I think. Growing up, books were an escape. Books about magic were forbidden. But I read them anyway. They saw me through dark times and moments of fear. From a young age, I knew I wanted to write books like the ones I read in secret. Today, I write about magic and love and broken things. And I wrote this story about Elizabeth, who is also broken but determined to heal. If you've ever felt broken, whether from religious trauma or something else, know that you are not alone.

"There is a crack in everything, that's how the light gets in." — Leonard Cohen

1

I stood in my closet doorway, gnawing my bottom lip. There they were: three new uniforms covered in plastic. I'd pushed my work dresses and church clothes far to the sides, so the uniforms had their own special place in the middle of the rack. They weren't anything special—just standard scrub pants and three scrub tops printed with various designs. To me, though, it was what they represented that made them worthy of center stage in my closet.

A little zing of nervous excitement shot through my stomach. Was I really going to do this? I cupped my hand over my mouth and blew out a huff of air. My lips curved against my palm. *Yes, I am definitely doing this.*

"Elizabeth?" Dinah's voice floated up the stairs leading to my loft apartment. "What are you doing?" Her tone was impatient—which it usually was when I was involved.

I walked out of my bedroom and leaned over the stair railing so she'd hear me. "Coming, Dinah!"

Quick footsteps, then she appeared under me, her round face shining with perspiration. "You're not even dressed? We're meeting in five minutes." She looked me up and down, shook her head, and then walked away. A muttered complaint drifted up, but there was too much noise downstairs to make out the words. Which was probably for the best. My husband's first wife had never been shy about her feelings toward me.

On any other day, I would have slunk back to my room, my stomach in knots over the prospect of facing Dinah across the big family table for our Monday morning meeting.

But not today.

I slapped a playful drumbeat on the railing, then rushed back to the bedroom. In a way, it was good I only had five minutes. It kept me from agonizing over which uniform to wear. I shrugged out of my bathrobe and let it drop to the floor as I walked to the bathroom. I'd braided my hair while it was still damp from my shower, so it only took me a few minutes to brush my teeth and slick some tinted lip balm on my lips.

I saved the scrubs for last. I'd worn a uniform during the clinical part of my training, but this felt different. The top was blousy enough to feel similar to my usual dresses, but the pants hugged my legs. I twisted around in front of the big mirror above my dresser, straining to see if they were too tight around my butt. Were pants supposed to feel like this? I turned in a full circle until I faced the mirror again. A few blond wisps of hair had escaped my french braid. I combed them back with my fingers.

The clock on my dresser caught my eye in the mirror, and I gasped. I might not have to spend the day under Dinah's thumb, but it was never a good idea to tick her off by showing up late to her meetings.

After one final glance in the mirror, I grabbed my shoes and purse and ran down the stairs to the main house.

Light, feminine chatter reached me as I hurried down the long hall leading to the kitchen. I passed the island, where stacks of dirty breakfast plates waited to be loaded into the dishwasher, and entered the dining room. My fellow sister-wives were already gathered around the big oak table.

The talking stopped and all eyes turned to me as I slid into a chair. "Sorry, Dinah," I said, my voice breathless. "First day jitters. I couldn't decide what to wear."

Dinah's dark brown gaze flicked over my scrub top. "Kittens?"

"The health center sees a lot of kids."

She pursed her lips.

Leah half stood and reached across the table, giving my hand a quick pat. "It's cute, Elizabeth." She smiled. "You've worked so hard for this. You really deserve it. I'm happy for you."

I beamed at her. "Thanks, Leah."

To her left, Patty offered me a more lukewarm smile. "It's good you're doing something to bring some cash into the family."

My smile faltered, and I looked down. *Never let them land a blow.* It was something my mother had said. The advice hadn't made much sense until I married Thomas . . . and three other women.

Dinah cleared her throat and snapped open the three-ring binder on the table in front of her. "Right. Ladies, we have a busy week ahead of us."

I listened with one ear as she doled out chores and responsibilities. My gaze drifted to the sliders leading to a large patio off the kitchen. It was already getting too hot to eat meals around the big table. Soon, we'd have to move everything outside, where the breeze made for more comfortable eating. With nineteen people in the family, the kitchen quickly got overheated.

"Did you hear me, Elizabeth?"

I looked at Dinah. "What? I mean, I beg your pardon?"

She tapped the table with her pen. "I asked what your temperature was this morning."

"Ahh . . ." I looked around the table. Patty watched me, arms folded, an irritated look on her face.

Leah offered me an encouraging smile.

"Ninety-eight," I said, and Dinah started writing.

"No, no, wait. Ninety-eight point two"—her pen moved again—"I think."

She looked up, a frown pulling her thick, dark eyebrows together. "Which is it?"

I tucked a stray strand of hair behind my ear. "Ninety-eight point two."

"You're positive?"

"Positive."

She studied the chart in front of her, then flipped a few pages back in her binder. Finally, she said, "Well, you're almost definitely ovulating. I'll mark you down for tonight."

I glanced at Patty. "Oh. No, Dinah. It's Patty's night."

Dinah shook her head, making her brown braid slide over her shoulder. "It doesn't matter. Your cycles are like clockwork, Elizabeth. You'll take tonight."

I tried to catch Patty's eye, but she kept her gaze on Dinah.

"Well, I think that about does it," Dinah said. She leaned back in her chair. "Any questions— Oh, hello, Father!" In an instant, her tone transformed from dour drill sergeant to what I liked to call her "lady of the manor" voice.

As one, we turned toward the square entryway connecting the kitchen and dining room. I fought the urge to stand as Thomas swept in. It was a bit like having the president drop by a PTA meeting. Dressed in his work clothes, with his white construction supervisor hat tucked under his arm, he exuded confidence and power. At fifty-two, he was still muscular and fit, his dark brown hair touched with gray at the temples, his strong jaw still square and firm.

He must have come from Patty and Leah's house, because he wore his shoes. Dinah hated shoes in the house, but she couldn't dictate what Patty and Leah did in theirs. She certainly couldn't tell Thomas what to do. She glanced at his feet and pressed her lips together.

I bit the inside of my cheek so I wouldn't smile.

"How are my beautiful ladies?" he asked, stopping by each chair to give us a chaste peck on the cheek. The smell of his aftershave wafted around me as he leaned down to kiss me, then stood beside my chair. "I don't know if I like these meetings you girls have," he teased. "It makes me think you're plotting my demise."

Dinah rewarded him with a big smile, revealing a charming dimple in her left cheek. It was a shame she didn't smile more often. It was a reminder there was a pretty woman under her usual, forbidding expression.

"Father, you know our little meetings are harmless," she said. "And they're for your own good." She looked around the table, her brown eyes twinkling. "My sisters and I are just trying to take care of you, aren't we, ladies?"

We all obliged her by making affirmative sounds. Patty even cracked a small smile.

"I've come to request a special dinner for tonight. I want the whole family to eat together." He placed a hand on my shoulder. "Elizabeth here is embarking on a new adventure. Her first day at a real job." He shifted his hand so his palm covered the back of my neck. His thumb feathered the tiny hairs at my nape. "We're all very proud of you, Elizabeth."

Dinah's beaming smile faded a little, but she covered it by saying, "Of course, Father." Which was the only thing she could say. Thomas might have phrased it as a request, but we all knew it was an order.

"Excellent." He passed his hand down the back of my head

and murmured, "Remember, Elizabeth, we are in the world, not of the world."

I bowed my head under the subtle pressure of his hand. "Yes, Father."

"Good girl." He gave my braid a playful tug before heading for the door leading to the patio. "Best of luck today, Elizabeth," he said over his shoulder. "Make us proud."

A tense silence fell over the table while we listened to his car door slam and the engine turn over. When the crunch of tires on gravel drifted through the sliders, Dinah looked at me. The accommodating, flirtatious expression she'd worn for Thomas vanished, replaced by the face she usually wore when he wasn't around.

"Well, this means we'll all have to take on more work today." She flipped her binder back open.

My stomach clenched. "I'm sorry, Dinah. We don't have to do the dinner. I don't want anyone to make a fuss." The family only ate together on Sunday afternoons. It was too difficult to prepare such large meals, and the older children were accustomed to fending for themselves anyway. We all took turns cooking for Thomas, who normally ate wherever he was sleeping for the night.

Unless it was my night. My kitchen—if it could be called that—was limited to a minifridge and a hot plate. Dinah fed him on the evenings he was scheduled to spend the night in my bed.

She snorted as she crossed out items on her menu page and scribbled in new ones. Without looking up, she said, "Okay, then you can be the one to explain to him why you canceled his plans."

I looked across the table, where Patty and Leah sat side by side. In a way, they were each other's opposite. Leah was short and curvy, with bright red hair and creamy white skin. She was thirty-five but looked ten years younger.

Patty was tall and thin to the point of gauntness. Like Dinah, she was forty-five, with brown hair and eyes. But where Dinah had a vivacious prettiness when she chose to display it, Patty's face was all angles and sharp corners. She was striking, with her olive skin and dark eyes, but she didn't fit any typical standard of beauty.

She tossed me a scathing look before turning to Dinah and saying, "Since I'm going to have the children all day with no help, I don't know how much assistance I can offer you."

"That's fine," Dinah murmured, still writing. "Leah can pick up whatever slack is left behind." She looked at Leah.

"Oh!" Leah sat up straighter. "Right. Yes. Yes, I can."

"And you'll take all the garbage down to the street? I'd do it, but I am swamped today. I've *got* to get some work done."

"Absolutely. I'll take care of it. The girls can help." At the mention of her daughters, a soft smile touched Leah's mouth. Anna and Ariel were thirteen and twelve, and little Aurora had just turned ten. They were all miniature clones of their mother, with red hair and warm brown eyes. Only her son, Simon, had Thomas's coloring.

"Good," Dinah said, sounding like Thomas. She put down her pen and leaned back. "We'll serve dinner at seven sharp. Please be on time, along with your children." She glanced at me before adding, "Or alone, as it were."

LEAH CAUGHT UP TO ME AS I PULLED OPEN THE DOOR OF THE truck.

"Elizabeth, wait!"

I threw my purse inside and turned. "What is it?"

Her caramel-colored eyes were pained when she said, "Don't pay any attention to Dinah, okay?"

I looked back at the house, imagining Dinah glowering at

me from her kitchen window. She was probably mad about the breakfast dishes. Normally, that was one of my jobs.

Leah was waiting for a response, so I forced a shrug. "I'm used to it."

She grabbed my hand and squeezed. "Don't let those two get to you." She lowered her voice. "I think she's going through *the change*. It's probably why she keeps bringing the baby thing up."

I almost laughed out loud. The way Leah said *the change* made it sound like Dinah had developed bubonic plague. On impulse, I hugged her. "It's okay, Leah. I promise it doesn't bother me. Maybe it used to, but not anymore."

She pulled back, doubt in her face. "Are you sure?"

"Totally sure." I released her, then climbed in the truck—something that was way easier in pants. Through the windshield, I saw Jackson walking over from Patty's house. "That's my ride," I told Leah.

"Okay. Well, good luck today." She closed the door, then put her chin against the bottom of the open window. "Just remember, anything is possible with Heavenly Father on your side. Sarah was ninety when she conceived Isaac."

I gave her a solemn nod. It was a nice Bible story, but something told me Thomas wasn't willing to wait that long.

But Leah's expression was so sincere, I forced a smile and said, "I'll keep that in mind."

She returned the smile, then backed away from the truck and started for her house, waving to Jackson as she went.

He climbed in the cab and slammed the door. "You ready?"

"Yes. What have you been doing?" I leaned away from him. He had huge sweat stains under his armpits, and his face was streaked with dirt.

He swiped an arm across his forehead, then stared down at his plaid shirt sleeve. "Dad had me pouring concrete at four this morning." He drew himself up and said in a low, measured voice, "Nothing builds character like manning a pump hose, son."

"I hate to break it to you, but that's just his way of getting cheap labor."

Jackson slanted me a skeptical look as he started the truck. "You mean *free* labor."

I just shook my head. That definitely sounded like Thomas. He owned one of the most successful construction companies in Jefferson City, and the secret to his success was that he employed mostly family members. Dinah ran the office from home and handled everything from payroll to zoning permits. Leah helped with accounts receivable and general bookkeeping tasks. At some point, all the boys in the family had worked various jobs—for little or no pay.

"So how'd you talk him into letting you take this job, anyway?" Jackson asked as we drove down the long gravel driveway away from the houses.

"It was Dinah's idea. She said times are tight, so it made sense for me to work." What she really said was that it made sense for me to work since I didn't have any children to care for, and that I should at least cover my room and board so I wasn't a burden on the family.

Jackson didn't need to know that, though. It was too embarrassing.

He turned the truck onto the main road leading out of town. We passed a few groups of boys walking along the sidewalk, probably on their way to work detail.

Jackson drummed his fingers on the steering wheel. "It doesn't add up," he said suddenly.

I looked at him. "What doesn't?"

"What Dinah said about times being tight. I've seen what Dad makes, and there is no way he's hurting for money."

"Well, he has to tithe. A lot of it goes to the faith."

He shrugged. "I guess. Not that they're doing anything

productive with it," he said, nodding to the old school building. At one time, the town had operated a small public school, but the state shut it down after some sort of audit claimed too many kids were being passed through grades despite missing months of school at a time. Families had gone back to homeschooling, and the building had fallen into disrepair.

We passed the town center with its small grocery store and town hall. Jackson slowed the truck to a crawl, glanced left and right, then rolled through a stop sign without stopping.

"Hey!" I exclaimed.

He glanced at me. "Do you want to be late on your first day? Besides, that's Theron and Bragg." He jutted his chin toward a white extended-cab truck idling near the intersection.

I squinted at the truck's dark windows but could only make out two shadowy figures in the front seat. "Since when are they working security?"

He gave a humorless laugh. "Since they went crying to their mom about being given shitty jobs. Now they're living the dream."

I wanted to scold him for swearing, but I heard the pain and confusion under his bravado. It was an open secret in the family that Thomas favored Dinah's children over all the others —a situation that had only grown worse since her oldest son, Thomas's namesake, had been excommunicated and forced out of the community. The night he left was the only time I ever heard Dinah raise her voice to Thomas. She'd begged and pleaded with him to intercede on their son's behalf, but he stalked from the house and slammed the door, leaving her sobbing on the kitchen floor.

Thinking to comfort her, I'd crept downstairs and placed my hand on her shoulder, only to jump back when she jerked away.

"I don't need pity from *you*," she spat.

"It's not pity, Dinah. I just—"

"What? Come to gloat?" She glared at me with such malice, I stumbled back a step.

Then she stood and smoothed her skirt. She squared her shoulders, the broken, weeping woman of seconds before replaced by the cool, dominant head wife. "Go back upstairs," she said. When I turned to go, she added, "And remember, he might want you in his bed, but *I've* borne his children."

The white truck grew smaller in my side mirror as we drove out of town.

Jackson gripped the steering wheel with tight fingers. I didn't blame him for being jealous. His half-brothers were driving around in air-conditioned comfort, enjoying power and prestige, while he toiled at construction sites and ferried his father's wives around.

"Thanks, by the way," I said.

He looked at me. "For what?"

"For driving me into the city." I dug in my purse and pulled out my driver's license. "Even though I'm official now."

"No kidding?" He leaned over so he could see the picture. "You need that for work or something?" When I nodded, he said, "You gonna start driving yourself into the city now?"

I sighed and tossed the license back into my purse. "I doubt it. Thomas said it's a waste of resources to leave a car in the city all day."

"Yeah, I guess. So what will you be doing, taking care of cats or something?" He cast a pointed look at my scrub top.

"Very funny." I reached over and gave him a playful punch on the arm. "It's an urgent care center. Like a mini emergency room and doctor's office all in one. They do drug screenings for employers, too, so I might help with administering those sorts of tests."

"Sounds cool, Liz."

I smiled. He was the only one who ever called me that. He'd been just ten when I married Thomas. Back then, my main job had been helping Patty, who homeschooled all the children. She'd been pregnant with her youngest at the time, so I took over her teaching role in that first year. Jackson had Patty's dark eyes and hair, but he was nothing like her in temperament. He was a jokester and something of a troublemaker, but he was so kind and lovable it was hard to get mad at him.

We drove in companionable silence for a few minutes, then he asked, "Want some music?"

"Sure."

He turned the radio on, filling the cab with Taylor Swift's "I Knew You Were Trouble."

He nodded his head to the beat for a second, then glanced at me. "I can change it if you want."

"It's okay."

He shrugged. "Well ... if you like it."

I hid a smile. "I don't mind it."

"Then I don't, either." He gave me a knowing look, a little grin tugging at his mouth.

I lost the battle with my smile and let out a laugh.

After a second, he joined in.

IT TOOK ANOTHER TWENTY MINUTES TO REACH THE OUTSKIRTS OF the city. The urgent care was actually located in Doverton, an affluent suburb of Jefferson City. I peered out the window as we passed upscale strip malls, car dealerships, and fast food restaurants.

There was so much to see, and everything was so vividly colored. The difference between this place and back home, just thirty minutes apart, was hard to believe. The seven Priesthood Council members who ruled the Righteous Brethren discouraged bright colors, especially for clothing. Looking around Doverton, I guess I knew why. Everything felt busy and overwhelming. A woman hurried across the street as we waited at an intersection, one hand clutching her skirt as it fluttered around her thighs.

I reached across the center console and put my hand over Jackson's eyes, which made him laugh. "It's only April," he said. "Just wait until the real hot weather hits. You'll be scandalized."

The urgent care loomed up ahead—a large square building made of dark brown bricks and lots of windows. As I stared at it, I caught a glimpse of my own reflection in the window. My eyes were like two saucers. I tried to rearrange my face into something less timid and awestruck, but I just ended up looking even more terrified.

"Where should I drop you?" Jackson asked as we pulled in. The parking lot wrapped around the entire facility, making the building look like a monolith on an asphalt island.

"Um, I'm not sure . . . right here is fine." I pointed to a spot near the front of the building. Jackson parked and turned off the engine. I looked up at the building and swallowed. It was way bigger in person than it appeared in the glossy brochure the recruiter had given me at my vocational school's job fair. I'd been thrilled to land a job just before graduation. Seeing the place now, up close like this . . .

How could I ever walk in there?

"Hey." Jackson was watching me. "Don't be nervous, Liz."

I looked at Patty's son. If a sixteen-year-old could see how scared I was, what would the people inside think?

My heart thumped. "I don't think I can do it."

He looked at the building, his expression thoughtful. After a minute he said, "The first time Dad sent me to work, I was thirteen. Have you ever seen the guys who work on those job sites?"

I shook my head. Thomas didn't like me hanging around his work.

"Well, let's just say they can be rough. Most of them are

decent, but they don't cut anyone a break. It's hard work, and they don't have any patience for newbies. It slows them down, you know? So, anyway, I was so terrified I went behind the office trailer and puked my guts out."

"Oh, Jackson."

He waved a hand. "It's okay. I actually felt better after that. The foreman—I think he saw me barf, to be honest—walked up to me, grabbed the back of my shirt, and put me right to work tying steel. For the next eight hours, I was so busy I forgot to be nervous." He flashed a lopsided smile. "This looks like a busy place. I don't think you'll be nervous for long."

I blinked back tears. Something made me lean over and give him a peck on the cheek. "Thank you."

His face reddened, but he smiled and said, "Go save some kittens."

I let out a watery laugh. "You are horrible." I grabbed my purse from the floor and hopped out of the truck. Then I took a deep breath and crossed the half-circle drive in front of the center. When I reached the door, I turned. Jackson's farm truck stood out like a sore thumb among the sea of sedans and SUVs.

He waved, then made a shooing motion with his hands.

I faced the automatic doors.

Now or never.

A pair of women in blue scrubs passed me. The doors whooshed open, spilling cool air onto the walkway.

I followed the women inside. The antiseptic scent of hospital swirled around me. I stopped, unsure where to go next.

A tall reception desk stood in the center of a bright lobby. Workers in scrubs and white doctor's coats streamed around it, headed toward what looked like an open atrium.

"Can I help you?" a voice rang out.

It took me a minute to realize it came from the head peeking over the reception desk. A woman regarded me curiously, her face visible from the nose up.

I walked to the desk, and the rest of her came into view. From this angle, I could see the bank of computer monitors on the counter in front of her. She wore street clothes and a little headset with a microphone near her mouth.

"Yes. Hi. I'm Elizabeth Grant, the new medical assistant. It's my first day."

She smiled and looked down at a clipboard by her elbow. "*The* new medical assistant, huh?" Her tone was teasing, so I returned her smile even though I had no idea what was funny.

"Ah. Here you are." She pointed to some black squiggles on her paper. "I'll get Brittney for you, one second," she said, pushing a few buttons on one of the phones on her desk. "Hey, can someone send Brittney down here?" she said into her mouthpiece. "Yep. New hire. Thanks." She looked up at me. "She'll be right down."

"Thank you."

Careful not to stray too far from the reception area, I wandered a little way into the atrium, trying not to gawk like a country bumpkin having her first big-city experience. The sunny space was two stories high, with hallways running around the perimeter at each level. People, some dressed in scrubs, others in regular clothes, strode down the hallways and through doors that must have led to doctors' offices.

"Elizabeth?"

I turned. A slim, dark-haired woman in blue scrubs approached. She wore a pink stethoscope around her neck, the bright tubing a sharp contrast to the more sedate color of her scrub top.

My stomach flipped over as I held out my hand. My mother's voice floated through my head. *You can't go wrong with a smile.* "I'm Elizabeth."

She shook my hand. "Brittney," she said, revealing beautiful white teeth. She had jewel-bright green eyes. In books, characters sometimes have jewel-bright green eyes. In real life, people's eyes were usually blue or brown. But Brittney's were the color of leaves after days of rain.

"I'm the nurse manager," she said. "We're actually located upstairs. We can get some paperwork out of the way, then I'll show you around, okay?"

"Sounds great," I said.

2

"Cute scrubs," Brittney said, taking a seat behind the desk in her office. "Do you like cats?"

"Oh. Um, no," I said, glancing down at my shirt. "I mean, yes, I do. I don't have one, though."

Good grief, I'm babbling. I took a deep breath. "The recruiter who hired me said you work with a lot of kids? I tried to pick something that would put them at ease."

Brittney smiled. "That was a good idea. She should have told you not to buy uniforms, though. We supply freshly laundered scrubs every day, right here in the building."

I nodded.

"Anyway," she continued, "what was your full name again?" She took out a stack of forms and pulled a pen from her shirt pocket.

"Elizabeth Hy—ah, Grant." I cleared my throat. "Grant," I said, giving my maiden name. "Sorry. Nerves, I guess."

Brittney laughed. "No worries. My last name is Creighton, by the way." She lifted the bottom of her scrub top, revealing a little plastic badge clipped to her waistband. "Crate like the wooden box, ton like the unit of measurement. I can't tell you how often people screw that up." She gave me a commiserating look and lowered her voice. "I swear, I will marry the first eligible bachelor I see with Smith for a last name."

I laughed, because she expected me to.

"Are you married?" she asked. I must have given her a blank look, because she tapped her paper with her pen. "It's a question on the form."

I shook my head. "No. No, I'm not married."

She sighed. "Join the club." She filled out a few more items on her form, biting her full lower lip as she wrote.

Her teeth were toothpaste-commercial white. She could be anywhere between twenty-five and thirty-five. I always had a hard time guessing the ages of women outside Riverview Heights, since so many of them wore makeup.

Brittney's makeup was flawless. Her lids were smeared with a dàrk gray color, and her eyelashes were so long and full they reminded me of the perfectly curled eyelashes on one of those baby dolls whose eyes open and close when you sit them up and lay them down. They swept like two perfect crescents across high cheekbones as she finished filling out her forms.

At first glance, her hair looked black. Up close, though, it was a very dark brown, with a glossy sheen that seemed to move every time she turned her head.

After a minute, she flipped the form around and held out the pen. "Okay, look it over and make sure everything is right. Then sign. Oh, and I also need to make copies of your driver's license and social security card."

I gave the form a quick once-over and signed my name, then pulled the two small cards out of my purse. Fortunately, Dinah had connections with several clerks in local government offices through her work for the construction company. She'd managed to get me all the official documents I needed for school and a job outside Riverview Heights. Before that, I'd never even had a birth certificate. As far as the state of Missouri knew, I'd just popped into existence six months ago.

Brittney held my license up, her eyes darting between my face and the square piece of plastic. "Twenty-five? Yeah, right. I bet you get carded everywhere you go."

I frowned. What did she mean?

She looked at me for a second, then laughed. "Elizabeth, I'm *kidding*. I'm sorry, I shouldn't have said that. You don't know me well enough yet for jokes."

"It's okay. I'm not offended." How could I be? I still didn't understand.

"Thank goodness. The last thing I need right now is HR up my butt."

I didn't know what HR meant, either, so I just continued smiling and hoped I didn't look like a complete idiot. My cheeks ached. If I had to fake smile like this much longer, I was going to get a cramp.

"Where exactly do you live in the Jeff?" she asked, looking at my license again.

Finally, something I understood. I'd heard people back home refer to Jefferson City as "the Jeff" before.

"It's just a little apartment," I said. I hated lying, but it was inevitable. For as long as I could remember, I'd been taught to fear and distrust the outside world. My grandfather and great-grandfather had both lived most of their lives in hiding, on the run from prosecution because of their faith. To keep our secrets, Dinah had listed the construction company's downtown headquarters as my home address. It made things easier, since Thomas would end up depositing my paychecks in a family account anyway.

Brittney gave me a bemused look. "Is it new? I'm familiar with the area, and I don't think I've ever seen apartments there."

"It's newish."

She looked like she expected me to elaborate. When I didn't, she sort of shook her head and cleared her throat. "Well," she said, looking around her desk, "I think we're all done here. I'm sure you have questions, but I can probably answer a lot of them as I show you around."

Crap. Had I offended her? Ten minutes into my new job, and I'd already messed it up. My mother's advice surfaced in my mind again, and I smiled. "That sounds great. Thank you for taking the time."

She waved it off. "No problem. It's my job." She stood and walked around the desk to the door. "If you'll follow me, I'll show you all the sights."

I followed in Brittney's perfume-scented wake as she introduced me to staff members and showed me around the center. The urgent care part of the building took up the entire second floor. It was a large space, but it was impossible to get lost, since the layout was basically a large square with exam rooms and supply closets on one side and offices for management and high-ranking staff on the other.

There were three doctors, two part-time and one full-time. There was also an addiction counselor, a dietitian, and a physical therapist.

"We have five beds," Brittney said as she swung open a door and flipped on a light. She gestured for me to follow her in. "This one and the one next to it are for acute patients."

I gazed around the room, which held a standard exam table covered with a white paper runner, two guest chairs, a doctor's stool, and a cabinet and table combo bolted to the wall. A framed poster of the human respiratory system hung above the guest chairs, which sat next to a defibrillator and a bag valve mask.

Brittney folded her arms. "According to the law, we can't refuse care to these people, but between you and me we have our ways of getting them out of here if they don't have insurance. Usually, we just call the guys from the charity hospital to come get them." She led us back out and down to a set of double doors with push handles.

"And here are the locker rooms. Men on the left, women on the right." She walked down a short hall that opened into a locker room ringed by wooden benches and narrow red lockers, some with combination locks hanging from the metal latches. At the center of the room sat a big wooden table and chairs. Judging by the small thermal bags and travel mugs scattered across its surface, this was where the staff took their breaks.

Brittney stepped back and looked me up and down, a bright pink fingernail pressed against her lips. "I think a medium will work. Wait right here, I'll grab you some scrubs." She turned and headed through another doorway.

Just then, a pretty, petite woman entered the locker room, then stopped short at the sight of me. Her hair was covered by a thin, blue cap, and she wore a surgical mask pulled down around her neck. "You look lost."

"Ah, I'm just waiting for Brittney. Brittney Creighton? She's getting me some new scrubs."

She looked amused. "I've heard of her," she told me, smiling. She crossed to one of the lockers and opened it. She looked in a little mirror clipped to the door and pulled her cap off, revealing light brown hair in a messy ponytail. She pulled the elastic out of her hair and put it between her lips, mumbling, "This your first day?"

"Yes. I'm a medical assistant."

"Welcome to the jungle." She combed her fingers through her shoulder-length hair and began sweeping it back up into a ponytail, her movements assured and efficient. Like Brittney, she wore an ID tag, except hers was clipped to her breast pocket. "I'm Natalie. I work downstairs, in outpatient, but I moonlight up here sometimes. Where did you work before?"

"This is my first job out of school."

Ponytail complete, she pulled a stretchy headband from her scrubs pocket and turned back to the mirror. "I can believe it," she said, her gaze on mine in her mirror. "You look young enough to be friends with my daughter, but once you're my age, everyone looks like a baby. The girl who cuts my hair isn't even old enough to drink. I'm waiting for her to offer me blue dye and a perm."

Before I could reply, Brittney returned with an armful of blue scrubs, which she dumped on the table. "Here, Elizabeth. Oh, hey, Nat. Have you met Elizabeth?"

Natalie closed her locker and faced us. "Yes, I was just telling her how wonderful this place is."

Brittney raised an arched eyebrow. "Don't listen to her, Elizabeth. She loves it here. Don't you, Natalie?"

"Are we on the record?"

"Ignore her," Brittney told me. "I got you two sizes because I wasn't sure about the length." Her gaze traveled down my body. "How tall are you, anyway?"

"Five nine."

She ran her hands over her perfect figure. "What I wouldn't give for a couple of those inches." She gestured to the pile. "Well, get changed, and then I guess you can hit the floor. Come find me at the nurses' station when you're done. Sound good?"

"Great," I said.

She tossed us a big smile, then breezed out of the room.

I walked to the table and picked through the scrubs.

Natalie watched me for a minute, then asked, "What do you think so far?"

I looked up. "Everything is great."

The friendly look on her face faded, and concern took its place. "Just . . . be careful with her, okay?"

I froze, a scrub top in my hand. "You mean Brittney?"

She nodded.

"But she's been so nice. She seems very kind."

Natalie walked to the table, flipped through the scrub pants, and pulled a pair out. "Here, these will work."

I hesitated. If I changed in front of her, she'd see my garments, which I'd worn every day since I'd become a member of the church. In the nine years since then, I'd never had to worry about an outsider seeing them because I'd never worn anything but long sleeves and long skirts or dresses.

Natalie would probably assume they were some modified form of long underwear. But that could raise uncomfortable questions. It wasn't exactly stifling outside, but it was far too warm for long johns. I'd worn a turtleneck under my scrub top, so I didn't have to worry about revealing anything there. My pants, on the other hand, presented a problem.

She seemed to sense my dilemma, because she wadded up her surgical cap and mask and tossed them in a nearby trash can. Then she grabbed one of the small bags off the table.

"I've got a thirty-minute break, so I'm gonna go smoke." She rolled her eyes. "They make us drive off the property now."

I clutched the pants to my chest. "Okay. Well, maybe I'll see you later?"

"I'm pulling a double today, so you definitely will." She walked to the doorway. Before she left, she turned back. "About Brittney . . ." A cloud fell over her perky face. "I didn't mean to scare you. Just watch your back, okay? When she sees someone as a rival, they usually don't last long."

I nodded. I seemed to do a lot of that around this place. It was safer than coming up with a suitable response.

Natalie glanced around the room. "Oh, and definitely get a

combination lock for your locker. These people are a bunch of thieving animals."

THE SCRUB PANTS WERE A LITTLE SHORT, BUT I MADE THEM WORK by tying them low on my hips. As I walked to the nurses' station, I mulled over my conversation with Natalie.

Why would Brittney see me as a rival? She had a BSN after her name, which meant she'd gone to a four-year college for her nursing degree. I had a certificate that said I'd completed a six-month training program at the local technical school. She was beautiful and accomplished. The idea of her seeing me as any kind of threat was laughable.

I sighed. Less than two hours into my job, and I was already being confronted with drama. Reluctant amusement made me smile. I'd been worried about fitting in, but maybe I shouldn't have. This place might not be so different from home, after all.

I was nearly to the nurses' station when a door opened, and a man in a doctor's white coat stuck his head out of one of the acute patient rooms.

"You! I need you."

I stopped, my hand splayed on my chest. "Me?"

"Hurry," he said. "I need another set of hands." He disappeared into the room, leaving the door ajar.

The nurses' station was too far away to see if anyone was there. A glance in the other direction revealed nothing but a deserted hall with an empty gurney shoved against one wall. With no other options, I pushed the door all the way open and stepped in.

The man stood over a metal instrument tray, his hands moving quickly as he sorted through several pairs of scissors and pliers. Behind him, a small boy in a white T-shirt and Spider-Man underwear lay on his side on the exam table. A nasty gash on his upper thigh oozed blood, the flesh around it already turning a dark purple. His face was tear streaked and red. A frazzled-looking woman—obviously his mother—stood at his side, stroking his head and murmuring, "It's okay, Sam. It's okay."

The doctor looked up as I hovered in the doorway. "Come on over. I need a little help keeping Sam's hands away from his leg while I suture."

I looked at the mother, who regarded me with an expression somewhere between curious and expectant. The little boy had his eyes screwed shut and wasn't looking at anything. His breaths came in short gasps that shook his whole body.

I had enough experience with kids to know he was on the edge of a full-blown tantrum.

I opened my mouth to tell the doctor I couldn't help, but he swung around and motioned me toward the boy's head. "Just block his view, okay?" he said in a low voice.

I nodded and moved where he pointed, angling my body so I obscured the child's view of his lower half. "Um, hi, Sam." I lay a hesitant hand on his arm. "I'm Elizabeth."

The shuddering breaths continued.

The doctor spoke behind me, his voice calm and assured. "The worst part is over, Sam, okay? I put medicine in your leg to numb it. You might feel a little bit of pressure, like someone is tapping your leg, but you won't feel pain."

I bit my lip. Should I tell him a story? Sing to him? When the younger children at home were sick, I usually sang. It didn't seem right in this setting, though. Behind me, the doctor's coat made quiet shushing sounds as he prepared his instruments.

The mother wiped a tear off the boy's cheek. "Our dog bit him," she told me in a loud whisper. She shook her head. "I swear, Minnie is the nicest, sweetest dog on the planet. Never in a million years would I have thought she'd tear into one of the kids. Just took a chunk right out of his leg. I've never seen so much blood in my life."

I racked my brain for something to talk about—anything to stop her from recounting the gory details of the injury in front of the boy. My eye caught the bright colors of the cartoon Spider-Man on his briefs.

"So, Sam," I said in a conspiratorial tone. "I heard you like Batman. I like Batman, too. Batman is probably the best super-hero out there."

His eyes flew open, big and brown, reminding me of the spaniel puppies my stepfather had raised for hunting. His little mouth turned down in a pout. "Batman is only cool because of his suit. Spider-Man can swing from webs."

"Hmm." I pretended to consider it. Behind me, the doctor's arm brushed my back as he placed the first suture. I leaned my hip against the table to keep Sam's attention on me. "You may be right. But Batman has the Bat-Signal. That's pretty cool, don't you think?"

He shook his head. "There's nothing special about his body, though. Spider-Man can shoot webs out of his hands!"

"Really? Where on his hands? Can you show me?"

He extended one arm, wrist out. "Like this," he said, and made a whistling sound.

We debated various superheroes for the next few minutes, pitting each one against Spider-Man, with Spider-Man emerging victorious each time.

"One more," the doctor murmured behind me. His arm brushed my back again as he made a twisting motion to tie off the thread.

I smiled down at Sam. "You've been very brave. I think Spider-Man would be proud. And what's cool is you have your very own spider web, right on your leg."

"I do?" His face lit up, and he craned his neck to get a glimpse of his leg.

"Give it just one more minute." I gave his arm a gentle squeeze.

"All done," the doctor said. He turned and dropped his tools on the tray and pulled a cloth over it.

I stepped out of the way so he could strip off his gloves and wash his hands. Unsure if I should stay or leave, I hovered near the door in case he needed something else.

He hooked the rolling stool with his foot and sat so he was lower than the child, who was now sitting up, examining his leg with the sort of morbid fascination common to little boys.

"You did great, Sam," the doctor told him. He held out his hand for a high five, then shook it and blew on it as if Sam had hurt him, prompting a delighted giggle from the little boy.

"Keep it as dry as possible for the next ten days," he told the mother. "He can shower, but no baths. You don't need to put anything on it. Just keep it clean."

She looked relieved. "Thank you for all your help."

His expression grew grave. "He's a lucky boy. I have to report the bite. Someone from the health department will be in touch." He glanced at me before telling her, "Now, there's just one more thing we need to do. Sit tight, and we'll be right back."

I took that as my cue to leave, so I slipped through the door and waited for him in the hall. Now that the moment of crisis had passed, my heart pounded. Would he be mad at me for not speaking up about it being my first day? I was qualified to help in such situations, but maybe the protocols were different here.

My throat went dry. If I got fired on my first day, I'd never live it down. I pictured Dinah and Patty smiling smugly around the dinner table tonight.

The doctor stepped into the hallway and pulled the door shut behind him. He grimaced and, pitching his voice low, said, "Every time I see one of those, I hope it'll be the last. Unfortunately, it never is."

"Will he be okay?" I looked at the door.

"Oh, yeah. It was pretty superficial, which means the dog was probably just excited or scared." He put his hands in his coat pockets. "I, uh . . . I'm really sorry about this, but for the life of me, I can't remember your name."

My cheeks heated, and I looked down at the toes of my white soft-soled shoes. "We've never met. It's my first day."

"Oh, man." He scratched his cheek and let out a soft chuckle. "I'm sorry. I really threw you into the deep end of the pool, huh?"

Wait, he was apologizing to me? Pink tinged his cheeks, but he couldn't be embarrassed. He was a doctor. An hour ago, I had never been within twenty feet of a real patient.

I smiled. "I didn't mind. This is what I trained for. I loved it, actually." I bit my tongue before I continued gushing like an idiot.

"Here, let's meet properly." He stuck his hand out. "Evan Adgate."

A little thrill shot through me. I took his hand. "Elizabeth Grant."

"Nice to meet you, Elizabeth."

"Same." Looking up at him, I realized he had to be over six feet tall to tower over me like he did. It made me feel small, but not in a bad way. He had a lean build, but his shoulders and upper body were well defined, which kept him from looking too rangy. His dark blond hair was straight and thick—the kind of hair women want for themselves. His eyes were a curious shade of blue, almost grayish, which should have made them look cold but somehow didn't.

"What is going on?"

We turned in unison. Brittney walked toward us at a fast clip, her ponytail bouncing. She didn't look happy.

"Elizabeth, I thought I told you to come find me once you changed." She stopped and glanced at a large, square watch on her wrist—one of those smart watches that sends emails and tells you to get up and walk when you sit around too long. "That was half an hour ago," she added.

Dr. Adgate stepped in before I could speak. "I'm afraid that's my fault, Brittney. I yanked Elizabeth into room two and put her straight to work." He shot me a smile. "The juvenile dog bite," he told her.

"Evan, this is Elizabeth's first day—"

"I know, I know. My mistake." He put up his hands in a defensive gesture. He grinned at me. "She rose to the occasion, though."

I couldn't help grinning back. Warmth curled through me.

But Brittney wasn't done. "She's also a medical assistant," she said, making *medical assistant* sound like *serial killer*. She focused on me. "I don't know how you did things at your school, Elizabeth, but assistants don't do patient care here. Maybe in the future you can help us with intake, but that depends on you." She crossed her arms. "How well you follow directions."

The warmth from Dr. Adgate's approval faded. I didn't know the rules, of course. But maybe every health center was like that? "I apologize, Brittney," I said. "It won't happen again."

"Brittney, really," Dr. Adgate said, his voice light. "Elizabeth did a great job."

Brittney turned to him. "Evan, could I speak to you in private?" She didn't wait for an answer. She just turned on her heel and stalked into an empty exam room.

He tipped his head back and closed his eyes for a second. When he looked back down at me, his expression was unreadable.

Was he angry at Brittney? She'd spoken as though she were the superior and he the subordinate. I'd watched enough *General Hospital* to know the medical hierarchy didn't work that way.

"Please wait right here," he said, his gray-blue eyes earnest.

"I will." I had nowhere else to go, except maybe back to the locker room. Or home. Given Brittney's reaction, I might be headed there anyway.

He entered the exam room and closed the door with a soft click.

I leaned against the wall as angry voices drifted out. I couldn't make out much, but I caught a few words and phrases —things like "my authority" and "in charge" and "rules and procedures." Dr. Adgate's low, moderate tone was a slow rumble compared to Brittney's higher, more agitated voice.

Finally, the door swung open, and he walked out without glancing in my direction. His coat billowed behind him as his strides ate up the white linoleum floor.

Brittney followed a few seconds later. She watched him go, then turned her attention to me. "Elizabeth, follow me, please."

THIS IS IT. I'M GETTING FIRED.

I trailed behind Brittney, my heart in my throat. How was I going to tell Thomas I got let go on my first day?

Dinah was going to love it.

We passed the deserted nurses' station and turned down a little hallway that ended in a set of wooden doors. Brittney pulled a key from her pocket and unlocked them, revealing half a dozen deep shelves lined with glass vials, big plastic pill bottles, and small cardboard boxes.

"This is our main med cabinet." She swung one door closed so she could access a big, white refrigerator set into a nook in the wall next to the closet. "This is where we keep meds that need to be refrigerated," she said, opening the door. She leaned down and peered inside for a second before pulling out a box and removing a small clear vial from inside, which she handed to me.

"It's DTaP," she said. "For the boy in two."

The vial was cold against my palm. I stared at her, my thoughts turning like rusty gears. "You're not firing me?"

She rolled her eyes. "Really, Elizabeth, no need to be so melodramatic." Her cold, angry tone was gone. Now, she was teasing and sarcastic, like she'd been in the locker room.

Wait. I was being melodramatic? Hadn't she just thrown a temper tantrum because I helped Dr. Adgate?

She must have seen the confusion in my expression, because she took a deep breath. "I'm not mad at you. But you report to me." She pointed a polished pink finger down the hallway. "Not him, and not any of the other doctors. I can't have my staff undermining my authority."

"I would never try to do that."

"Then there's nothing to worry about." She took the vial from me, smiling the same friendly smile from earlier. "I have to give the kid in two this injection."

Sam. Should I tell her he loved Spider-Man more than any other superhero?

But I bit my tongue. She didn't need any reminders about my involvement in his care.

She led me back down the hall and around the corner to the nurses' station, which was still unoccupied. "We're a small crew most days," she said, rolling the vial between her hands. She leaned against the tall, white counter that shielded a long desk and three rolling chairs from view.

"Besides me, there's usually just one other nurse, although we can always call down to the ambulatory surgery suite for a couple of extra hands when we're swamped. The part-time doctors work evenings and weekends mostly." Her face tightened. "And you've already met Dr. Adgate, obviously. He's full-time." She grabbed a clipboard from the station's counter and gave it to me.

"The nurses' time is really eaten up by charting. That's where you come in. I need you to handle a lot of the tasks we just can't get to. This is just a rough list of items off the top of my head. I'm sure I'll be able to add more as you settle in."

I ran my gaze down the list.

"Any questions?" she asked.

I hugged the clipboard to my chest. "No, I think I can handle these."

"I'm glad to hear it." She pushed away from the counter and headed toward room two. Halfway down the hall, she turned and spoke over her shoulder. "By the way, the cleaning supplies are in a closet in the locker room."

3

I suppressed a groan as I climbed in the truck after work.
"Rough day?" Jackson asked me. He tossed his comic
book on the dashboard as I buckled my seat belt.

"I guess you could say that." I'd spent the majority of my
shift on my hands and knees, dusting behind the exam tables
in the patient rooms. By the end of the day, I'd filled up two
garbage bags with grimy paper towels.

I leaned away from my seat so I could rub the small of my
back. "You were right, you know. I was too busy to be nervous."

He was smug as he pulled out of the center's parking lot and
onto the road. "Told you."

My smile faded as the center grew smaller in the rearview
mirror. Brittney's list had contained a dozen or more cleaning
tasks. Just a handful of items could be considered medically
oriented, and even those involved zero patient interaction.

I frowned as the truck went over a hill and the center disappeared from view. Had she planned my role from the beginning, or was this retaliation for helping Dr. Adgate?

I was probably just being paranoid. She said my level of
involvement depended on how well I followed directions.

Maybe this was just her way of getting an idea of my attitude and abilities.

I reviewed the day in my head. I hadn't seen the doctor again, but I'd heard him speaking to patients in the exam rooms every now and then, his deep voice muffled behind the thick wooden doors. Brittney had checked up on me a couple times, once to make sure I'd found the supplies I needed and again to tell me I could take a lunch break. I ate my ham sandwich at the table in the locker room, where I met a few of the nurses from the surgery center where Natalie worked.

"Come down and introduce yourself one of these days," a stocky woman named Carla had told me. "We might even try to steal you away. I promise we have a lot more fun."

I'd also met Gloria, the other full-time RN who worked in the urgent care center. A heavyset, older woman with iron-gray hair cut into a bob, she'd switched from hospital nursing to working at the center about five years ago after her knees went bad. The pay was lower, but she preferred the more reasonable hours and less stressful environment. She did most of the patient intake, while Brittney assisted the doctors.

As Jackson turned into Riverview Heights, I resolved to give Brittney the benefit of the doubt. After all, she'd just met me. I had to earn her trust. Once she knew I was capable and willing to work hard, she'd give me more rewarding job duties.

By the time we pulled up the driveway, optimism replaced the dread I'd felt leaving the center.

I thanked Jackson for the ride and slipped into the house, then watched the truck pull away as I washed my hands in the kitchen sink.

The house was quiet, but Dinah had been busy. Three Crock-Pots simmered on the island, filling the kitchen with the smell of pot roast. There was a big pie in the oven, and the counters held empty serving dishes waiting to be filled with sides. She'd probably given Patty and Leah a list of dishes to prepare.

I changed into a skirt and fitted button-down, then went back downstairs to do my chores.

When I got the job at the Doverton Urgent Care, Dinah made it clear I'd still have most of my regular responsibilities at home. It was only fair, she'd said, since I didn't have children to care for.

I entered the kitchen, careful not to make too much noise. Dinah's office was on the other side of the dining room. I stopped at the basement door, one hand on the knob, and listened.

There it was—the faint sound of muffled voices. Dinah's afternoon soaps.

The ones I wasn't supposed to know about.

Television wasn't exactly forbidden, but I knew Thomas would have disapproved. That meant Dinah knew it, too.

I opened the basement door and went down the stairs, ignoring the soreness in my back. I flipped on lights as I crossed the big, empty space and headed for the laundry room.

When Thomas had built the house, he'd finished the basement with a fourth wife in mind. There were three bedrooms, a living room, a kitchen, and a full bath. After years of sharing a bedroom with four stepsisters, it had seemed like a paradise to me.

But I'd been kicked out of paradise, with Dinah playing the role of the angel with the flaming sword.

"It doesn't make sense for you to have all that space," she'd said. "Not until you have children."

So I'd moved upstairs, to the loft apartment her two oldest sons had used before leaving home. It was small, but it was mine. That made it better than anything I was used to.

I pulled a load of clean clothes out of the dryer and folded them, then filled the washer with more and started it. The counter against the wall held stacks of Thomas's shirts and pants waiting to be starched and ironed.

I hummed while the iron heated up. Like the other men in the community, he tended to plain colors. I ironed several white oxford button-downs, pausing every now and then to spray starch on the sleeves. By the time I got to the pants, my face was damp with sweat, and the ache in my back had blossomed into a stabbing pain that radiated down my legs.

I switched the laundry, started a new load, and bundled the shirts and pants together on hangers so I could carry them upstairs in one trip.

Dinah turned from the kitchen window when I emerged from the basement. "Did you turn off all the lights down there?"

"Yes." I blew a hair out of my eyes. "I'll come back down once I get these upstairs."

Her gaze moved over the clothes in my arms. "He doesn't need that many shirts up there." She held out her hand. "Give some to me."

"I can take them for you." She had the first-floor master suite at the back of the house. The other two bedrooms belonged to her teenage daughter, Daria, and her ten-year-old son, Jonah.

"No." Her tone was firm. She motioned for me to hand them over.

I peeled off three shirts and shifted the heavy stack of clothes in my arms so I could hold them out to her.

She folded them over the back of one of the barstools ranged around the island and turned her back.

Dismissed.

I'd lived with her long enough to know when she was in one of her moods. When I'd joined the family a few months shy of my twentieth birthday, I thought I could win her over by helping with the endless chores that pile up in a house with six children.

Stupid.

I should have known better. I witnessed my own mother struggle to please my stepfather's first wife. As a child, I hadn't understood the complicated undercurrents that ebbed and flowed between sister-wives.

I hadn't known that what goes unsaid is what matters.

At nineteen, I would have offered to help Dinah with the dinner, and I would have spent the night sobbing into my pillow when she rebuffed me.

Now, I just hefted the clothes higher in my arms and made my way upstairs. The unsaid things between us had built up so high, I couldn't even see my way around them anymore.

Upstairs, I hung the clothes in the tiny section of my closet reserved for Thomas, then flopped on my bed. It was heaven to finally be off my feet. The sharp pain in my back faded back to a dull ache. I must have dozed for a while, because I jerked when I heard Dinah call my name from the bottom of the stairs.

I rolled over and pressed my face into the quilt before raising my head and yelling, "Coming!"

She was back at the sink when I walked into the kitchen, but this time her fists were on her hips. "Just look at that garbage blowing everywhere!" She thrust an arm toward the window. "Didn't you see that when you came up the driveway today?"

I went to the sliders and peered out. Sure enough, the grass near the end of the driveway was strewn with garbage. "One of the cans must have tipped over."

"I'm calling Leah right now. I don't care how busy she is with Simon."

I turned. *Crap.* At our meeting that morning, Dinah had

asked Leah to take all the cans to the end of the driveway. She must have forgotten to bring them back up to the house.

Dinah picked up the phone.

"It's my fault," I said.

She lowered the phone.

I licked my lips. "I'm sorry. Leah and I talked this morning before I left. I told her I'd bring them in."

Dinah frowned. "We agreed Leah would do it. I put it in the book this morning. You can't just go changing things around like that, Elizabeth." Her voice rose as she warmed up to a full-blown lecture. "With this many moving parts, we have to stay on schedule. I know you don't always appreciate what I do, but I'm telling you there is real value in organization. It's not just a couple of garbage cans that's the problem. It's people forgetting what they're supposed to be doing, which means vital tasks don't get performed, which has a ripple effect across the whole family."

I chewed the inside of my cheek as she veered from the garbage to all the times I'd done something like this before. My laziness was only matched by my carelessness, and even that wasn't as bad as my lack of respect or my inability to follow directions.

On and on it went, a litany of traits that spun around me in a slow circle. My knees hurt from kneeling on the floor all day, and the ache in my back fired into a sharp, pinching flashpoint.

Without warning, something inside me snapped.

"I get it, Dinah, okay?" My voice was loud. Abrupt. Like a slap.

Dinah's jaw dropped.

Satisfaction zipped through me. She was speechless. *First time for everything.*

"I'll get the stupid cans," I said, "and I'll clean up the stupid mess." I jerked open the slider and stepped outside, then turned back.

Dinah shut her mouth. The shock on her face was morphing into something more ominous, but I didn't care.

"They're *trash cans*," I said, letting sarcasm drip from my tone. "Worry about something important for once." Before she could reply, I pulled the slider shut and stalked from the house.

THE SATISFACTION OF SILENCING DINAH ONLY LASTED AS FAR AS the end of the driveway. As I grabbed a trash container and tipped it upright, anxiety knotted my stomach.

No good could come of speaking to her that way. A gust of wind raced across the lawn and up my skirt. Goose bumps formed on my arms, and I gritted my teeth.

It was stupid to anger Dinah, but I didn't regret covering for Leah. Her nine-year-old son, Simon, was a handful most days. He'd been born with a condition that was becoming more common among children in Riverview Heights. It had also shown up in a handful of children born in my hometown in Illinois, which was even more rural and isolated. Because members of the Righteous Brethren were required to marry someone from the faith, the gene pool shrank every year.

Simon's disorder was similar to autism, but it was almost unique to our community, which meant outside doctors had almost no opportunities to study it. He was temperamental and prone to bursts of emotion that kept Leah on her toes.

Even worse, there was no rhyme or reason to what might set him off. One day, a passing car horn would throw him into a screaming fit. The next day, a similar noise had no effect at all. He also suffered from asthma, which grew worse when he got agitated.

Thomas had consulted with his fellow Priesthood Council members, who'd authorized him to take Simon fifty miles south to be evaluated by the only doctor who shared our faith.

I'd met him once, when he traveled to my stepfather's farm to treat my mother. He seemed competent, but I knew he couldn't help Simon. The boy needed intervention from specialists trained to accommodate his needs. I tried telling Thomas as much.

Once.

I grabbed the trash can's plastic handle and started up the driveway.

A plastic milk jug blew across the grass like a tumbleweed. I left the can in place, then walked to the jug and grabbed it. There was also a smashed fast food bag. When I picked it up, cola-colored liquid leaked from the side.

Gross.

Patty's three teenage boys were notorious for sneaking cheeseburgers and sodas while they were on construction sites. They got rid of the evidence before Thomas could find it.

I grabbed an empty water bottle, a soiled paper towel, and a plastic detergent container from the lawn and tossed them in the empty can. Then I resumed my trek up the driveway. It was slow going, despite the wheels on the bottom. The lid bumped open as I pulled the container over the gravel, making the whole thing wobble. I was halfway back to the house when I heard the crunch of tires behind me.

Thomas pulled his work truck next to me and rolled his window down. I stepped onto the grass. He looked me up and down, a slight frown wrinkling his broad forehead. "You're not dressed for this wind. What are you doing out here?"

Wasn't it obvious? I patted the top of the big green can, which made a hollow sound. "Just bringing the cans back up to the house. One tipped over and blew some leftover stuff around."

He looked in his rearview mirror, his gaze on the four identical cans sitting at the end of the driveway. "Well, be quick about it," he said, his voice laced with displeasure. "You'll delay dinner."

As he pulled away, his truck's red taillights made the driveway look like a river of blood.

It was dark by the time I rolled the last can into place at the rear of the house. A burst of light and noise hit me as I slid open the heavy glass door and stepped into the kitchen.

"Elizabeth!" Leah passed, carrying a tray of roasted potatoes. "You're just in time. Thomas is about to say the blessing." She set the tray on the counter and bustled into the dining room.

Apparently, they were content to have my celebratory dinner without me. I washed my hands and dried them on my skirt as I hurried to the dining room.

Everyone was seated around the dining room table, which had two long benches on each side to accommodate the younger children. Thomas sat at the head, with Dinah and Patty on his right. Leah waved me over to the seat beside her.

Thomas's gaze rested on me for a long, uncomfortable moment before drifting over the children. One by one, they fell silent. It was a useful trick, and one I'd never managed to successfully imitate. When he had everyone's attention, he said, "Let us pray." Everyone folded their arms and bowed their heads.

"Heavenly Father, we thank you for this food and for those who have lovingly prepared it. Please bless it so that it will nourish and strengthen our bodies. We thank you for the gift of family and ask you to watch over those who have left us to do work in your name. We also thank you for your servant, Elizabeth, who has embarked on a new journey. We say these things in the name of Jesus Christ. Amen."

"Amen," we all echoed. Dinah dabbed at her eyes.

Was she thinking about her oldest sons? Thomas's mention of family members who had left home to "do other work" might have dredged up unhappy thoughts for her. Although Theron and Bragg seemed to have fallen into favor with their father and the rest of the Priesthood Council, they hadn't lived at home for close to five years. Once boys reached their early teens, they were put to work—the idea being that young men were too hormonal and unpredictable to be left idle for any amount of time.

The church assigned them to work crews and housed them in military-style barracks on the edge of town. They kept a grueling schedule that had them up before dawn, with little time for hobbies or entertainment.

Jackson had let it slip that this was the reason Dinah's oldest, Tom, had run away. Thomas had forbidden anyone to so much as say Tom's name. He'd even been the one to stand up in meeting and ask the prophet to excommunicate his oldest son.

Dinah met my gaze. The softness fled her face. She lifted her chin and turned to Thomas. "Thank you, Father. Let's eat, everyone, before it gets cold."

I WAS STANDING OVER THE SINK, SCRUBBING KETCHUP OFF PLATES, when I remembered it was my night with Thomas.

"Damn," I muttered, stripping the heavy plastic gloves off my hands.

"Better not let Brother Stafford hear you say that," Leah said as she passed behind me with a stack of clean bowls. Ermon Stafford, the oldest member of the Priesthood Council, was notorious for his dislike of swearing. He doled out repentance assignments to anyone who uttered even the mildest curse in his presence. I avoided speaking altogether when he was around, just to be safe.

Leah's bright red braid swayed against her back as she lifted the bowls over her head, aiming for one of the upper cabinets.

"Here," I said, taking them from her and placing them in the cabinet.

She grinned. "Show off."

"What's going on in here?" Dinah stood in the doorway, hands on her hips. "The children are finishing up homework. The noise is distracting them."

"Sorry," Leah and I said together.

As soon as Dinah stalked off, Leah and I hunched our shoulders and broke into stifled giggles. After a second, she grew abruptly serious.

"Elizabeth, are you sure about taking the fall for me with her?" She had cornered me as soon as dinner was over, worry plain on her face.

"Of course. Don't even worry about it."

"But you know how anal she is about sticking to the schedule."

I laughed. "I can't believe you just said anal."

Leah clapped a hand over her mouth. "I did, didn't I?"

"You did, but I promise I won't tell anyone." A rush of gratitude overwhelmed me. She had plenty of worries of her own, with Simon and her girls, but she'd never treated me like a burden or an interloper.

She grabbed the dish towel from my hands. "You better go." She glanced at the clock on the oven.

I nodded and untied my apron. She knew as well as I did that Thomas was a stickler for staying on schedule. He kept track of everything—even personal time with his wives—in his phone.

I rushed through the house and up the stairs to the loft. If I hurried, I'd get at least an hour to myself to read or knit before he arrived.

I was three chapters into a new book when his footsteps sounded on the stairs.

"How are you, dear?" he said, bending and kissing my

cheek. I caught a whiff of his signature aftershave, still present even after hours at a job site.

"Good." I smiled up at him, even though it felt strange to talk like this after we'd just seen each other at dinner.

He sat in his chair by the sofa and pulled a stack of paperwork out of the small bag he'd brought. He kept clothes in all four bedrooms, but he always liked to have a few essential items with him wherever he went. In a way, I felt bad for him, living like a nomad in his own houses.

"Do you mind if I do a little work?" he asked, crossing one leg over the other. He still wore his dress pants and crisp white oxford, but he'd rolled the sleeves up—his one concession to comfort. He pulled out his reading glasses and flipped open a beige file folder.

"Not·at all," I murmured, happy to get back into my book. He'd come for sex, and we both knew it, but we had to play out the fiction that we were an ordinary married couple enjoying a relaxing evening together. It was a rare night that we didn't make love during one of his visits. I suspected he viewed me as something of a challenge, since he'd never gotten me pregnant.

After a while, he looked up from the papers he was reading, which was my signal to stop reading, too.

Fatigue swept me, and I yawned.

"Are you tired?" he asked.

I shot him an apologetic smile. "Sorry. Yeah."

He got up and sat beside me on the sofa. "Long day?" He placed a hand on my kneecap. His manicured fingers were long and brown on the plain white cotton of my nightgown. He was meticulous about taking care of himself. For as long as I'd known him, he'd gotten his nails and eyebrows trimmed every two weeks at a men's salon in Jefferson City.

"Yes," I said. "But I liked it."

"Was it challenging?"

I thought it over. It was on the tip of my tongue to tell him about Brittney and Dr. Adgate and the long list of cleaning chores, but something made me keep it to myself. "Yes, but not in a bad way."

"Hmmm." He caressed my knee.

"What about your day?" He rarely spoke to me about work. I always got the sense he didn't think I'd understand what he did for a living. It seemed straightforward enough, but maybe I was missing something.

He tapped my knee. "I'd rather talk about your day." Another tap. "Specifically, what happened to cause you to neglect your work at home."

My stomach clenched. "What did Dinah tell you?"

His expression hardened. "Why don't *you* tell me what happened," he said.

I thought about telling him the truth but almost immediately discarded that idea. I couldn't do that to Leah. And he wouldn't believe me anyway. His blue eyes bored into me. No matter what I said, he'd already made up his mind that Dinah was right and I was wrong.

My cheeks heated. I hated never knowing when Dinah would strike. The worst part was, I'd have to face her in the morning, and I'd have to pretend I didn't notice her smirking at me, reveling in the fact that she could make my life miserable any time she chose. Thomas *never* sided against Dinah, never.

I mumbled my way through the story, my head bowed so he'd know I was contrite. And I was, not because I cared about lashing out at Dinah, but because I knew I wasn't getting out of this unscathed.

A warm hand lifted my chin. "You were disrespectful," he said.

I nodded, forcing myself to meet his eyes. My jaw moved against his fingers. "I'm sorry."

He released me and patted my hip. "Apologize to Dinah in

the morning." He stood, then gestured toward the bedroom. "Go get it."

My heart seized, then kicked into a furious rhythm. "Thomas, please," I said, hating the pleading note in my voice.

"Go get it, or I will."

I rose, and my nightgown fell to my ankles as I walked to the bedroom. I opened the top drawer of my dresser and removed the long, thin switch that lay nestled between pairs of socks and rolled up tights. It was light and springy, the kind of thin branch that made a whistling sound when it whipped through the air.

I returned to Thomas and handed him the switch. "Where?" I asked, my voice low and hoarse.

He exhaled. "Since this new job seems to have given you idle hands at home, the hand seems fitting, don't you think?"

I didn't answer. I just extended my right hand, palm up.

He waited about thirty seconds, which felt like thirty minutes. I flinched when he drew his arm back, then hissed when he brought the switch down once, twice on my open hand. It took a second for my brain to register the burning stings. As soon as it did, I curled my hand into a loose fist and cradled my arm to my middle.

Thomas stepped past me so I could recover in private. I blew on my hand and shook it a little, my breaths fast and uneven. When I heard the bathroom door shut and the shower turn on, I walked to the bedroom and slid under the covers. Tears ran down my temples and into my hair.

I wiped them away.

It wasn't the pain that made me cry, although a switching was certainly painful enough to justify tears. It was the whole humiliation of being punished by my husband like a naughty child. I knew it was wrong to feel that way. I certainly wasn't the only one in the family to feel a branch on my hand or backside on occasion. Thomas regularly took a switch to all the children, even the teens. I closed my eyes. Did he ever swat Dinah?

I tried not to think about such things. Picturing Thomas and Dinah together in any kind of intimate setting seemed wrong . . . like a voyeur spying on something sacred.

But I couldn't help wondering if he treated me differently than his other wives. I could have probably asked Leah, but we sort of had an unspoken pact to never discuss personal things like that.

The shower cut off. I kept my eyes closed and turned my head to the side. My hair, still damp from my shower earlier, was soaking my pillow, but I didn't care. A few minutes later, the mattress dipped by my hip.

"This pouting is unbecoming, Elizabeth."

I rolled to my back and turned my head so my gaze was even with Thomas's chest. It was impressive for a man his age: broad and muscular, with a sprinkling of black hair that was just enough to be masculine without straying into Sasquatch territory.

"I'm not pouting," I told his pecs.

He reached over and untied the silk bow holding the neckline of my nightgown together, then slipped a hand inside and cupped one of my breasts, weighing the plump swell in his palm. "Yes, you are," he said, his voice soft. He raised his blue eyes to mine and thumbed my nipple. "Why can't you mind your tongue with Dinah? You know how volatile she is."

I blinked. Was he actually acknowledging that Dinah was difficult? He never spoke badly of his first wife. "She doesn't like me."

He chuckled, a low warm sound in his throat. "She's jealous."

"Of what?" She held all the power. If Thomas was the dictator in the family, Dinah was his trusted lieutenant. *Which probably makes me a peasant.*

He was silent a moment while he tugged my nightgown down my shoulders, exposing my breasts and belly. He lingered over my chest, circling a fingertip around each nipple. The cool air made my nipples contract, and he plucked at the puckered tips.

He made an appreciative sound, then dragged the nightgown to my ankles.

Now I was bared to him.

Goose bumps broke out across my arms. I wanted to rear up and grab the covers, but I forced my hands to stay at my sides while he looked his fill. He traced a fingertip around one areola, then the other, before leaning over and taking a nipple into his mouth. "Of this," he said against my skin. He sucked lightly, his teeth teasing the peak to a hardened point.

It took me a minute to realize he'd answered my question. I looked down at the top of his dark head. We never discussed sexual jealousy. It was a taboo topic in the community. Wives were supposed to fight and conquer those ugly feelings on their own.

He moved his mouth to the other breast and repeated the same treatment. "Of this," he said again. I lay still as he trailed his mouth down my stomach, then held my breath when he hovered over my pubic bone.

He rolled so his shoulders wedged between my thighs, then he forced them wider with his elbows. He lifted his gaze to mine. "Of this," he said, then lowered his head and kissed the soft flesh between my legs.

4

I winced as I picked up a bucket of hot, soapy water and race-walked it to the nurses' station. I'd grabbed the handle with my right hand without thinking. The cleaner stung my palm, which still smarted from last night's switching.

I clenched my jaw and hung on long enough to set the bucket down without spilling water everywhere.

I leaned out over the chest-high counter and looked up and down each side of the hall. There was no sign of Brittney, so I plopped in one of the chairs.

Thanks to yesterday's cleaning spree, my body ached in just about every place possible. I studied my palm. The skin was welted, but not broken. It would heal in a couple days, leaving me with nothing but a memory of the consequences of crossing Dinah.

Surprise, surprise, she'd been gracious at breakfast.

Of course, that was after I apologized for my outburst over the garbage cans. The children had bustled around in the nearby kitchen. Their presence usually stopped her from being outright cruel. Still, they knew how she felt about me—the older boys especially. Before they'd left home for their mission work, Theron and Bragg had taken to treating me with the same thinly veiled condescension. But the gleam in their eyes had taken on a more sinister feel. I'd grown up with enough stepbrothers to know their interest wasn't brotherly. It was a relief when they finally moved out.

I sucked in a breath, then stood and began clearing the desk attached to the nurses' station. I paused, stapler in hand, so I could yawn into my elbow. Thomas hadn't let the incident with Dinah stop him from performing his marital duties. We made love three times over the course of the night. I woke sore and sticky between my legs, my head fuzzy from the night of broken sleep.

When I was ovulating, he always insisted I stay in bed after he finished to maximize my chances of conceiving. I wanted to tell him the chances of that happening after five years of marriage were slim, but I knew he wouldn't appreciate my opinion.

I crouched and put the stapler in a cardboard box on the floor. I could expect at least two more nights of his company. Dinah's meticulous ovulation charts were never wrong. If she said this was the best time for me to get pregnant, Thomas would have already put it in his calendar.

Just then, a familiar light brown ponytail bobbed into view.

"What are you doing?" Natalie peered over the counter.

I straightened. "Hey! I'm just . . ." I looked at the mess. "It's not as bad as it looks." I waved my sponge around. "I'm just giving it a spring cleaning."

"This pigsty probably needs it. When's your lunch break?"

I jiggled a computer mouse so I could see the time on the monitor. "Right now, actually."

"Excellent. Come on, I'll show you the cafeteria." Then she put up a hand. "One second, let me grab my purse." She took off down the hallway before I could say anything.

I stood, sponge in hand, soapy water dripping onto the

counter. Maybe lunch was a bad idea. What if Brittney came looking for me?

Natalie returned, a sparkly black tote slung over her shoulder. She looked at my face and stopped. "What's wrong?"

"I don't know." I swallowed. "Brittney said to take a lunch at twelve, but . . ."

Natalie raised an eyebrow. "Did she say, 'Elizabeth, you are absolutely forbidden to go to the cafeteria with Natalie'?"

"No, but—"

"Then move your ass. I'm starving."

"IT'S REALLY NOT A CAFETERIA, SO MUCH AS A GLORIFIED SNACK bar," Natalie said as she led me across the sunny atrium.

"It's beautiful," I murmured, slowing so I could look up at a huge leafy tree. Its big branches stretched all the way to the second-floor railing. There were a dozen others just like it scattered throughout the atrium, which featured a glass ceiling that poured sunlight over everything. Here and there, park benches sat in the shade of the giant trees. A rectangle-shaped planter dominated the center of the space. It was filled with tall green stalks topped by tightly furled flower buds.

Natalie followed my gaze, then gave me an odd look. "Yeah, I guess it's not so bad, if you like mall decor or something. It's a good place to park surgery patients while they're waiting for their ride. If they puke out here, it's maintenance's problem."

She tugged the short sleeve of my scrub top. "Come on, nature lover. I need coffee."

The "glorified snack bar" turned out to be a sunny, spacious room just off the atrium. Instead of trees and benches, it was filled with small round tables and comfortable chairs. People in various colors of scrubs waited in line for food and sat around eating and talking.

Natalie dumped her bag on a table and announced she was "off to raid the coffee bar." I watched her go, then opened my brown paper bag and pulled out my sandwich and apple.

As I bit into my sandwich, I let my eyes drift shut. Domineering and unpredictable she might be, but Dinah was a fabulous cook. She would have died before allowing store-bought bread in her house.

The cafeteria wasn't quiet, but it was still peaceful. Having spent all my life surrounded by people, there was comfort in the soft swell of chatter, the beeping sounds of the cash register, and the other random noises of a bustling common area.

I was halfway through my sandwich when a shadow fell over me, and a familiar deep voice said, "Mind if I sit down?"

I looked up. Dr. Adgate stood at my side, a red plastic tray in his hands. I swallowed, and my bite stuck in my throat.

Then I started coughing.

He sprang into action, setting his tray down and rounding the table in one smooth movement. He struck me between the shoulder blades.

I waved a hand. "Not . . ." Another violent coughing fit seized me.

He struck again, harder this time. Any second, he was going to haul me up and try the Heimlich maneuver.

"Not . . . choking." I gasped between coughs, my eyes watering uncontrollably. "Just . . . went down . . . the wrong way."

"Here." He grabbed the soda from his tray, popped the tab, and handed it to me.

I took a few sips, which forced the food down. Look at that, I managed a whole ten seconds without coughing.

Maybe if I sat very still, a hole would open under my chair, and I could disappear.

"She okay?" A heavyset black woman in purple scrubs

looked between me and Dr. Adgate. She and a few other people had rushed over as soon as I started coughing.

Dr. Adgate sent me a questioning look, and I nodded. I turned to her and managed a raspy "yes" between sporadic coughs. She gave me a lingering, concerned look before dispersing with the others.

"Are you really all right?" Dr. Adgate asked. He pulled out a chair and sat, his body angled toward mine. His hand hovered in the air near my shoulder for a second, but he withdrew without touching me.

I put my elbows on the table and leaned my forehead against my hands. "I'll tell you after I'm done dying of embarrassment."

His soft chuckle brought my head up. He regarded me with kind grayish eyes and a lopsided smile that showed even, white teeth. "Look on the bright side. If you had to pull a Mama Cass, at least you did it in the right place. There are at least twenty people in here qualified to perform the Heimlich."

I must have given him a blank look, because he added, "Cass Elliot? The Mamas and the Papas."

For the life of me, I had no idea what he meant. "I'm sorry . . ." I shook my head.

He waved a dismissive hand. "Sorry, it was a bad joke. They were a band in the sixties." He gave a little laugh and ran a hand through his hair. "There was this rumor the lead singer died from choking on a sandwich."

"That's horrible." I looked down at my half-eaten sandwich. "What a way to go."

"Yeah."

We stared at each other for a few seconds. Then, as if on cue, we both burst into quiet laughter. My eyes watered all over again, and I clutched my stomach. The whole situation was so absurd, it just made me laugh harder.

He recovered before I did, his laughs winding down until he just smiled at me.

Eventually, I got control of myself. He waited, amusement still evident in his eyes. The sun streaming through the windows lit up his face and made his blond hair shine. He was boy-next-door handsome, with even features and a squared-off jaw.

There was nothing boyish about him, though. His broad shoulders were proof he was all man.

And I was staring at them.

I jerked my gaze away as heat crept up my neck. I gestured to the soda. "I'm sorry about your drink."

"What?" He looked at the can as if he'd never seen it before.

"I drank some of it." I gave a little shrug. "I mean, you can't have it now."

He grinned. "Don't be silly. I don't care about that." As if to prove his point, he picked it up and took a big swig. "You don't have cooties, do you?"

"No, I think I'm cootie-free."

He winked at me. "I thought so." He took another sip, then set the can down and stared at it, his expression thoughtful. "I, uh . . . I wanted to apologize. For yesterday." He glanced at me. "What happened with Brittney."

I waved my hand. "Oh. It was nothing."

"No, you don't understand." He hesitated. "It's . . . Well, there's a backstory there. I'm sort of new here. I started about six months ago. Brittney, on the other hand, has worked at the center for ten years." He smiled, but this time there was no humor in it. "She has something of a reputation for running people out of here."

I rubbed my throat. "You mean, like she fires people a lot?"

"Yes and no." He seemed to think for a minute, as if trying to choose his words carefully. "She's very good at her job.

Someone in her position has to be tough, you know? But I think sometimes she can be too tough on people."

I'd definitely experienced that firsthand. It helped, though, to know it was just Brittney's personality and not anything I'd done.

And I could handle a little adversity, couldn't I? I'd learned how to navigate around three other women—each with her own unique traits and quirks—without losing my mind. If I could share a house with Dinah, surely I could manage six hours a day with Brittney.

"Anyway," Dr. Adgate said, "the real reason I approached you today was to start over." He gave a self-deprecating laugh. "I definitely didn't give you the best first impression yesterday, dragging you into that dog-bite case."

"Oh, no." I leaned forward. "I loved it. I mean, I obviously didn't love that Sam was hurt, but I loved helping out."

He smiled. "How did you know, by the way? About him loving Spider-Man?"

"Just a lucky guess. He had on Spider-Man underwear, so . . ." I shrugged.

"Well, you handled the situation perfectly. Not everyone in our profession is good at connecting with patients. Really, that's what this job is about."

It was like someone turned on a heat lamp above my head. His words wrapped around me like a warm blanket. He said "our profession" as if the work each of us did was equally important. After two days of scrubbing floors on my hands and knees, it was a welcome sentiment.

He stuck out his hand the same way he'd done outside the exam room. "Now that I got my apology out of the way, let's start over—for real this time. I'm Evan Adgate."

The gesture surprised a laugh out of me, and I took his hand without thinking. The second he squeezed, pain shot through my palm and up my arm. I tried to cover my wince, but he saw it and immediately loosened his grip.

"What is it? Did I hurt you?" He started to turn my hand over.

"Nothing." The word jumped from my mouth. I tugged, but he captured my hand with both of his. The welts were angry, red slashes on my palm.

His expression went from teasing to clinical.

"You've injured yourself." He looked up. "How did this happen?"

I rolled my eyes. "It's silly. I lifted something heavy at home."

His gave moved over my hand. "It doesn't look like a stress injury." His touch was featherlight but assured as his fingers examined the raised skin.

I tugged harder, and he released me. "It's not a big deal."

He looked like he wanted to say more, but Natalie chose that moment to reappear, two steaming cups of coffee in her hands.

"Hey, sorry that took so long. I went outside to smoke and decided to run next door." She sat one of the cups in front of me. "Trust me, I'm doing you a favor. The coffee in this place is like flavored cat piss." She flopped in one of the chairs and turned her attention to the doctor. "I would have gotten you one, too, if I'd known you were going to grace us with your presence."

"Actually," I said, "he can have mine." I shot an apologetic glance at Natalie. "I don't drink coffee."

Natalie gave me a look like I'd just announced I didn't breathe oxygen. "What kind of sick freak are you?" She looked at Dr. Adgate and circled her finger around her ear in a "crazy" gesture.

He laughed. "The surgery department runs on caffeine," he told me. "It's something of an occupational hazard."

"You got that right," Natalie said.

We spent the next half hour listening to her describe every person in the surgery department in hilarious detail. The way she told it, each one was either incredibly annoying or mentally unhinged.

She had an especially poor opinion of the anesthesiologist who handled most of their cases, calling him "a misogynistic a-hole." Although I suspected most of her tales were exaggerated, they were definitely entertaining. I laughed until my sides hurt.

Dr. Adgate just shook his head. He cast me the occasional exasperated look, but the small smile playing around his mouth told me he liked Natalie.

The time flew, and I felt a pang of regret when the cafeteria started to clear out.

Natalie checked her watch. "Ah, back to the old grind." She stood and piled all her trash onto a plastic tray. "I have to assist with a vasectomy in twenty minutes." She made a little snipping motion in the air.

I wadded up my brown paper bag. "I should go, too."

"I'll walk you up," Dr. Adgate said, standing with his own tray.

Natalie raised her eyebrows at me while his head was turned. I braced for a teasing comment, but she simply gathered her purse and coffee and gave us a friendly wave on her way out.

"Are you sure you don't want me to take another look at that hand?" Dr. Adgate asked as we rode the elevator to the second floor. It felt much smaller than all the other times I rode in it. The sleeve of his white coat brushed my arm.

"Oh, no. It's fine, I promise." I changed the subject before he could insist. "Thank you again for helping with my coughing fit."

He smiled down at me, warmth in his grayish eyes. "No problem. You'll just have to buy me a soda at lunch tomorrow."

My stomach did a little flip that had nothing to do with the lurch of the elevator as it reached our floor. He stepped out and held the door while I exited.

He fell into step beside me as we moved down the hall, his hands in his scrub pockets.

After a period of silence, he glanced at me. "How's it going around here? I didn't get a chance to ask at lunch. Do you like it? I'm usually so busy running from patient to patient, I don't get much time to slow down and talk."

"It's an exciting experience," I said. Anything, even scrubbing floors, was more exciting than Riverview Heights. "I have a lot more to learn, but I like the work—" I stopped short at the sight of Brittney. She was behind the nurses' station, which was now piled with all the supplies I'd moved.

"Excuse me," I told Dr. Adgate, then went to the nurses' station as fast as I could without running.

"Hey," Brittney said at my approach. "Did you have a nice lunch?" Her voice was crisp and professional.

"Yes." My stomach knotted. She had finished the cleaning and was now putting all the office supplies back in place. "Brittney, I can do this."

"It's fine. I'm almost done." She flashed Dr. Adgate a smile as he walked up. "It's my mistake, really," she said, her voice now directed more toward him. "I should have told you to save this task for when you had enough time to finish it without any breaks. We can't run this department without a functioning nurses' station. I assumed you would know that." She reached for one of the flat screen computer monitors on the tall counter in front of her.

"Here, let me." Dr. Adgate lifted it out of her grasp. He

carried it around the station and set it on the desk. Brittney thanked him and caught his sleeve before he could turn away. "We got two new ones over lunch. A migraine and a sprain that might be a break."

I waited while they discussed the two new patients she'd put in exam rooms for him to treat. Their conversation was easy and familiar, and it was obvious they had worked together long enough to develop a rapport. She rattled off a stream of unfamiliar medical terms, and he nodded and scribbled down notes on a small pad he pulled from his coat pocket.

"Call radiology and let them know I might be sending someone down, will you?" he told her as he headed in the direction of the exam rooms, sparing a brief nod for me as he passed, a closed, focused look on his face.

Brittney resumed straightening up.

I gnawed my lower lip. "Can I help with anything?"

She threaded the wires protruding from the back of the monitor through a small hole punched in the desk. "I'm just about finished here. Gloria can hook all this up. We were forced to chart on paper while everything was down."

"I'm really sorry about leaving it like this during lunch."

She straightened. "I hope you're sincere about that." A ghost of a smile touched her lips. "Listen, Elizabeth, I know it's exciting to get attention from someone like Dr. Adgate, but I trust you won't let that interfere with your responsibilities."

My cheeks burned. "Brittney, I assure you—"

She put up a hand. "I'm not interested in hearing excuses. Your private life is your own. This isn't the place to discuss such things."

"I'm not making excuses." Was she accusing me of something? If so, what, exactly? Her tone made it sound like I had a habit of divulging inappropriate details about my personal relationships, which was ridiculous, considering she'd known me

for two days. I took a deep breath, but she spoke before I could
say anything.

"You have nothing to worry about as long as your work gets
done." She handed me the clipboard with my list of tasks.
There were two items that hadn't been there before lunch.

"I thought of a couple more things for you to do," she said.

I bet you did. I looked up from the list. "That's fine."

She bustled from behind the nurses' station. "Also, Elizabeth. I should have mentioned this before, but you need to pin
up your hair. That long braid is unacceptable in a medical
setting. Try some bobby pins or something."

I touched the back of my hair, which I wore in my
customary french braid. The tail reached my lower back, but it
usually stayed well out of the way. She held my gaze until I
dropped my hand and nodded, then she smiled and walked off
toward the exam rooms.

5

I was so busy the rest of the week, I didn't have much time to worry about Brittney or her mind games. Determined to work my way through every one of the items on her list, I ignored the aches and pains that reminded me how much time I spent cleaning instead of using my training.

It was fitting I wore scrubs, I thought as I wiped down the cabinets in one of the exam rooms, since most of my tasks involved scrubbing something.

But there was one bright ray of hope.

After that second day, Natalie had appeared promptly at noon and pestered me until I agreed to lunch. I told myself not to look for Dr. Adgate. But he'd been there, right at the same table, the same warm smile on his handsome face.

As we approached, he stood and pulled out two chairs in an old-fashioned gesture that made my heart pound.

"Ladies," he said, "I enjoyed your company so much yesterday, I propose we make this a daily event."

Since then, my days had fallen into distinct halves: there was the time before lunch, when I looked forward to seeing him, and there was the time after lunch, when I reviewed everything he said and did when we were together.

A little voice of caution in the back of my mind warned this was a dangerous habit, but I pushed it aside. It was one hour a day, nothing more. And it wasn't like he was interested in me as anything other than a friend. He showed the same gentle, courteous attentiveness to Natalie—a happily married woman with a teenage daughter.

Still, I couldn't help but notice how gray and dull the weekend was without that magical hour.

Saturday passed as it usually did, with a steady rotation of chores, most of which took place in Dinah's kitchen. The prophet was joining us for the Sunday meeting the following day, so she was on a one-woman mission to cook everything in Missouri.

Everyone in the community would be there to hear him speak and bring news and announcements from our headquarters in Illinois. Although he sometimes returned home directly after, there was a chance he would stay the night. Because Thomas was unofficially his second in command, he'd almost certainly stay at Dinah's.

All of this meant she was beside herself, turning the house upside down in a fit of cleaning. She ordered me to take down all the curtains, wash and iron them, then hang them back up. As soon as I finished, she had me flip every mattress in the house.

"Does she think he's going to try out all the beds and decide which one he likes best?" I asked Leah.

She laughed. "Maybe we should make porridge instead of ham and fried chicken."

On the bright side, Dinah was so busy cooking and baking and cleaning, she had no time to scrutinize everything I did. After I finished with the mattresses, I sneaked upstairs and relaxed on the sofa with a book.

I'd just turned to the final chapter when a car door slammed outside. I dog-eared the page and went to the window.

Thomas helped an elderly man in a white cowboy hat up the front porch steps. I hurried to the bathroom and washed my hands and face, then unraveled my hair and rebraided it. I was snapping an elastic around the tail when I heard Dinah yell up the stairs.

"Coming," I said under my breath.

I'd rolled up my sleeves to do dishes, so I hastily unrolled them and buttoned the cuffs as I made my way downstairs.

"Ah, here's Elizabeth," Thomas said. He stood with the prophet in the living room. Dinah, Patty, and Leah sat on one of the sofas behind them. Dinah's mouth formed into the thin white line she always wore when she disapproved of something.

I stepped forward, my hands clasped, my gaze directed at the men's feet. "Prophet Benson, I hope your journey was comfortable."

The old man's chuckle brought my head up. "Looks like an angel, doesn't she, Thomas? But there's a devilish streak behind those pretty blue eyes."

Thomas's smile was wan. "Elizabeth is spirited, Prophet, but I have her well in hand."

Hands clasped, eyes down. It's what my mother always whispered when the prophet visited. Or my stepfather. It was better to go unnoticed, to blend into the background.

But that was hard to do when Thomas and Prophet Benson talked like I was an unruly child . . . or a prize cow.

I stared at a spot on the carpet until my vision blurred. Prophet Benson's gaze was like a spotlight on the top of my head. He'd known my parents—had been the one who ordered my mother reassigned to my stepfather after he excommunicated my biological father.

My sad, beautiful mother had lived in desperate poverty, the eleventh wife of a man old enough to be her grandfather, because she'd angered the prophet.

She'd protected me as much as possible from her sister-wives, but the whole community had known about us. Once you fell out of favor with the prophet, you were treated like the lowest creature on earth. There was no escaping the knowing looks and loud whispers.

After my mother died, I'd assumed he'd forgotten about me —but I was wrong. He remembered, and he treated me like any other commodity. As soon as I became useful, he traded me for something more valuable.

I dared a glance at Thomas, who had turned toward the prophet as they continued talking. Did he remember the prophet warning him about my supposedly tainted blood? As a member of the Priesthood Council, Thomas was a frequent visitor to the faith's headquarters.

The night Prophet Benson announced he'd found me a husband, I'd been astonished to find myself standing in his immaculate living room, face-to-face with the most handsome man I'd ever seen. He was older, yes, but I'd expected that. Few girls got to marry a man their own age, and if they did it was because they were the privileged daughters of powerful men in the community. Those kinds of girls became first wives, with all the legal protection and authority that came with such status.

No, I was never going to be a first wife. I'd assumed I would end up like my mother, forced to sleep with a man more interested in me as a nurse than a spouse.

But Thomas had exceeded all my expectations. He'd cupped my chin and lifted my head, forcing my gaze to his. "Are you frightened of me?" he'd asked in a soft voice.

"No," I'd whispered, because how could anyone so beautiful be bad? "Not of you."

He'd seemed to understand, even without me looking toward the corner, where the prophet watched us. "Are there any questions you would like to ask me?"

"Um . . ." Dozens, but he didn't really mean for me to ask anything I wanted. Normally, when people asked if you had questions, they just wanted to make sure you understood what they expected of you. So I settled for the one that seemed the most important. "How many wives do you have?"

He smiled. "You will be the fourth. Is that acceptable to you?"

Fourth. It was better than eleventh. It was better than living at the prophet's mercy. Better than avoiding my stepfather every time he came around, hoping he didn't notice me.

I looked at the handsome, distinguished man who smelled of soap and spice and nodded. "It's acceptable."

There was no courtship, no dates, not even a minute alone prior to the ceremony. We said our vows in the prophet's home, in front of a handful of witnesses. Prophet Benson informed everyone that I was a sinful woman from a bloodline of sinners, and that it was a mercy Thomas had agreed to take me on.

Despite the three hundred or so miles between my old home and my new one, that attitude had followed me. Dinah had taken one look at me and decided I would bring the whole family down if given the chance.

She watched me now, her lips pressed so firmly together they were in danger of disappearing altogether. Even after five years, I think she still hoped my marriage to Thomas was temporary.

The prophet clapped Thomas on the back. "You're a lucky man, Brother Thomas, to have so many beautiful wives. Heavenly Father has shone you his favor."

An interesting observation, considering the prophet was the one who decided when and whom men in the faith were

allowed to marry. I lingered in the living room as the men left
and Dinah tossed out orders to Patty and Leah.

Finally, she turned to me. "What are you doing just
standing there, Elizabeth? There are a thousand more things to
do before dinner."

I swallowed a sigh. "Just tell me what you need, Dinah."

She narrowed her gaze. "A little less attitude for a start," she
said, but there wasn't much heat behind it. She looked
distracted for a minute, then rattled off a list of things for me
to do.

I HAULED THE LAST BAG OF ICE UP THE BASEMENT STEPS AND
dragged it across the kitchen floor.

"Careful with that, Elizabeth," Dinah barked over her
shoulder. "You'll rip the bag doing it that way."

I almost stuck my tongue out at her long, dark braid, but I
saw Patty look at me from where she stood peeling carrots over
one of the side counters. She flicked an orange shaving off her
knife, her knowing gaze telling me she'd read my thoughts.

"This lemonade is ready, Elizabeth," Dinah said, placing a
big glass pitcher on a metal tray. "Take this into Father's study
and come right back."

I wiped the sweat off my forehead with the back of my hand
before sliding the heavy tray off the counter. As I walked toward
the back of the house, my steps slow and measured to keep
from spilling the sloshing yellow liquid, I tried to calculate how
many times Dinah said my name out loud on an average day.
*Elizabeth, go make the beds. Elizabeth, you're doing that wrong. Eliz-
abeth, put that down. Elizabeth, Elizabeth, Elizabeth.*

After a while, it just became part of the constant background noise of the house.

Low, muffled, masculine voices drifted from beneath the

closed door outside Thomas's study. This was a place I rarely ventured, since it was right next to Dinah's bedroom. She didn't like me anywhere near her private space.

I knocked the toe of my boot against the bottom of the door. At least Dinah hadn't balked at me wearing shoes while I lugged heavy bags of ice up from the basement. She probably realized I'd be no good to her as a servant if I broke my foot.

Thomas called out for me to enter.

I looked at the knob . . . then at the tray. How on earth was I going to hold this thing and open the door at the same time?

Thomas called *enter* again.

I shifted the tray so it rested against my hip. With one hand, I turned the knob and flung open the door. It slammed into the doorstop, then bounced off with a shudder.

Thomas gave me a disapproving look from behind his desk. "Well, Elizabeth, you certainly know how to make an entrance."

"I'm sorry." I walked to his desk and plunked down the tray before my arms gave out. A little lemonade sloshed from the pitcher onto the small, white paper napkins Dinah had arranged in a fan shape off to one side. I grabbed a few and blotted the dots of liquid off the tray.

Prophet Benson observed me from his chair in front of Thomas's desk.

"You cut a fine figure, Elizabeth. Nearly as fine as your mother." His eyes roved up and down my body. He'd removed the cowboy hat, revealing a thick head of black hair.

It had to be dyed. He was at least seventy-five years old. Age had caught up with him since the last time I saw him. The hands resting on his thighs were gnarled and bony, with thick knuckles and prominent veins.

I stepped back from the desk and met his gaze. "I'm surprised you remember, considering we didn't attend meetings after she was reassigned."

His pale, rheumy eyes glinted, and his expression shifted

from one kind of assessment to another. Where he'd been focused on my body before, now he sized me up as an actual, thinking person.

We both knew I referred to his ban on my mother attending meetings. He hadn't excommunicated her, but his edict had cut her off from any support she might have received from the community. Without money or access to medical care, she died far sooner than she should have, and under miserable conditions.

His fault. His hand twitched on his thigh. Would he strike me for speaking out of turn? Rumor had it he was quick to discipline his wives.

Thomas cleared his throat. "As you were saying, Prophet?"

The tension broke. I lowered my gaze and let out an unsteady breath.

Prophet Benson slapped his thigh. "What's that, Thomas? Ah, yes, your girl, Daria. I think she'll do well in Utah."

I jerked my head up. "You're marrying off Daria?" I looked at Thomas. "She's too young."

"Elizabeth." Thomas scowled.

"Does Dinah know about this?"

"Out." His voice was whisper soft, which meant he was furious. Thomas never yelled. He got quieter. His cold, seething hisses were somehow worse than yelling.

I grabbed the tray without making eye contact. The men were quiet as I walked to the door. Heart pounding, I closed it with a soft click and returned to the kitchen.

Dinah still bustled about, bending to stick a meat thermometer in a ham. She straightened, one hand flinging her braid back over her shoulder, then froze when she saw me standing in the doorway.

"What's wrong?" she asked, her forehead wrinkling. "Are you sick?"

"I . . . maybe." I pressed a hand against my stomach. "I don't know. May I be excused for dinner?"

Her gaze went to my midsection. Then she nodded. "All right. Go on up."

I fled upstairs before she could change her mind. Thomas was scheduled to be with Patty tonight. If I could avoid him for the next twenty-four hours, he'd be so busy with Prophet Benson, he'd probably forget all about the conversation in his study.

MY HEART RATE SLOWED AS I REACHED THE SAFETY OF MY bedroom. What was I going to do with all this free time?

I turned around in slow circle, and my gaze landed on my small bookshelf.

Oh yeah. Happiness was like a firework in my chest. Thomas and the others would be at dinner for hours. I could read a whole book without anyone interrupting me.

First, though, I needed a bath. After the long day of standing in a steaming kitchen, my skin itched all over. I'd worn my hair in two french-braided pigtails, so I pinned them up, dumped half a bottle of bath oil in my tub, and soaked until my fingertips wrinkled.

Afterward, I didn't even bother picking up my dirty clothes and wet towel off the floor—I just dropped a nightgown over my head and climbed into bed. I dug my book from under my pillow and relaxed back with a contented sigh.

I was so engrossed in the story, my brain didn't even register the footsteps on the stairs until Thomas crossed the threshold.

"Feeling better?"

"Thomas!" I closed the book without marking my place and stuffed it under the pillow. "Yes. Th-Thank you." My heart jumped into my throat. He wasn't due to visit me until tomorrow night. That meant he'd come for other reasons.

Judging from his face, I could guess what for.

He stared at me from the foot of my bed, his hands resting on his hips. "What were you thinking, Elizabeth, speaking like that to the prophet?"

"I'm sorry—"

He slashed a hand through the air. "I don't want to hear excuses. I should tan your backside, girl."

My heart stuttered. He'd only done that a couple of times, early in our marriage, and each time had been almost too humiliating to bear. I clenched my hands in the quilt. A surge of nausea burned the back of my throat.

A long minute passed before he sighed, then ran a hand through his hair. He left his hand on the back of his neck and said, "Is it this new job that's made you so bold?"

"What? No!" My heart threatened to pound from my chest. He could stop me from working. He could do anything he wanted.

His gaze drifted over me. "Dinah said you weren't feeling well. Is that true?"

"It was just my stomach. I'm feeling better."

He rounded the bed and sat, his hip pressed against mine. I drew my knees up, and the quilt draped over them like a tent. The light from my nightstand highlighted the gray at his temples. He looked tired. The lines bracketing his eyes and mouth appeared deeper than usual.

He pulled the quilt down to my feet and wrapped a warm hand around my ankle, preventing me from straightening my legs.

"You still have hate in your heart about what happened in Illinois." He gave my ankle a squeeze. "Elizabeth, the prophet is God's representative on earth. You shame your mother's memory by holding on to this anger."

I stiffened. "He shamed her enough while she lived."

"Consider for a moment that you don't know the whole story. Don't you think it's possible your judgment is clouded by your love for your mother? Sometimes, we allow our affection for others to blind us to the truth."

I figured I knew enough. I was ten years old when my father was forced to leave town, leaving my mother and me at the mercy of Prophet Benson. I still dreamed of her sobbing as she packed the few belongings we were allowed to take from our home. I'd never told Thomas anything about my childhood, and he'd never asked. As close as he was to Prophet Benson, he had to know the story. If anyone's judgment was clouded, it was his, not mine.

But I couldn't say that. So I gave him the answer he wanted to hear. "I guess anything is possible."

"That's a start." His hand moved up my calf, taking my nightgown with it. "My stubborn Elizabeth." He dropped his voice to a murmur, and he cupped his palm over my knee. "You are an unfailing champion of those you love. I've always known that. Do you love me, I wonder?"

"Yes, of course, Thomas." I watched his hand through the veil of my lashes. What was he doing? He was rarely seductive, and then only if he was scheduled to be in my bed.

My nightgown puddled around my waist. I pushed it down.

He continued his path up my thighs, then dipped his hand between them.

"Thomas." I wore nothing beneath the plain cotton nightgown, and he had a clear view between my legs. I tried to press my thighs together, but he shook his head.

"Be still." He rucked the nightgown up to my waist and rested a warm hand over my flat belly. His blue gaze met mine. "Do you think you might be pregnant?"

"I . . ." I cleared my throat. "It's still too early to tell." This was why he'd reined in his anger over Prophet Benson. My lie to Dinah had saved me this time.

He made a noncommittal noise in his throat, his gaze still on the private place between my legs.

I took a deep breath. "You're supposed to be with Patty tonight."

His black brows snapped together. "You think I don't know that?"

A wild, humorless laugh bubbled up my throat as I pictured the phone in his back pocket buzzing with a reminder of which bedroom to sleep in. What happened if he rearranged the schedule without updating it? The laugh threatened to spill out as I imagined a thin trail of smoke seeping out of the phone as it self-destructed.

I tried to think of something else—anything to stop myself from bursting into inappropriate laughter and riling his anger again, so I said the first thing that popped into my mind.

"Thomas, what are you planning for Daria?"

He pulled back. The glow of desire fled. "How is that any of your business?"

I pulled my nightgown over my legs. "I don't mean to pry." I arranged my face into what I hoped was a sincere expression. Which wasn't hard, considering I was truly sincere about my concern for his seventeen-year-old daughter. "Prophet Benson said Utah. It's so far . . . and she's so young."

He stood. He was silent a moment, as if considering how much he should tell me. "She and Kelly have always been close," he said finally. "Daria sees her sister wed and happy. She longs for the same."

I couldn't disagree with him about the sisters' closeness. Born just one year apart, they had grown up together—the only girls in a house with four active boys. Kelly seemed content. She already had one child and another on the way. But she lived a few miles down the road and spent half her time with Patty or her mother. Thomas was talking about shipping his teenage daughter to Utah, where she'd be surrounded by extended cousins who were little more than strangers—and a husband who might not be as indulgent as her father.

Thomas stepped close and pinched my chin between his thumb and index finger. "Dinah doesn't know yet, and I want to keep it that way. Understood?"

I nodded, but I couldn't help picturing the fallout that was likely to happen once Dinah learned he planned to send her daughter a thousand miles away. The Utah community was near a thriving metropolitan area, but it was the farthest in distance from the other four communities that made up our faith.

Dinah wasn't going to like this.

Thomas released me and started for the door.

"Who is the man?"

He stopped and turned, irritation stamped all over his face. "That is none of your concern, Elizabeth." His gaze dipped to my midsection. "I suggest you focus on what's important in your own life instead of meddling in the affairs of others."

The rebuke stung. How was it meddling to ask basic questions about the marriage of a teenager? The outside world didn't always view our lifestyle as positive or healthy. The Righteous Brethren made a lot of effort to integrate as much as possible with nonbelievers.

Avoiding underage marriages was a big part of those efforts. The Priesthood Council made a show of being open with outside authorities. Thomas was personal friends with nearly every major politician and administrator in Jefferson City. His company had built a new public building downtown just last year.

Why he would jeopardize those connections by marrying off Daria so young? What did he gain by that?

But I'd pushed my luck enough tonight. And he'd made it clear he didn't value my opinion.

No, my value lay in reproduction. I folded my hands over my stomach. "What if I'm not pregnant?"

His gaze flicked to the empty space on the bed beside me. "Then we'll just try again. I'll see you tomorrow."

6

Over the next month, I didn't have much time to think about secret weddings or anything else going on at home. Thrown right back into the hectic pace of work, I existed in a kind of repetitive haze: work, eat, sleep, repeat. Even Jackson noticed I was dragging.

"What do they have you doing at this place, anyway?" he asked on one of our drives into the city. "You look bad, Liz." He blanched. "I mean not *bad*. You never look bad. Tired, I meant. You look tired."

I laughed at his attempt to take back the insult. "It's okay. I *am* tired." As if my body wanted to prove my point, I yawned so big my jaw cracked. "It's busy work, mostly. They don't have a lot of staff, so we all have to pitch in when needed. There's always something to do."

No matter how tired I felt, I was determined to conquer Brittney's list. The problem was, it kept getting longer.

At first, I dismissed the additions as a temporary thing. Hadn't she said she jotted down the first few items off the top of her head?

The longer I worked with her, though, the more I suspected

the list was her way of wearing me down until I gave up and quit. It didn't make sense, because the center was woefully short-staffed, but I couldn't shake the feeling she wanted me gone.

She never said or did anything outright. I couldn't point to any one incident as definitive proof of her goal. It was more a death by a thousand cuts—little digs here and there that let me know she wasn't happy with my presence.

Late last week, for example, I found a package of hairpins in my locker, with a note reminding me to pin up my hair. I wouldn't have thought anything of it except I seemed to be the only person required to comply with this rule. Gloria's bob brushed her neck, and she was constantly pushing it back over her ears. Brittney herself usually wore her hair in a ponytail, but I'd seen it loose around her shoulders a couple times.

In the truck, I touched the double coronet I'd braided around my head. I'd stuck so many pins in the heavy mass, I wouldn't have been surprised if I started picking up radio signals.

As Jackson pulled into the center's parking lot, I gave a mental shrug.

I couldn't do anything to change Brittney's attitude, just as I couldn't do anything to change Dinah's . . . or Patty's.

I wasn't helpless, though, and I wasn't alone. My friendship with Natalie was new, but it felt real.

And there was Dr. Adgate, too. I had him, didn't I?

A smile tugged at my mouth. Our lunches had become the most important part of my day.

My life.

I bit my lip. It was so very dangerous to keep seeing him— even if it was just for an hour over a sandwich and a piece of fruit.

So very, very dangerous. I knew that.

Jackson pulled up to the center's door, and I looked at the building.

Yeah, I had no business having lunch with Dr. Adgate.

But I knew I wasn't going to stop, either.

～

ON TUESDAYS, THE CAFETERIA OFFERED A SPECIAL—TWO SOFT tacos for five dollars. They were huge and filling, with ground beef, fresh lettuce, and a liberal sprinkling of shredded cheese. Fixings were fifty cents extra. The whole building turned out for Taco Tuesday, and there was usually a line stretching out the door.

"I swear, I will start exercising, right after I'm done stuffing these in my face." Natalie moaned as she took a healthy bite of taco. Beef and cheese spilled out the other end and plopped on her plate.

Evan, who finally threatened to stop talking to me if I didn't start calling him by his first name, chuckled and patted his stomach. "I'm not embarrassed by my food baby. I flaunt it, loud and proud."

I looked down. My period had come and gone. Again.

Thomas seemed especially annoyed this time. I was due to ovulate in a couple days.

"Elizabeth, are you okay?" Evan's voice jolted me from my thoughts. He and Natalie wore identical concerned expressions.

I smiled, an excuse on my lips, when I saw Brittney approach our table, a tray in her hands. My smile froze.

"Mind if I join you today?" She sat before anyone could answer.

Natalie raised her eyebrows. "This is a surprise."

Brittney shrugged. "I guess I just wanted to see what all the fuss is about."

"You've never tried the tacos before?" Natalie asked. She

scooped a blob of beef off her plate with the edge of her tortilla and popped it in her mouth.

Brittney waved her hand. "Oh, probably a while ago." She looked at me. "I wanted to see why lunch is so popular now that Elizabeth is with us." She glanced at my brown bag lunch. "You don't like the tacos?"

"I'm not a big fan of Mexican food." It was the same lie I offered Natalie and Evan when they asked why I didn't partake in Taco Tuesday. Dinah gave me twenty dollars for any incidentals I might need for the month. I couldn't risk spending everything on lunch, no matter how good it tasted.

Skepticism burned in Brittney's kohl-lined eyes, but she let it go. She turned her attention to Evan. "I'm surprised to see you eating like this. Aren't you doing a race next week?"

"Two weeks." He looked at me. "I run a couple marathons a year."

Brittney bit into one of her tacos, somehow managing to make the otherwise messy act look ladylike and delicate. She swallowed and said, "Don't be modest, Evan. You're only one of the premier marathoners in the state." She leaned toward me, as if imparting a juicy secret. "You should see the medals in his condo. I was nearly blinded the first time I saw them."

My heart sank. In just a few sentences, she'd managed to tell me two important things: she knew private details about Evan no one else did, and she'd been to his home more than once.

I concentrated hard on my sandwich.

Evan's laugh had a sharp edge. "Yeah, well, that was a long time ago, Brittney. I doubt you got a very good look, considering you only stopped by a couple times."

"Not so long ago." Her voice was light.

Natalie looked between them and frowned. "Anyway," she said loudly, "now that you've been here a month and some change, what do you think of the place, Elizabeth? Is it everything you hoped it would be?"

"Everyone has been really kind."

Natalie snorted. "You should move to Washington and become a diplomat, because that was a bullshit answer if ever I heard one. This place is exactly like high school and you know it."

Brittney spoke up. "Oh, Elizabeth wouldn't know, actually. She didn't go to high school."

An uncomfortable silence descended over the table.

My cheeks burned. Then my throat burned. I took a sip of water.

Brittney clapped a hand over her mouth. "Oh gosh. I really put my foot in it, didn't I?" She touched my arm. "Elizabeth, I'm so sorry I let that slip."

"Really, Brittney?" Natalie said. She shook her head.

"What?" Brittney frowned. "I said I was sorry. Listen, this is why I'm not in HR."

I swallowed. "It's all right." I looked at Natalie and Evan. "It's true. I didn't go to high school. I do have my GED, though. My mom got really sick when I was about twelve. I took care of her." I lifted my chin. "I don't regret it. She died when I was sixteen. I'm glad I had those four years with her. That time is more important to me than anything I may have missed in school." I fixed my gaze on my lunch. "I tried to keep up with my education as best as I could. There was a library close to our house. The librarian let me check out as many books as I wanted."

The silence persisted. My cheeks were on *fire*.

Evan spoke, his voice quiet. "I lost my grandfather when I was in college."

I looked up. His gaze was kind, his gray eyes sincere.

"I know it's not the same," he said, "but we were close. He was like a second dad to me." He leaned forward, as if he wanted to make sure I knew his next words were for me alone. "There is no shame in making a sacrifice like that for someone you love. I envy you that time, Elizabeth. You made the right choice."

I stared into his eyes, my own filled with tears. "Thank you."

Brittney's light laugh intruded. "Well, I didn't mean to bring up bad memories."

Evan gave her a stony look. "I don't think it's necessary to keep talking about it." He rose and extended a hand to me. "We should get back. Can I walk you up, Elizabeth?"

As I let him help me up, Brittney's stare threatened to burn a hole in the back of my head. I murmured goodbye to the table in general and let him lead me from the cafeteria and across the atrium.

It was nice, walking with someone capable of matching my strides. One of the things Dinah complained about was what she called my "rangy walk." With Evan, I didn't have to shorten my steps. His long legs ate up the marble floor.

"Mind if we take the stairs?" he asked. The sunlight streaming through the windows touched the lighter pieces in his hair, turning the dark blond nearly as pale as mine.

I smiled. "Not at all."

"I hate elevators." He gave me a lopsided grin—the one I'd started to crave without realizing it.

He held the stairwell door. As I slipped past, he put a gentle hand in the small of my back, making the spot tingle.

"Listen, I'm sorry about what Brittney said back there," he said as we climbed the stairs. He shoved his hands in his coat pockets. He'd stuffed a stethoscope in one, and the silver binaurals caught the reflection of the overhead lights.

"It's okay. It doesn't bother me." Some impulse made me add, "I'm fully qualified. I mean, I have my certificate and everything."

He glanced at me. "I'm not worried about that. I knew from

that first encounter with Sam that you know what you're doing."

Warmth spread through me. "I'm the only one in my family who went to college." Sure, it was junior college, but holding that piece of paper in my hand had been like Christmas and my birthday at the same time.

When we reached the second floor, Evan paused, one hand on the latch of the center's door. His eyes were really more gray than blue. Like a clear winter sky.

He cleared his throat. "You said you used to check out books."

I nodded.

"There's a bookstore right next door. A big one."

"Yes, I've seen it."

He grinned. "It's kind of hard to miss. I thought maybe we could try lunch there tomorrow. It has bottomless coffee if you buy a mug." He held up a hand. "I know you're not a coffee drinker, but I'm pretty confident I can convince them to bend the rules and do the same thing for hot chocolate."

I almost said no. Brittney had sent quite a message by showing up at lunch today. She might have fooled the others with her story about letting my GED slip, but I knew better. I also knew there would already be hell to pay for walking out of lunch with Evan.

Staring up at him, though, I was overcome with a longing so intense it hurt. A physical hurt in my bones.

I'd never, not once, in my life had anything just for myself. I knew I couldn't have him—not really—but I could have some part of him, even if it was just stolen minutes in a surgery center cafeteria. The selfish part of my brain overrode the part that warned me I was walking directly into danger.

Then he smiled that lopsided smile, and I knew I was lost.

"Okay," I said. "I'd love to."

7

The bookstore was actually a three-story behemoth with several seating areas, a music section, and a big cafe that put the surgery center's cafeteria to shame. It took up most of the second floor and overlooked a children's wing on the ground level.

I smiled down at a trio of chubby toddlers sitting in a semi-circle on a colorful rug while a store employee read them a story from a rocking chair. Evan had gone to grab a coffee and a sandwich, which left me plenty of time to wonder just what I thought I was doing, meeting a man for lunch outside of work.

My stomach had been fluttering since I woke up—a feeling that had intensified when Evan instead of Natalie had shown up to escort me to lunch. He'd said she was too swamped to break for lunch today, so she told us to go ahead without her.

Suddenly, an innocent lunch among coworkers had turned into something suspiciously close to a date. Evan must have sensed my hesitation, because he offered to postpone our trip to the bookstore for another time.

"I just thought it might be nice to get away from this place, even if just for an hour," he said.

He didn't say Brittney's name, but I knew he had her in mind. A wave of anger had washed over me. Was I really that much of a doormat that I was content to let someone dictate who I talked to on my own time?

I'd accepted her objection to me working closely with Evan, because there was a rational reason behind it, even if I didn't necessarily agree with it. But there was no justification for her meddling with my break time—or whom I spent it with.

If I let her get away with that, I might as well quit right now, because my job would start to look exactly like my life at home.

As Evan waited for my decision, I wadded up the paper towel I'd been using to wipe down the patient beds. "Let me grab my purse."

Still, I hadn't been able to stop myself from glancing up and down the hall to make sure she didn't see us leaving. At the time clock by the locker room, it had taken me two tries to swipe my employee badge through the little card reader slot. The small beep had sounded as loud as a gunshot, and I'd expected her to appear out of nowhere and bar me from leaving the building.

Or for Evan to change his mind and say he'd rather not go to the bookstore after all.

None of that had happened, though, and now I sat at a small table, the smell of roasted coffee and pastries filling the air. I leaned my chin on my hand and let the sounds of the bookstore wash over me—the quiet buzz of conversation and the occasional cash register beep on the busier sales floor below. From the hushed reading area above came the soothing whisper of books being slid on and off shelves.

"Here, you look like you could use this." Evan set a steaming steel mug in front of me. "Not as much kick as coffee, but there's enough sugar in there to wake you up."

The mug was huge—one of the bottomless refill kind sold

by the bookstore's cafe. It was a soft purple, with a green *E* in script on two sides. I couldn't accept a gift from him.

"Evan . . ."

"I know you're not a coffee drinker, but who can say no to endless hot chocolate? It's probably the best in town. Besides, I've been eying that mug for myself, but it's not quite masculine enough for me." He raised sandy-blond eyebrows over the rim of his own mug as he took a sip.

I smiled and shook my head. "You shouldn't have gotten it. I still owe you a soda."

"You do not." His voice was firm. "Anyway, are you sure you don't want something to eat? My treat."

"Next time." I nudged the brown paper bag that held my sandwich and a granola bar. Then, to distract him from insisting on paying for lunch, I tried the hot chocolate. Sugar, cocoa, and a hint of vanilla hit my tongue.

I put down the mug. "This is amazing."

He looked smug. "Told you so."

I curled my hands around the mug, savoring the warmth. The temperature had been all over the place lately, as if the weather couldn't quite decide whether it wanted to be spring or summer. Today was unseasonably chilly for the first week of June, and I'd worn a dark gray turtleneck under my scrubs. "It's so peaceful here," I said, smiling as the toddlers downstairs began dancing to a song led by the employee who'd read to them.

"I thought you might like it," Evan murmured.

I looked back, and he was watching me, a smile in his eyes.

Pleasure curled low in my belly. "I love libraries. Anything to do with books, really. The one near my house as a kid was small, but the librarian was a kind woman. She used to give me the books they had pulled out of circulation. I guess I like the quiet . . . and the smell of old books."

He opened the plastic container that held his salad and

began rooting through it with a fork. "You would have loved the library at my college. I didn't appreciate it at the time, but I'd kill to go back there now. It was this old private school in Connecticut, and the library building was the oldest on campus —one of the oldest libraries in the country, actually."

"Is that where you're from originally? Connecticut?"

"Born and raised."

I tilted my head to the side. "Is it very different from Missouri?"

"At first, yeah. I was like a fish out of water." He hunted through the lettuce and speared a piece of grilled chicken. "I was really homesick the first couple months. Everything is different. The people, the terrain . . . even the buildings. It's the same with any big move like that. You know, the culture shock."

I didn't know, but I nodded, unwrapping my sandwich.

"I think it's just the pace of everyday life," he continued. "Things move a little more slowly here than they do on the coast. It hasn't taken me long to adjust, though." His face lit up. "I'm definitely in love with the land. Flat, even roads for miles. It's heaven on earth for a runner."

"I can't even imagine," I said. "The only time I run is when I'm being chased by bees."

He chuckled, and little laugh lines formed at the corners of his eyes. Far from taking away from his attractiveness, they lent his face a ruggedness when it might have otherwise been too smooth and clean cut.

He ate another bite of salad. "You might be surprised how well you do, if you ever give it a shot. You have the build for it."

"I do?"

He nodded, his eyes still amused, but now there was something else. "You're all legs and long lines . . ." He took a drink from his bottled water. "I'm sorry, Elizabeth. I didn't mean—"

"I'm not offended." I wanted to hear more. The compliments were like water on the desert of my soul.

I didn't know how to tell him that, though—not without sounding desperate or crazy. I looked back downstairs, where the children wandered through the brightly colored juvenile section. One tiny boy tugged his mother along by the hand, a determined look on his face.

Evan followed my gaze. "Do you like children?" he asked quietly. "You did so well with Sam."

"I do." I turned back to him. It was on the tip of my tongue to tell him I'd been surrounded by children my entire life, but that might open doors I'd rather not walk through, so I said, "What about you?"

His expression softened. "They're my best patients. I almost went into pediatrics, but I really wanted a chance to see a broad range of acute cases, so I stuck with family medicine." He grimaced and added, "Much to my father's chagrin."

I frowned. "Your dad didn't want you to be a doctor?"

Evan laughed, but there was little humor in it. "Oh, he was more than fine with me being a doctor. He just wasn't impressed with my choice of residency." He stabbed at a cucumber with his plastic fork. "Dad's a well-known cardiologist in New Haven. He always wanted us—my brother and me —to follow in his footsteps. He was very, ah, vocal about his disappointment when I chose not to."

Although he tried not to show it, I could tell his father's attitude still bothered him. It was there in the rigid set of his shoulders and the tightness of his mouth. I tried to think of something encouraging without sounding trite.

"I can't imagine any parent being disappointed by their son choosing to help people," I said.

Evan's eyes warmed. "My mom would like you. She was always supportive, no matter what we chose to do. She's a middle school guidance counselor—or at least she was. She retired a couple years ago. She was the one who stood up to dad when I chose cross-country over Yale."

"Yale." I gripped my mug. "As in, the college Yale?" Country bumpkin or no, even I knew Yale was one of the most prestigious universities in the country.

"The very same. It's something of a family tradition to go there." He gestured with his fork. "My grandfather, my dad . . . even my mom did her undergrad there. But I broke the mold. A tiny little school near my mom's house in Hartford offered me a full ride for cross-country." He shrugged. "My dad didn't talk to me for two years after I told him my decision."

My mouth fell open. "I'm so sorry, Evan." My heart hurt for him. I knew how it was to be without a parent. I just couldn't imagine any parent willingly giving up contact with a child, especially over something like that.

"It was a long time ago." He seemed to shake off a bad memory, because his expression brightened. "What about you? Did you always want to go into the medical field?"

I'd hoped to keep the conversation away from my private life, since there was so much I couldn't tell him. I kept my reply as vague as possible. "I took care of my mom for a long time. My parents divorced when I was ten. Mom died almost six years later. I wish I could have done more for her."

"It sounds like you did everything you could," he murmured. "Besides, you were just a child. May I ask how she died?"

Something in his eyes compelled me to say more than I normally would, and I found myself telling him things I'd never told anyone. Like how my mother had been diagnosed with MS shortly after I was born, and how her symptoms had been mostly nonexistent . . . until my father left.

I told him how I read to her out loud when her eyes failed, walking the three miles to the tiny town library to get new books after we exhausted everything on the shelves.

"She went downhill after my dad left," I said. "I think he kept her healthy. Once he was gone, she sort of gave up."

He'd placed his hand on top of mine as I spoke, and he gave it a gentle squeeze. "Divorce is hard, even when it's the right decision."

It wasn't her decision. But I couldn't reveal the truth without divulging all my secrets, so I nodded.

Then something he'd said made me ask, "You said you went to school near your mom's house. Were your parents divorced, too?"

"They separated when I was five, but they didn't make it official for another three years. According to my mother, Dad couldn't be bothered to drive forty minutes to sign the papers. She always said he was too busy saving lives to save their marriage. I guess she had a point."

"He sounds . . ." I searched for the right word.

"Conceited?" Evan's smile was tight. "Formidable? Domineering? He's all of those things, I assure you. But I've learned to find the good in him. It took the better part of thirty years, but I'm getting there."

We both looked down at the table, where his hand still covered mine. When I started to pull away, he grasped my fingers. "Elizabeth, would you meet me here again? Just us?"

"Just us." I tested that out, as if saying it out loud would help me decide how I felt about it.

"I don't want to pressure you, or make you uncomfortable. I can talk to Brittney, if that's what you're worried about." The interest he'd shown earlier returned, and he lowered his voice. "But I see no point in pretending I don't want to know more about you."

"I want to know more about you, too," I said before I could stop myself.

His lips curved into a lopsided smile, and I knew then that I would meet him again, even while the cautionary voice in my head warned that nothing good could come of it.

8

The more time I spent with Evan, the harder it was to tolerate being at home. The evenings dragged by, and I literally counted the hours until it was time to go to work again. We spent the rest of the week eating lunch at the bookstore, then a week turned into a month, and suddenly it was July.

He told me more about his family, which was small and quirky but close-knit. His older brother, Brian, had conceded to their father's wishes and specialized in cardiology. Like Evan, though, he'd forged his own path by moving to South Carolina, where he worked at a teaching hospital.

"I visit him a couple times a year," Evan had said over another salad. He'd grimaced at it when we first sat down, explaining that his diet was only this disciplined because he was preparing for a half marathon near Table Rock Lake, which he considered a "fun run."

He spoke fondly of his brother, who was five years older. "He and his wife have a beautiful home on the water."

"I'd love to see the ocean," I said. "The Missouri River doesn't quite cut it."

"Maybe I'll take you someday." The look in his eyes made it clear he wasn't just saying it to be polite.

Little things like that let me know I was getting in far over my head. Every day, I resolved to put some distance between us, or to find a way to let him know I wasn't exactly available.

And every day, I failed.

On the last Monday in July, he'd pulled a paperback from the black messenger bag he usually carried.

"I know you said you're into medical history." He placed it on the table. "I just finished this, and I think you'll like it." He tapped the glossy cover. "It's about a country doctor in World War Two. It's a fast read." He paused, then added, "I thought maybe we could talk about it over dinner later this week."

My gaze jumped from the book cover to his face. "Dinner?" My voice sounded half strangled.

He leaned back, a hesitant smile on his handsome face. "I'm still sort of new to town. I just thought . . ." His smile faded. "Elizabeth, if I've read you wrong, I'm sorry."

"No," I said quickly. "I mean, not no, I won't go with you. I meant, no, you haven't . . . No, you haven't read me wrong, I mean." I closed my eyes. "Can you please pretend you didn't just hear the foregoing sentence?"

He laughed. "I take that as a yes, then?"

"Yes," I said breathlessly, my eyes open now and staring into his. "I would love to go to dinner."

Leah's voice broke through my thoughts, jerking me into the present. "What is that you're reading, Elizabeth?"

I looked up.

She smiled at me from the other end of the sofa. We were in the big family room at the back of the house, waiting for the oven buzzer to sound so we could pull the lasagna out to cool and start making the rest of the meal.

Normally, Dinah would have never allowed anyone else to prepare the main dish, but she'd spent the last two days locked in her room. Thomas had finally broken the news about Daria's marriage, and it had gone about as well as I'd predicted, which wasn't well at all.

At least Daria was happy about it, I thought, watching her play with Kelly's one-year-old daughter on the floor. Kelly had spent the past few days at the house, trying to coax their mother into accepting the marriage. To say her efforts had been unsuccessful was an understatement, considering Dinah would only speak to her through the locked bedroom door. Thomas had threatened to take it off the hinges, and even that hadn't budged her.

Leah waited for my answer, so I waved the book around a little. "Just a novel. It's about a doctor."

"Something for work?" She grabbed the remote and turned down the volume on the television, where the von Trapp children sang goodnight to their father's dinner guests.

"Just for fun." I smiled. "How's Simon?"

She sighed and put her sewing to the side. "No better." She glanced at Daria and lowered her voice. "Thomas won't let me take him to the doctor."

It was my turn to sigh. Thomas didn't like acknowledging Simon's health problems, which meant he mostly ignored the child. Now that the weather had turned warm for good, everything was blooming, and the boy's asthma was acting up.

"He needs an inhaler," I told Leah.

"I know. Try telling Thomas that, though. Every time I bring it up, he lectures me on indulging Simon."

"It's not indulging him to treat a serious medical condition."

When she blinked back tears, I moved down the sofa and put an arm around her. "Do you think one of the doctors you work with could help?" she asked softly.

I gnawed my lower lip. "I don't know . . . Usually, they want to see you in person before they prescribe anything." I didn't tell her I had no idea what the center's policy on dispensing medication was, since Brittney had never let me near a patient after that first day. But I assumed it was similar to what I'd been taught in school.

It sounded right, anyway.

She nodded. "Well, since you'll see Thomas tonight, maybe you could say something? He'll listen to you."

"Of course." I moved back to my end of the sofa.

Her confidence was seriously misplaced. Thomas didn't respect any of my opinions, let alone my so-called medical opinion.

I gazed across the room, where Daria lay on her stomach, coaxing the chubby baby into a crawl. Her husband-to-be was thirty years old—the son of another Priesthood Council member. Thomas had gathered everyone to announce the news, a stone-faced Dinah on one side, a beaming Daria on the other.

Would her husband treat her well? And how would she treat the wives who came after her? Daria was gorgeous, with her flawless skin and mahogany hair. She was used to being pampered. Since the older boys had left, she was usually the center of attention. It was easy to see her resemblance to her mother. Would she tolerate another woman sharing her husband? Or would she be like Dinah, making the unfortunate women who came after feel like indentured servants?

On the television, the blond baroness watched with narrowed eyes as Captain von Trapp danced in the courtyard with Maria. "If the captain had lived in Riverview Heights," I said, "he could have just married them both."

"What?" Leah shot me a confused look.

Kelly breezed into the room, saving me the effort of coming up with a response. Her body had bounced right back into pregnancy. Even though she was only a couple months along, her midsection swelled softly under her flowered dress.

"Don't do that, Daria!" she scolded her sister as she crossed the room. In one movement, she stooped, grabbed a plastic fly swatter from the floor, and struck the crawling baby on the arm. The little girl froze, her round face shocked. A second later, she burst into tears.

Leah and I exchanged a look. Like me, she didn't believe in the merits of blanket training. It was one of the first things that had united us against Patty and Dinah.

I stood and walked quickly to the baby, then picked her up and settled her on my hip. "Here, precious thing," I murmured. "You're all right."

The baby gave me a gummy grin, then grasped at the braid on my shoulder.

Kelly rolled her eyes. "You're too soft, Mother Elizabeth." She rested a hand over her small belly and smirked. "It's easy to tell you never raised children."

"I helped raise *you*," I said lightly. I scrunched up my face at the baby, who laughed and waved her arms.

"Yeah, right," Daria said from the floor. "We were practically grown when Father brought you home."

As flattered as I was to be spoken of like a stray cat Thomas had found, I decided to let it pass. "You're right," I said, and handed the baby to Kelly. "I don't know much about kids, so I guess I'll just go read or something." I winked at Leah as I grabbed my book off the couch and walked out of the room.

She lowered her head to hide her smile. She knew I'd be back down to help with dinner as soon as the oven chimed. My only regret was not seeing what I hoped were the confused expressions on Kelly's and Daria's faces behind me.

I TRIED TO GET BACK INTO MY BOOK AFTER DINNER, BUT I KEPT losing my place when I glanced at the clock.

Where was Thomas? After dinner, I raced upstairs so I

could shower before he arrived. My hair took so long to shampoo and condition, I usually ended up shaving my legs huddled in the corner to avoid an icy waterfall of water on my back.

And hairy legs weren't an option. Not with Thomas scheduled to share my bed. He'd once run a hand up my leg, a frown on his face at discovering a little bit of stubble I'd missed.

"Really, Elizabeth," he'd said, disgust thick in his voice. "Is it really too much to ask you to look after yourself the one or two times a week we're together?" Later, I found a little bottle of women's shave gel on my bathroom counter.

The hour hand inched a notch closer to nine. It had been a quiet dinner without Dinah at the table. She normally kept conversation moving by asking all the children what they'd done during the day. Her absence had been a palpable thing, like a heavy blanket thrown over the dining room—a feeling intensified by Thomas's obvious anger at her refusal to leave the bedroom.

He'd sat at the head of the table like usual, but he'd been short-tempered, complaining that the lasagna was bland and snapping at Ariel, Leah's twelve-year-old daughter, for spilling her drink. Everyone had eaten quickly—eyes down, forks constantly moving.

My stomach rumbled. I shouldn't have eaten a second helping of lasagna. I pulled my blanket over my cold toes.

Another rumble. I lowered my book and closed my eyes. What was wrong with me? I was never sick, and it was unlike me to get indigestion. Leah joked I had a cast-iron stomach that could handle even Patty's cooking, which was usually overloaded with salt.

It was nine thirty when I finally heard Thomas on the stairs. He entered the living room, a dark cloud over his face.

Crap. He'd been talking to Dinah.

I put my book aside.

He stopped at the foot of the sofa. "It's almost ten o'clock. What are you doing out here?"

"Um, just reading. A book."

"Yes, I can see that." His voice held an uncharacteristic edge of sarcasm.

This is going well.

His gaze wandered over me, then fell on the book at my side. "What's it about?"

Faint alarm bells sounded in my mind. "It's just a story about a doctor during the war. World War Two."

He held out his hand. "May I see it?"

We stared at each other. He'd phrased it as a question, but we both knew it wasn't a request.

"Of course." I gave it to him.

He looked at the cover for a second, then flipped through a few pages, pausing to read here and there. He turned it sideways and ran a finger down the spine. Blue eyes lifted to mine. "This isn't from the library. Where did you get it?"

"Just someone at work. One of the nurses."

He sighed, a short exhalation that was more disapproval than exasperation. "Elizabeth, I know you love to read, and I indulge this hobby because it brings you joy." He thumped the book against his open palm. "But this material isn't appropriate."

I swung my legs to the ground and stood. The blanket dropped to the floor. "Why? You barely looked at it."

"I'm not going to argue with you about this." He gestured to the bookcase next to the television. "You have plenty of books to choose from. I've made my decision." He turned toward the bedroom, Evan's book tucked firmly under his arm.

"Your decision is unfair!" He didn't care what I read. He was doing this just to be mean.

He spun.

The alarm bells blazed in a screeching warning.

Thomas advanced on me.

I stepped back, but the sofa bumped my legs. I had nowhere to go.

He grabbed my upper arm, capturing a few loose strands of hair.

My stomach dropped.

Thomas was always self-controlled. He never did anything without thinking it through, without examining the possible consequences from all angles. Even when he meted out punishments, he did so with deliberate calculation.

The cold, furious man who held me now was capable of real violence. The threat of it vibrated down my arm.

"I'm sorry." I ducked my head. Tiny pinpricks of pain fired across my scalp. I'd pulled my own hair out when I lowered my chin.

Thomas pulled me toward the bedroom. "I will not be henpecked in my own house," he said under his breath. He shoved me toward the bed. "Get in."

I stumbled against the mattress. My heart pounded, and I yanked back the sheets and scrambled under the blankets.

He turned away. For a moment, he just stood there, his hands on his hips. His gold watch winked on his wrist, and his back rose and fell with his breaths, showing the outline of his garments.

After a minute, he stalked to the bathroom and shut the door with a bang that wasn't quite a slam.

I let out a shaky breath. There was the buzz of his electric razor, followed by the muffled hiss of the shower.

My stomach lurched.

He was here for sex.

No. He was here to impregnate me. Like a specimen in a lab.

I placed a hand over my unsettled stomach. If I got pregnant, I'd be bound to him forever. No woman had ever left the faith with her children. It was the reason my mother had willingly divorced my father. She could have stayed with him, but she'd refused to leave me behind.

I studied the bathroom door. Thomas had fathered fourteen children, but the last one, Ginny, had been born shortly after our marriage. Patty had been pregnant with her when I'd moved to Riverview Heights. Since then, none of my fellow sister-wives had conceived.

The door opened and Thomas emerged, a towel wrapped around his hips. He had a scar on one shoulder from a scaffold collapse when he was a teen. Although it had been years since he lifted so much as a hammer on a construction site, his body was still toned and muscular. Over the past two years, he'd thickened around his middle, but he still put men a decade younger to shame.

Ordinarily, the sight of him in a towel would have made me stop and take notice. Now, his bare chest was a reminder of his purpose for being here.

He tossed the towel at the foot of the bed, and I averted my eyes while he lifted the quilt and settled next to me. Propped on one elbow, he gazed at me a moment, then twirled his index finger around one of the golden curls coiled over my shoulder.

"Did I frighten you before?"

"Yes." My voice was a rasp.

He pulled my nightgown off my shoulder and pressed a warm kiss against my collarbone. "I would never hurt you, Elizabeth," he whispered. "You know that."

But you have, said a small voice in my head. He'd switched me for offending Dinah. At least that time he spared me the indignity of baring my backside and lying across his knees, or stripping to my garments so he could take a switch to my back —punishments he knew I hated.

He pulled my chin toward him and kissed me, his tongue dipping into my mouth. When I failed to respond, he drew back, his brows knit. "Is there a problem?"

Of course there was a problem. He was angry at Dinah, so he'd taken it out on me, stealing Evan's book and shoving me into bed. Now, he expected me to be okay with it.

Was his admiration of my body his version of an apology?

"There's no problem, Thomas," I said in a low voice. "My stomach hurts a little, that's all."

He pursed his lips. "I don't want to miss this opportunity in your cycle."

Of course not. Because this month could be the month, right? Couldn't he see it was pointless?

I took a deep breath. "Do you think we can skip tonight?" My hand fluttered above the quilt. "There's always tomorrow, and the next night."

He shook his head. "I'm driving Dinah and Daria to Provo tomorrow. I won't be back until Friday. Jonah is coming with us."

I blinked. That must have been what he talked to Dinah about tonight.

And the reason he was in such a bad mood.

"So Dinah agreed to the marriage?"

"She will," he said, his tone grim.

Sympathy rushed over me. It was unlikely Dinah would have another child. With the three older boys gone, and now the girls married off, she was left with ten-year-old Jonah. The transition from a full house to a nearly empty nest had happened in less than two years.

For a woman whose life revolved around motherhood, it had to be a blow.

I laced my fingers together over the quilt. "Do you think maybe you should postpone the trip until she's fully on board with the wedding?" I pictured a tight-lipped Dinah in the car next to Thomas for the eighteen-hour drive to Provo.

His jaw tightened, but his touch was gentle as he brushed my hair off my shoulder. He undid the little row of buttons running down the front of my nightgown, his movements deft and sure. He spread the halves apart. Cool air hit my breasts.

"I think," he said, his eyes following his fingers, "you should relax and let me make love to you."

I opened my mouth, but he placed a finger over my lips. Up close, his eyelashes were long and spiky, which made his eyes brighter. Since he'd shaved, his jaw was smooth and well defined, the black and silver hairs almost invisible against his tanned skin.

"I know you struggle with your inability to conceive," he said. "No, don't say anything. Just listen. It's a spiritual struggle for you. But I still believe you're meant to be part of our family, both now and for eternity."

He moved over me, his body supported by his elbows on either side of my body. The little hairs on his chest brushed my bare breasts.

"Heavenly Father has promised children to the faithful. It's not up to us to dictate when they come. All we can do is make sure we do everything we can to welcome them into this life." He leaned on one elbow and used his free hand to tug my nightgown down my hips.

I lifted my butt so he could pull it free.

He settled back over me, his penis hard against my leg. He kissed me again.

I opened my lips under the pressure of his mouth. He plunged his tongue inside, stroking it along mine. His hand snaked between our bodies, and he slid a thick finger inside me.

I turned my head to the side, breaking off the kiss. "Thomas, wait—"

"Elizabeth, enough of this!" He jerked one of my legs up and wedged his hips between mine.

I sucked in a breath. *Hands clasped, eyes down.* It was better to go unnoticed.

But Thomas noticed me. He slid the finger in and out, then turned his wrist so his thumb brushed the tiny, sensitive spot above my opening.

I closed my eyes.

"Good girl," he said. "I know what my girl likes." His touch was light, his thumb flicking back and forth, back and forth.

I couldn't close my legs. Not with his hips between my thighs, his body pressing me into the mattress.

His thumb continued its circuit, teasing at my sex until a little fire ignited.

Warmth curled low in my belly. A restless ache built between my legs.

Thomas withdrew his finger, then spread moisture over my sex, rubbing it into the folds, circling the little nub over and over again.

My heart pounded.

"That's it," he said. "I like you wet like this."

He was distracted, so I turned my head to the side, my gaze on the window. The fire built higher, the ache more intense.

Thomas pushed my legs apart, gripped himself, and slid inside. He dropped his forehead to my shoulder.

"God, Elizabeth," he gasped. "You feel so good."

He filled me, stretching and pushing, a hot, insistent presence.

The fire flickered. Faded.

I stared at the window.

He pulled back, then slid forward again, a little grunt escaping him. He thrusted half a dozen times, his breaths short and harsh, each one forcing an explosion of mint-scented toothpaste over my face.

My head shifted up and down on the pillow. Up and down. Up and down. The window slid back and forth, like a movie reel stuck on the same scene.

Thomas shoved a final time and held. Wet flooded me. The fire was long gone, its remnants like ash in my gut.

He rolled to his back, an arm flung over his eyes.

I turned my head and stared up at the ceiling. Warmth trickled between my legs. I sat up and snatched the discarded towel from the foot of the bed, then wiped at myself.

The covers rustled, and Thomas spoke behind me. "If you don't get pregnant this month, I want you to see a doctor. Someone in the city."

I looked over my shoulder. "Don't you think Heavenly Father will provide?" The cynicism in my voice was as clear as a bell. Now he would blow up all over again.

But he didn't notice. "It's your destiny to be in the celestial kingdom with me, Elizabeth. With all of us. Dinah and Patty and Leah. There are souls waiting to be born. It's our obligation to do everything we can to make sure that happens."

Lucky me. Because who wouldn't want to spend an eternity with Dinah?

I frowned. I'd never really questioned our faith before. But now . . .

As far back as I could remember, I'd been taught that living a faithful life meant you got to dwell in the highest level of heaven after death, surrounded by your earthly family. It was the fundamental tenet of our faith, and something everyone aspired to.

So why did it fill me with something close to despair?

9

"I'm sorry, but we don't have this in stock," the girl behind the counter said. Like all the other bookstore employees, she wore a dark green T-shirt with a white cartoon worm on it that encouraged everyone to "be a bookworm." I'd approached her as soon as she unlocked the big glass doors out front. At this hour, other employees were still filtering in for the morning shift.

Disappointment shot through me. "Are you sure?"

She shook her head and angled the screen of her computer toward me. "See here?" She tapped the book's title, which had a red zero beside it. "It's on back order. I could order it for you, though. You'd have it by next Monday."

My heart sank. That was too long. Evan wanted to do dinner this week. What was I supposed to tell him? That I'd lost it? I couldn't tell him the truth—that my husband had confiscated it like a teacher who caught a student passing notes in class.

Yeah, no. That wasn't happening.

"Do you want me to order it?" The girl raised black eyebrows behind bright purple glasses. The lower half of her hair was the same shade of purple, which should have looked awful but somehow worked on her.

"No, I need it before then, unfortunately. But thank you."

I left the store and crossed the parking lot, my gaze on the center.

As soon as Thomas left the bedroom that morning, I turned the loft inside out looking for Evan's book. I looked under the bed and sofa cushions. I ransacked the closet. I searched the bathroom.

Then kicked the door in a burst of frustration.

Of course Thomas had taken it with him. He didn't care what I read. He just wanted to assert his authority over even the tiniest parts of my life.

The only thing that bothered me about it was that it hadn't really bothered me before. It was as if someone had thrown a bucket of cold water over my head, and I'd woken from a fog of routine and complacency.

As I'd stared at the scuff mark on my bathroom door, I realized I had become two people: the old Elizabeth and the new.

The old Elizabeth still existed, but only at home, and only out of necessity.

I wasn't exactly sure what the new Elizabeth was like—I just knew something had snapped apart inside me, and I didn't think I could put it back, or if I even wanted to.

The book was gone, but I still had an entire bookstore at my disposal, so I'd run downstairs and hurried next door to Patty's, where I knew I'd find Jackson in the kitchen. He'd looked up from his bowl of cereal.

"What's up, Liz?"

"Hey," I said, my wave taking in a frowning Patty and the other three kids sitting around the big breakfast table. "Sorry to barge in. Jackson, could you run me into the city a little earlier today?"

He glanced at his mother. "Sure, no problem."

"Did Thomas and Dinah leave already?" Patty asked me. She wiped her hands on a towel and tossed it on the counter.

"About a half hour ago." When her face fell, I realized he hadn't said goodbye to her. "He seemed distracted this morning."

I caught the eye of Ginny, Patty's five-year-old daughter. She offered me a shy smile.

I returned it, then went to Patty and spoke in a low voice. "I think he's still . . . you know, having trouble with Dinah about the marriage."

She sniffed. "Well, that's none of our concern. Father has made his decision. It's our duty to accept it."

And just like that, she let me know she neither needed nor wanted my sympathy.

Business as usual.

I walked faster across the parking lot. The bookstore had taken longer than I expected, and now I was running late. I jogged the last few steps to the center's main doors, an image of Brittney floating in my mind.

She would *salivate* at the opportunity to write me up for being late.

I nodded to the receptionist as I bypassed the elevator bank and pushed through the door leading to the stairwell. I took the stairs two at a time, sweat beading on my forehead.

It took me three tries to swipe my ID badge through the time clock, and I swore under my breath as the little light finally blinked green, clocking me in. In the locker room, I jerked out of my clothes and threw on scrubs in record time.

Back out in the hallway, I almost barreled into Gloria. "Oh! I am so sorry." I brushed the hair back from my temples, which had grown damp in the race to change into work clothes.

"I wondered where you were," she said, her round face kind. "It's not like you to be late." She bustled down the hallway. "By the way, Brittney was looking for you," she said over her shoulder. "She's in her office."

As soon as she was out of sight, I clenched my fists. "Dammit."

A forbidden thrill zipped through me.

"Shit."

Huh. No wonder people cussed. It felt *great.*

I took my time walking to Brittney's office. Why bother hurrying now? I was already in trouble. A few minutes weren't going to make any difference. I should have known I'd never get away with being late. She probably set a lookout near the time clock, just waiting for me to slip up.

Her door was slightly open, but she'd once snapped at me for not knocking, so I knew better than to walk right in.

I raised my hand to knock when Evan's voice drifted out.

"Brittney, you're being ridiculous."

"Oh, I don't know, Evan," Brittney answered. "You're looking pretty ridiculous yourself these days."

"What's that supposed to mean?"

She laughed—a short, ugly sound. "Since when did you develop a *Little House on the Prairie* fetish? We're all wondering."

"You're acting like this because I had lunch with her," he said, his voice low and angry.

The blood drained from my face. *Walk away,* a voice in my head urged. *Just turn around and walk away.* But I couldn't. I was welded to the floor. I had to hear the whole ugly thing out.

"Please." There was a squeaking sound, like someone had risen from a chair. "You think I'm jealous of your little fling with the pioneer girl?"

"That's exactly what I think."

"I wouldn't be so smug, Evan. Apparently, all it takes to get into her pants is a coffee mug."

There was a sharp intake of breath. "Listen, Brittney, you

are more than out of line. What happened between you and me has nothing to do with Elizabeth."

"That's fine, Evan, but don't expect me to be sympathetic when you're done with her. I'm not cleaning up your mess when you're finished."

"It's not like that—"

"It's not? I've never seen you move so fast. You've been on her since day one." Her voice dripped venom. "It must be frustrating to have to work so hard for it, to be so nice and accommodating."

"I'm nice to her because she's a nice person. She obviously comes from an underprivileged background."

Brittney gave a crack of mocking laughter. "So that's what this is? A pity fuck?"

His next words were delivered in a tone far nastier than hers. "You'd know a lot about that, Britt. But just because you're offering it to the highest bidder doesn't mean *anyone* wants it."

The sharp cracking sound of flesh hitting flesh made me jump back.

The door jerked open before I could move, leaving me staring at Evan. His face was white except for the clear outline of a handprint, which was rapidly turning red.

He froze, shock glazing his eyes. Then, before either of us could say anything, he pulled the door shut and stepped toward me. "Elizabeth . . ."

I held up my hands, arms extended like a barrier between us. "I heard enough."

I whirled, tears burning my eyes.

I WAS ALMOST TO THE LOCKER ROOM WHEN EVAN CAUGHT UP to me.

"Elizabeth, wait." He pulled me to a stop before I could walk through the doorway.

I tugged against his grip.

He released me, then raised his hands in apology. "Please, just hear me out."

"I don't think I want to hear anymore."

He hung his head, his hands on his hips. Today, he'd gone without his usual white coat and wore only a pair of light green scrubs, the pants tied with a red drawstring. He lifted pained eyes to mine. "I know what you heard, and it sounded bad." He grimaced. "There are a lot of things you don't know. About Brittney and me."

My throat was so tight, it hurt to swallow. "Evan, you don't need to explain anything to me."

"Yes, I do." He looked around, then stepped closer. Voice low, he said, "Elizabeth, I care about you. I care what you think. I understand why you're hurt, but please give me a chance to explain."

I glanced down the hall, toward Brittney's office. His ex-girlfriend's office.

I had no future with Evan. No future at all. Why should their past relationship impact me in any way? Why did it hurt so much to imagine them together?

"Please, Elizabeth. Have lunch with me today. I need to talk to you."

The mark on his cheek had turned a dull red. I knew how much a slap like that could hurt. More than anything, it hurt your soul. There was something about being struck that wounded you to your core.

"All right," I said.

He exhaled. "Thank you."

When I turned to go, he called out. "Wait. Dammit, I just remembered. There are pharmaceutical reps in all week, so we won't be able to do lunch." He sighed. "They always bring in a catered lunch. Sandwiches and stuff. They go all out. It would look strange if we missed it. Are you free for dinner tonight?"

"No." I needed time to arrange a ride. "It can't be tonight. I mean, I have other plans."

"What about Thursday?"

I hesitated. Was he asking me on a date? I couldn't boast much experience with dating. The only times Thomas had taken me out were for quick anniversary dinners at a little diner on the long stretch of highway between Riverview Heights and Jefferson City. We could never go anywhere too public, at least not together. People in the surrounding area knew about the community, but the Priesthood Council thought it bad for business to parade our lifestyle in front of outsiders.

"Please, Elizabeth. Say yes."

Thomas was gone for the week. This might be the only chance I'd have to spend time with Evan like this. And who knew how long I'd last at the center. There was no question how Brittney felt about me, not after what I'd heard. My days were obviously numbered.

And what did I have to look forward to at home? The minute Thomas returned, I would probably be shipped off to a fertility clinic and forcibly impregnated. If I conceived, he'd never let me work again.

I looked at Evan.

It was all hopeless.

He stepped toward me. "I promise I can explain. Have dinner with me. No strings. No expectations. Just let me explain a few things."

It's just dinner. And no one would ever know. I didn't even have to tell Jackson. I could just say I had to work late. There was no harm in having dinner with someone, even someone handsome and funny and smart.

"I'd have to be back by nine," I heard myself say.

"No problem."

I swallowed. "Okay, then. I can do it on Thursday. But we have to leave from here."

"Thursday, then." He looked like he wanted to say more, but two nurses from downstairs rounded the corner and walked toward the locker room.

"Thursday," I said, then slipped into the locker room before he could say anything else.

～

I REGRETTED ACCEPTING EVAN'S INVITATION ALMOST IMMEDIATELY after I talked to him.

Once the initial shock of overhearing his conversation with Brittney wore off, I realized what a stupid idea it was.

Even if he had a perfectly reasonable excuse for the things I overheard, it was pointless for us to see each other outside of work. There could never be anything romantic between us. The very idea of it was laughable.

Whatever explanation he revealed, it couldn't possibly be worse than the secret I was keeping.

And if Thomas or anyone from home found out, the consequences were unthinkable.

If I hadn't been so busy trying to keep up with Brittney's lengthening task list, I would have tracked him down and canceled. As it was, I barely had time to catch a breath.

She'd been especially vicious since her argument with Evan and seemed determined to vent all her anger and frustration on me. I started my shift on Wednesday morning by lugging all the center's trash down the stairs and out to the dumpster.

Apparently, all the spiteful, bitter women in my life lived to see me hauling garbage.

Brittney also made it clear how irritated she was that I hadn't reported to her office yesterday after coming in late. She retaliated by assigning me to cover any walk-ins who showed up during lunch throughout the week.

"That's total bullshit!" Natalie said when she found out. She'd been waiting by my locker and had demanded to know why I'd missed yesterday's catered lunch.

I'd shrugged and reached past her so I could open my locker. "I don't mind, really."

Natalie crossed her arms.

"I don't," I insisted.

"Elizabeth, this whole place shuts down at lunch. You know that as well as I do. If patients show up, they just have to wait."

I pulled my work shoes out of my locker. "I mean it, I don't mind. It's a chance for me to interact with patients instead of scrubbing floors and cleaning toilets."

Natalie uncrossed her arms, a frown making two tiny lines between her eyebrows. "What do you mean 'cleaning toilets'? Is that all you've been doing up here?"

I sat down so I could change my shoes. "Brittney is just making me jump through a few hoops before letting me get involved in real assisting stuff. It's nothing I can't handle."

She sat next to me. "You shouldn't have to handle it. Why didn't you say something before?"

I smiled. She looked so fierce. Natalie put on a good show, but her sarcasm was just a front. Underneath the eye-rolling and the occasional insult was a soft heart. If she thought I was being mistreated at work, she'd do whatever she could to put a stop to it.

I stood. "It's something I have to work through on my own."

Natalie looked doubtful.

"I've worked with people like Brittney before," I said. "I know what I'm doing."

"You don't know her, Elizabeth. Not really." She stood and leaned against the row of lockers. "At least let me talk to someone in surgery. I bet I could get you moved downstairs."

"I appreciate it, but I'm happy here."

"It wouldn't have anything to do with a certain Nordic-looking doctor, would it?"

"We're friends."

"That's not what my spies in the bookstore tell me," she said. I must have looked startled, because she put a hand on my arm. "I'm kidding! People do talk, though. You can't even take a smoke break around here without someone broadcasting it to the entire building. Anyway, you have my blessing. Evan is a great guy. Not to mention a tall drink of water." She made her hands into claws and mouthed *meow*.

"I've missed you at lunch," I said. "Have you guys been busy downstairs?"

She grinned. "Nice try. I can take a hint." Her smile faded. "Elizabeth, just be careful with Brittney, okay? She knows where you've been spending your lunch breaks. I'm sure that's where this new rule about you covering the walk-ins came from."

I'd figured as much. I took a deep breath. "I'll be careful."

But it didn't really matter. I couldn't go to dinner with Evan.

I couldn't see him at lunch anymore, either, no matter how much I wanted to.

So I had two tasks ahead of me. First, I needed to tell Evan dinner was off. Then, I had to find a way to get on Brittney's good side.

Assuming she had one.

∽

By the end of my shift on Wednesday, I'd already failed miserably at one of my goals. Brittney tracked me down at the nurses' station, a stack of papers in her hands.

"There you are, Elizabeth." She flashed her white smile. "I swear, I can never find you when I need you."

"I've been right here." Her comments about Evan having a *Little House on the Prairie* fetish still lingered in my mind.

She plopped the papers down on the desk. "I need you to put these insurance forms in yesterday's charts." Her eyes flicked over me. "I'm afraid I'm also going to have to write you up for being out of uniform."

"What?"

She propped a hand on one hip. "I've mentioned several times now that turtlenecks aren't part of the uniform. If you're cold, although I can't imagine how you would be, you can wear a scrub jacket over your top."

I touched the neckline of my shirt. She'd never said anything about my turtleneck before. "Brittney, I don't think—"

"Please don't argue, Elizabeth," she said, her voice gentle. "It's unprofessional." She looked pained, almost as if she were embarrassed for me. "It's fine for today, but I expect you to be properly uniformed tomorrow. Excuse me, I have a patient in room three."

So much for staying on her good side, I thought as she walked away. I tugged at my white turtleneck. It *was* warm, but it was the only way I could keep my garments from showing underneath the scrub top. I sighed and pulled the stack of paperwork toward me.

A few minutes later, Brittney's voice crackled over the phone's intercom. "Elizabeth? Are you still at the nurses' station?"

I reached over and pressed the button. "Yes."

"Good. Can you run down to room three and take vitals? I'm tied up with a patient in one."

I almost fell off the chair. She was letting me see a patient? I hit the button again. "No problem." I sprang out of the chair, grabbed a stethoscope and blood pressure cuff from an empty exam room, and headed down the hall.

Evan stepped out of room four and into my path as I approached room three.

"Whoa!" He steadied me with a hand at my elbow. "You okay?"

"Never better." I couldn't keep the smile off my face. "Just taking vitals. Brittney couldn't get to it."

"Okay," he said. He lowered his voice. "We still on for tomorrow?"

This was my chance to back out. Why encourage him by agreeing to dinner? Better to end it now.

But if I said no, he'd want to know why I changed my mind.

And my patient was waiting. *My* patient.

I nodded. "Yes, that's fine." I brushed past him.

"Meet at the bookstore at five?" he asked after me. "I thought it might be better to meet somewhere besides work."

I turned and walked backwards, a stupid smile tugging at my face. "Good idea."

I was still smiling when I walked back to the nurses' station. The patient had been a little old lady with symptoms of a bad cold. Between sneezes, she'd told me the names of all her grandkids and their various accomplishments. She hadn't seemed to notice that my hands trembled as I placed the cuff around her upper arm, or that I had to take her pulse twice because I lost count halfway through.

Brittney sat at the nurses' station, sorting through the stack of insurance papers.

"Thanks for letting me take that," I said as I walked up. "I left the chart on the wall outside for Evan. Was that right?"

"*Dr.* Adgate," she said without looking up.

"Yes, of course. Dr. Adgate."

Brittney stood, frowning. "I'm disappointed, Elizabeth."

"I apologize. I won't call him that again."

She held up a hand. "That's a problem, yes, but I'm talking about something else." She gestured to the paperwork. "You left these out in plain sight, where anyone could have picked them up. There is sensitive patient information here, Elizabeth. It's a clear HIPAA violation. You should know better."

I gazed down at the papers. "I'm sorry. I didn't realize."

"This is why I've been reluctant to give you more serious responsibilities. I'm not happy you proved me right."

"Really? Because you seem pretty happy about it."

Her mouth curved in an acid smile. "A bad attitude isn't helpful. Frankly, you're making me question whether you have a future here."

My heart pounded. She'd set me up on purpose.

I couldn't prove it, and I couldn't accuse her. But I knew. The smirk on her face was evidence enough.

I drew a shaky breath. "I'm sorry, Brittney. It was careless. All I can say is that it won't happen again."

"Well, I'm sorry to say you won't have the chance for it to happen again. At least not for a long while."

I nodded. "Is that all?"

"Yes, I think so." When I turned to go, she called out, "Please be on time tomorrow. I need you to wipe down the shelves in the medication closet."

Shoulders stiff, I nodded without turning around.

10

"Are you sure it's okay if you pick me up later tonight?"

Jackson and I sat in the truck outside the urgent care the next morning, a bag of fast food on the console between us.

He finished chewing his bite of sausage biscuit and wiped a hand across the back of his mouth. "Of course. I got nowhere to be."

"Thanks." I'd been nervous about asking him to drive into the city so late. The curfew in Riverview Heights was eight o'clock, but Jackson promised no one would say anything about me working late.

I glanced at him as he unwrapped his second sandwich, guilt almost making me blurt out the real reason I needed a ride so late at night. It wasn't fair to pull him into my scheme. If we were caught . . .

"Hey, Liz, it's fine, I promise." He put his sandwich on the paper in his lap and turned so he faced me. Concern made him look older. "Don't look so worried. You can't help it you have to work late." He smiled a little. "Although, if I were you, I'd take advantage of having the house to myself and throw a big party."

I snorted. Spoken like a true teenager. "What, and make more work for myself? I'm taking advantage of a few days with no chores."

I'd also slept better than I had in years. Even though I usually only spent a couple nights a week with Thomas, my subconscious must have always known there was a possibility of hearing his footsteps on the stairs. In the last month or so, since he'd become determined to get me pregnant, I'd spent most nights tossing and turning, even when he was scheduled to be with another wife. This morning, I'd woken refreshed and well rested for the first time in what felt like forever.

"You want a hash brown?" Jackson held up a paper-wrapped square.

"No, thanks." I pointed to the grease seeping through the paper.

He shrugged and tore into it.

"I should get going." I grabbed my bag from the floor. I'd stuffed a change of clothes in the bottom, along with the few bits of makeup I owned—mostly Daria's castoffs.

"I'll be here at nine," he called after me as I closed the door and waved to let him know I'd heard.

I clutched my bag to my side as I walked quickly toward the building entrance. No one could possibly know I had clothes inside it. Evan and I had told no one—not even Natalie—about our plans. Still, I half expected the bag to burst into flames to signify my guilt to the world.

The bad feeling followed me throughout the day. Not only was I deceiving everyone at home, I was deceiving Evan. At lunch, I didn't even mind being stuck cleaning out the medication closet, since it kept me from having to face him. I wasn't sure I was capable of not breaking down and confessing everything. Fortunately, half the building was downstairs eating subs brought in by the pharmaceutical sales rep.

I'd met her for the first time yesterday, when she'd stopped by the nurses' station to drop off some samples. She was tall and polished looking, with carefully arranged blond waves that cascaded over her shoulders and never seemed to move.

"They're all like that," Gloria confided to me in a low voice. "You'd think they were selling something more than Lipitor and Viagra."

I wrung out a sponge and swiped it down a long metal shelf. The sales rep's presence was a blessing in disguise. With an impossibly gorgeous woman in the building, Brittney was on full alert, which gave her little time to monitor my movements. She'd checked in once earlier to make sure I moved all the medication off the shelves—"don't just dust around it"— and then disappeared, presumably to make sure the sales rep didn't get too close to Evan.

I dried the shelves and began loading them back up with the hundreds of bottles and boxes of medication. The sheer amount of pills, blister packs, and vials was astonishing. I checked expiration dates and inventory against a list and wrote down the new samples the rep had dropped off.

When I knelt and opened the last box, I sat back on my heels and stared down at it. Dozens of small white boxes were tucked in neat rows, each one stamped with *80 mcg Inhalation Aerosol* on the side. I'd seen the same inhaler on the bathroom counter at Patty and Leah's house. Simon took it for his asthma.

My hand hovered over the box. They were just samples, and new ones at that. If I didn't add them to the list, it would be as if they'd never even entered the building. Gloria had said the sales reps treated the samples like they were boxes of candy. It was a marketing ploy to get doctors to offer a drug and then hopefully prescribe it once a patient tried it and liked it. No one would know if a few boxes went missing.

The back of my neck burned, and my heart thumped against my chest as I grabbed three boxes and stuffed them in the big square pockets of my scrub top. I hesitated, then took one more and put it in my jacket pocket before buttoning the jacket over my top.

Quickly, I stacked the remaining boxes on the shelf, added them to the bottom of the list, and closed the doors and locked them.

The four boxes felt like fifty-pound weights on the short walk to the locker room, and my hands fumbled with the combination lock on my locker. I turned the dial with fierce concentration. The lock clicked, and relief swept me. I dumped the boxes into my bag and slammed the locker shut again just as Gloria walked in.

"There's still a few subs downstairs if you're hungry." She went to her own locker and tossed her purse inside.

I plastered a smile on my face and headed for the door. "Thanks, I'll check it out."

THE REST OF MY SHIFT PASSED SWIFTLY. BY FOUR, I COULDN'T GET to the locker room fast enough. It was wrong to take the asthma medication. It didn't matter that they were just samples. I'd never stolen anything in my life, not even when my mother and I had struggled to buy food. I stood in front of my locker for a long time, indecision making my gut churn.

Since childhood, I'd been taught that bad decisions tend to lead to more bad decisions. Now, I realized it was true. I'd spent the past month having lunch with Evan, which had set me on a crooked path. I'd gotten swept up in the attention and the excitement, to the point where I was poised to compromise my vows to Thomas by sneaking off to have dinner with another man.

And taking the medication from the closet? That was just theft, plain and simple.

I opened my locker and pulled out the clothes I'd hidden at the bottom of my bag. My fingers brushed the inhalers, and a renewed surge of guilt washed over me.

I piled the skirt, shirt, and ballet flats on a nearby bench, then closed the locker with a click and leaned my head against the door. I had to put the inhalers back. And then I had to meet Evan at the bookstore and tell him I couldn't see him anymore. Our first dinner together would be our last.

"Elizabeth? What are you still doing here?"

I jerked my head away from the metal door, which had grown warm under my forehead. Brittney stared at me from the doorway, a puzzled look on her face. She checked her watch. "It's almost four. I'm closing up."

"I-I was just changing."

She smiled. "Okay. Well, go ahead, then." When I didn't move, she made a little "hurry up" motion with her hand.

"It's okay," I said. "You can go. I'll turn off the lights when I'm done."

She went to the table in the center of the room and collected a handful of empty coffee cups and soda cans. "I'm afraid not," she said over her shoulder, "but thanks for the offer." She dropped the cans in a recycling bin and faced me. "It's company policy. I need to physically see that the building is empty."

I couldn't change in front of her. Even if she didn't recognize my garments, she'd definitely wonder about them. I wasn't exactly an expert on women's lingerie, but I knew my garments would raise eyebrows even among the most modest outsiders. And Brittney was definitely not my friend. I couldn't give her any excuse to probe my personal life.

There were no other options. I scooped up the clothes and ducked into one of the bathroom stalls around the corner. At worst, she'd simply think I was shy about changing in front of another woman.

In the stall, I pulled the scrub top over my head and draped it over the door. When I reached for the plain white shirt I'd hung on the hook, I froze.

I closed my eyes. How could I have been so unbelievably stupid? I'd chosen it, along with a calf-length jean skirt, because it was the most normal-looking clothing I owned. Few people saw me coming and going to work. For a dinner, though, I'd needed something that didn't scream Riverview Heights.

The shirt was more fitted than my others, with three-quarter length sleeves and subtle pleats along the sides. It wasn't necessarily transparent, but the sacred symbols sewn on the bodice of my garments would definitely show through the material—something that wouldn't have mattered at home but absolutely mattered here.

"Elizabeth?" Brittney called from the locker room. "Not to be rude, but I have someplace I need to be."

I tugged my garment top over my head. "Sorry, just a second!"

Her feet appeared beneath the stall door. "Here, you forgot your shoes." She slid the ballet flats under the door.

My fingers fumbled over the buttons of my shirt as I tried to dress as quickly as possible. I untied my scrub pants and let them drop to the floor so I could stand on them while I stepped into my skirt. After a brief pause, I peeled off my garment bottoms, too. They'd be invisible under the skirt, but it felt weird to wear them without the top.

As I wiggled my feet into my shoes, Brittney spoke from the other side of the door. "By the way, I uploaded all the changes you made on the medication closet inventory sheet to the computer. I'll need you to do the same for the refrigerated stuff tomorrow."

I took a deep breath and opened the door. "Not a problem," I said, stepping past her.

"Is something wrong, Elizabeth?" she asked, her voice concerned. I wondered if she even heard the edge under the friendly tone.

I stopped at my locker. "No, why?" Maybe if I smiled and acted normal, she'd leave.

But she trailed after me and stood off to the side, watching as I turned the dial on my combination lock. I'd wrapped my garments in the bundle of scrubs, which I'd placed on the table. Somehow, I had to figure out a way to get the garments into my bag and the scrubs into the soiled laundry bin without Brittney noticing.

"You seem distracted." She leaned a hip against the table. "Listen, Elizabeth," she said, tucking a piece of hair behind her ear. "I want you to know you're doing a great job around here. I'm really impressed by you."

I turned, speechless. Was she serious?

My face must have given away my thoughts, because she laughed and held up a hand. "I know, I know, we've had our differences. I also know I'm tough to work for." She winked, as if she'd just divulged a fun and interesting fact about herself.

She seemed to be waiting for me to say something. "Brittney, I..."

"No, you don't have to say anything. I just want you to know it takes a strong person to pass my tests. You've risen to the occasion." She gifted me with a dazzling smile. "You should be proud of yourself." Before I could reply, she grabbed my scrubs from the table and tossed them in the laundry bin in the corner. "Come on, I'll walk you out."

I stared at the laundry bin for a long minute. She couldn't possibly know, could she? She'd turned around and was flipping off the lights. The locker room plunged into near-darkness, the only illumination a small security light that flickered to life above the door leading to the hallway.

"You coming?" She'd finished switching off the lights and stared at me with a curious expression.

"Yeah." I shook myself out of my stupor and closed my locker. Bag in hand, I followed her out of the locker room, sparing one final glance at the laundry bin.

THE BOOKSTORE BUZZED WITH CONVERSATION AND THE HUSHED sounds of the baristas preparing the seemingly endless variations of coffee people were willing to pay fifteen dollars for.

I sat in my usual spot overlooking the children's section. A mother watched her two children play around a train table. They pushed small wooden train cars up the grooved tracks, then squealed with delight when they careened down the other side.

Ordinarily, watching them would have been soothing. Right now, though, my thoughts were divided between worry over the medication I'd taken and guilt over meeting Evan, just to tell him I couldn't have dinner with him.

I propped my chin on my hand. There was nothing I could do about the samples. Brittney had made sure of that when she uploaded my notes to the center's computer system. If I returned the medication now, someone would eventually notice the discrepancy between what the computer said and how much was actually on the shelf.

And then Brittney would trace it back to me.

Evan, though . . . I heaved a sigh. He'd been so determined to explain his exchange with Brittney the other day.

I felt his approach before I saw him. The little hairs on the back of my neck lifted with awareness. He pulled out the chair and sat across from me. Out of his doctor clothes, he looked more approachable and more intimidating all at the same time.

As I puzzled over that paradox, he smiled. It was a slow, careful smile—a hesitant expression that told me he wasn't sure of his welcome.

"I'm really glad you're here," he said. He leaned his elbows on the table. His gray button-down made his eyes look more gray than blue.

"You didn't think I'd come?" I wondered if he sensed how close I'd been to canceling.

"I wouldn't have blamed you if you'd decided not to."

I took a deep breath. "Evan—"

"Wait, before you say anything more, just let me explain something. The past two days have been hell, knowing you're near and not getting a chance to talk about what happened." He swallowed. "What you heard . . ."

I had to stop him, break things off cleanly. "Evan, you don't owe me an explanation. We're friends."

"We are," he said. "But I'm not going to say I don't want to see if we could be something more."

I fell silent. What could I say to that?

He leaned forward. "Tell me you feel it, too. You do, don't you?"

My throat burned. "Yes. But it's complicated."

His smile was like the sun coming out from behind a cloud. "It always is."

Oh, Evan. You have no idea.

He licked his lips. "Elizabeth, I don't know what you heard, but I want you to know I have nothing but respect for you. Brittney brings out the worst in me—the worst in most people, I imagine." His mouth tightened. "When I first came here six months ago, I knew nothing about the place. Nothing about Missouri or the people." He huffed a laugh. "I got lost looking for the post office. Connecticut is filled with tiny towns.

Everyone knows everyone. Things are more sprawled out here. It's hard to make connections with people."

"And you connected with Brittney?" I had to ask.

"I did." He rubbed a hand over his mouth. "She was a little more aggressive than what I'm used to, but I was alone in a new place. And Brittney is . . ."

"Beautiful?"

He raised an eyebrow. "I was going to say relentless. We went out a few times, and it was okay at first. After a month, though, she started pushing to spend more time together. I—" He cleared his throat. "I never . . . slept with her."

Something flared in my chest. Hope? Relief?

Pink tinged his cheeks. "She took it hard when I broke things off. Before you came, I was ready to turn in my resignation."

I sucked in a breath. "Where would you go?"

"I haven't decided." His expression grew intense as he looked at me. "But now I think I've found a reason to stay after all."

It was my turn to blush, and I looked down at my hands in my lap. As much as I believed him, something still bothered me. "Evan . . ." I chewed my lip a second before working up the courage to continue.

"Yes?" he said softly.

I forced myself to look at him. "Do you really think I'm underprivileged?" I heard the pain in my voice, even as I tried to mask it. "You said—"

"I know." He stretched a long arm all the way across the table and pulled my hand into his. "Listen to me," he said in a low voice. His thumb feathered over my knuckles. "What you heard was a frustrated man talking to a jealous woman. I don't care where you come from, Elizabeth. If anything, I admire you for it. I had everything handed to me my whole life."

"That's not true. You worked to get through college, through medical school."

"Those things are a lot easier when you don't have to worry about money," he said, his eyes serious. He gave my hand a squeeze. "Forgive me?"

"There's nothing to forgive."

He lifted my hand and placed the lightest kiss on my knuckles.

I caught my breath.

"Will you have dinner with me, Elizabeth Grant?"

All thoughts of secrets and duty and faith and responsibility fled. There was just this man, holding my hand, asking me to spend time with him.

And there was only one response I could give.

"Yes."

11

The restaurant was a small Italian place that looked like it could have come straight out of a movie. Doverton didn't have much of a downtown area, but there was a tiny historical center with the typical handful of nineteenth-century brick buildings.

The restaurant was squeezed into one of these, and it looked like it hadn't changed much since the place was built. The floors were made of thick wooden planks worn smooth and shiny from more than a century of use. The tables were covered with red-and-white-checkered tablecloths and topped with large mason jars bursting with wildflowers.

Dozens of tea lights were scattered across the tabletops, the nearby bar, and the hostess's stand in the small waiting area. The only other illumination came from ornate gas lamps that hung from curving brass pipes. The hazy light reflected off the tin ceiling and lent the restaurant a soft, romantic atmosphere.

Evan had found it when he was still new to town. Homesick and tired of fast food, he'd stumbled on it during an evening jog.

"I sat down in full winter running gear," he said as he

twirled spaghetti around his fork. "Sweats, jacket, gloves—I even wore a little beanie on my head." He smiled when I laughed at the image his words painted. "The waitress didn't even blink an eye, just brought me the biggest plate of pasta and meatballs I'd ever seen."

I tilted my head. "How did she know that's what you wanted?"

"I wondered the same thing. When I asked her, she just shrugged and said, 'You looked sad. Mama says meatballs make everything better.' "

I looked down at my plate. I'd already eaten several marinara-covered meatballs.

Mama might be onto something.

We ate and talked our way through pasta, meatballs, salad, and calamari. He pronounced the latter "acceptable" but not as good as the seafood back home. I took him at his word, since I'd never eaten squid in my life.

I worried we would have nothing to talk about, but I shouldn't have. The conversation bounced easily from one subject to another. We spoke about our mutual love of books. Evan was currently reading a thriller about a serial killer at the 1893 World's Fair.

I told him I was reading a novel about a midwife in the heart of Pennsylvania Amish country. I'd always been drawn to books about what I felt were other misunderstood religious orders, but it was the emphasis on the woman's point of view that had hooked me. Women in Riverview Heights had little authority outside overseeing their children. It was so different from the outside world.

Evan said he'd finally decided on paint colors for his condo and had moved all the furniture to the center of each room so he could work. He described being late for work yesterday because he'd accidentally blocked access to his dresser drawers. His neighbor, an elderly woman who'd taken it upon herself to look after him, had nearly called the police because she'd thought he was being robbed.

"I don't know what shocked her more," he said, winking at me. "The language I used as I moved three pieces of furniture out of the way at six in the morning, or the fact that I answered the door in my boxers."

I put a hand over my mouth so I wouldn't laugh with a mouthful of spaghetti. When I swallowed, I said, "I'm sure she didn't mind seeing the handsome young doctor in dishabille." Heat blasted my face. Had I really just called him handsome?

He grinned, then let me off the hook by changing the subject. "I don't really see you much around work," he said, spearing a piece of meatball.

"Yeah, well, Brittney keeps me pretty busy."

He frowned. "Busy how?"

I waved a hand. "She finally admitted she's been 'testing' me. I've suspected it for a while, because she won't let me near the patients, so it wasn't a big shock or anything to hear her say it."

Evan put his fork down. "What do you mean by testing you? What have you been doing?"

I shrugged and turned my fork sideways so I could cut into a meatball. "Cleaning, mostly. It's okay, Evan," I said when his expression turned angry. "It won't be forever. I'm not afraid of hard work."

"I know you're not. But the center has a maintenance staff. You weren't hired to clean, Elizabeth."

From the look on his face, Brittney was in for some harsh words tomorrow.

I lowered my own fork. "Evan, I told you that as a friend, not as a doctor at the center. Please, promise me you won't say anything to Brittney."

His eyes softened. "Why? She doesn't have to know you told me. I could say I noticed it on my own."

I took a deep breath. "Just trust me when I say I've fought and won battles like this before. I know how to handle someone like Brittney." I looked down at my plate. "I know I seem like a pushover, but there's more to winning than being the strongest or the loudest."

He made a sound that brought my head up. "You are a remarkable person, Elizabeth," he said softly. The glowing light highlighted the angles of his face, giving his features a stark purity normally hidden by his ready smile and animated expressions.

We stayed that way for a moment, just staring at each other, both caught and wholly aware of it. The noise around us faded to muted voices and the muffled sounds of cutlery and people moving about. I was the first to look away, my face heating from the intensity surging between us.

"I'm just me," I said, fiddling with my water glass.

He leaned across the table and touched my wrist. "I won't say anything to Brittney. But promise me you won't ever hesitate to come to me for help, okay? For anything."

"All right." I nodded slowly. "I promise."

When the server returned, Evan ordered a piece of chocolate cake for dessert. "Two plates," he told her, and she smiled. With her thick, dark hair and liquid brown eyes, she bore a striking resemblance to all the other servers.

A short time later, she set a massive piece of chocolate cake between us.

"I really couldn't eat another bite," I said as he cut it in half and handed me a plate and fork. Even halved, the cake needed two hands to safely navigate it to the table. It was a rich, decadent brown so dark it was almost black.

"That's okay. You can just watch me eat it." He took a bite and groaned. He spoke around the mouthful of cake. "You're missing out."

"Fine." I sighed and took a bite. My eyes closed involuntarily.

"See? What did I tell you?"

I opened my eyes. "You were right. It's incredible."

Evan licked his fork. "I'm always right."

"I think you enjoy gloating over food," I told him. "First the hot chocolate, now this." I waved my frosting-covered fork at him.

He carved off another huge bite of cake. "It seems ungrateful to complain when you're the one directly benefiting from my superior knowledge of chocolate-based foods."

The server brought coffee, and Evan told me more about his family. His brother had gone into orthopedics after breaking his leg in a skiing accident in college.

"Mom always says doctors make the worst patients, and I have to say she was definitely right about Brian. He rigged up a broomstick suspended from the ceiling so he could bang on the wall between our bedrooms any time he wanted something."

I laughed, picturing it. "Why not just pound on the wall?"

Evan's eyes gleamed. "I probably should have mentioned his undergrad degree is in mechanical engineering. He calculated the precise spot where the sound of the broomstick would be the loudest in my bedroom. The vibration shook my bed."

"The joy of siblings," I said, nabbing another forkful of cake.

"What about you?"

I paused with my fork halfway to my mouth. "What?"

"Do you have any brothers or sisters? You haven't said much about your family."

"Um." What could I tell him? That my father had been forced out of our home when I was ten years old and my mother had married a man with ten wives? That I had more than fifty stepsiblings, many of whom I'd never even met?

"I'm an only child," I said. "I'm . . ." I frowned, struggling to think of something neutral to say. Finally, I settled on an extremely abridged version of the truth. "My family and I are kind of estranged."

"Hey," he said, his eyes concerned, his cake forgotten. "I'm sorry I was nosy."

"No, no, it's okay." I smiled. "I just . . . we don't talk much. Once my mom died, I sort of lost contact with everyone." That much was true, at least. I had plenty of cousins in Illinois, all of whom had broken off communication when my mother got reassigned. I didn't blame them. They'd just been protecting their families. That didn't mean it hadn't hurt.

Still hurt.

"I'm sorry to hear that."

I waved it off. "It's all in the past. I'm over it."

He looked like he wanted to say more, but just then the server reappeared with the check. Evan left several bills on the table and helped me up.

"I feel like I might tip over," I said as we walked to the front of the restaurant. "I don't think I've ever eaten that much in my life."

Evan waved a goodbye to the smiling hostess, then held the door for me. "Do you want to walk for a bit?" he asked once we were outside. "There's a cute little art gallery right down the street. It's closed now, but it always has new paintings in the window."

I had a half hour until Jackson was due to pick me up at the bookstore. If this was going to be my last time with Evan, I wanted to make every minute count.

"All right."

He proffered his elbow in an old-fashioned gesture. I curled my hand around his arm and let him lead me down the wide brick sidewalk.

The night was warm, with a cool breeze that stirred my hair. I'd worn it in a very loose braid that draped over one shoulder.

When I'd stood in the bookstore bathroom, turning this way and that to check my reflection, I'd pulled a few pieces forward to frame my face. Between the casual hairstyle and the fitted shirt and calf-length fitted skirt, I felt light and feminine.

I hadn't realized how much my garments and usual clothing weighed me down.

"What are you thinking about?" Evan asked, his head angled toward mine as we walked. In this part of downtown, the little stretch of street in the historical district was lit by gaslights spaced about every twenty feet. The soft light gave everything a dreamy quality and turned his hair the color of butterscotch. A few steps from the restaurant, a tall, two-faced post clock stamped with *Doverton, Missouri* in gold letters stood like a sentinel at the edge of the street.

"I was just thinking how pretty it is here."

He smiled. "I'm glad you like it. I guess the gaslights are kind of a pain to keep up, but they're trying to attract more people to the area." He gestured to a broad glass window up ahead. "Here's the art gallery."

There were three big paintings in the window, each propped on a wooden easel. Peering through the glass, I could see other paintings on the walls inside, each one a burst of color against the stark white. The large paintings were done in primary colors and featured geometric shapes. I tilted my head, trying to figure them out, when a small painting—no, it was a sketch—near the window caught my eye.

I leaned forward, straining to make out its details in the dim light of the gas lamps. It was a simple sketch, done in either pencil or one of those charcoal pens artists use.

In it, a house sat high up on a sloping hillside. It was clearly an older home—a little jewel box of a cottage with neat windows and a deep porch. Tiny cows dotted the hill in the distance. Unlike the prints around it, which were all in plain black frames, the sketch sat in an ornate, bronze-colored frame that looked too heavy for the delicate cord suspending it on the wall.

"What do you think?" Evan murmured.

I pulled my gaze from the simple sketch and looked again at the three paintings in the window. The display was obviously centered around them. The gallery's spotlights in the ceiling shone done on each one, like laser beams that said, *Look here, these are important.*

Only they didn't pull at me like the black-and-white cottage. Evan watched me, an expectant look in his eyes.

"I think," I said slowly, "beauty is in the eye of the beholder."

He threw back his head and laughed, then put a big arm around my shoulders and pulled me to his side. The movement was so natural, I melted against him as if we did this all the time. Tucked under his arm, his fresh, clean scent filled my lungs—a mix of soap and whatever hair products he used. He wore jeans and a button-down under a thin sweater, but he still managed to look dressed up, which was probably due more to the cost of his clothes rather than the style. His jeans probably cost more than my entire closet.

"You want to know something?" His voice was low and conspiratorial. "I'm almost positive I made something incredibly similar in second grade art class."

We laughed softly. His right hand slid from my shoulder down to my hand. He folded his fingers around mind and turned me toward him.

"I don't know anything about art," I said.

"I don't, either. I read once, though, that art is anything that moves you." He looked at the paintings. "Maybe that's why it means so many different things to so many people."

"Thank you for tonight." I stared at the little house so I could forever hold it in my mind. "It was beautiful."

"Yes, it was," he said, and when I looked up he was looking at me.

My breath caught.

His head descended, and his mouth brushed mine in a light, questioning touch.

I parted my lips.

He cupped my cheek and deepened the kiss.

Shivers coursed over my skin. His mouth was warm, his lips soft. He didn't demand entry, or charge in like a conqueror.

He teased. He held back, inviting me to follow. When I did, he was right there with me, his mouth moving against mine.

He broke away first, resting his chin against my forehead with a sigh, his fingers threaded in the loose hair above my ear.

A deep, doleful chime rang out.

The clock we passed had begun to chime the hour.

I turned toward the sound. Even if we left now, it would still take at least ten minutes to get back to the bookstore. Jackson was never late.

"What is it?" Evan's eyes were concerned. He still held my hand, and now he gripped my elbow, pulling me back around. "What's wrong?"

"I have to get back." I shrugged from his grasp, then turned and walked quickly toward the restaurant, where his car sat in the lot next to the squat brick building. The clock continued to chime, the solemn notes coming one on top of the other, each one louder than the next.

"Elizabeth?" He followed, his voice bewildered. He caught up to me easily, his long strides matching mine. "Is something wrong? Listen, if this is about the kiss—"

I stopped. "No! Please don't think that." I looked down the street toward the clock, which was still ticking off the hours. Anxiety bubbled up in my chest. I had to get back to the bookstore. The longer I was gone, the more Jackson would suspect something was off. The clock finished its chiming, and the last note hovered in the air before slowly fading.

I faced Evan. "I just . . . things are complicated. I wish I could explain."

"Is it because of work? Because I can find a position anywhere."

I blinked. "I would never ask you to do that." The fact that he'd even suggested it made me realize just how serious he was about us.

He must have read that realization in my expression, because he brushed the back of his hand against my cheek. "I know we haven't spent a lot of time together, but I intend to remedy that. There is something between us. I don't know what it looks like yet, but it's powerful. I want to see where it goes."

So did I. Heaven help me, so did I.

But he would hate me if he ever learned the truth. How could I even hope to explain it to him?

I couldn't, which was why I had to find a way to put an end to this madness before it got too out of control. I couldn't have him leaving his job at the center because he thought I was worried about our blossoming relationship interfering with our professional lives.

"Don't you want the same?" He stepped close, his body warming mind. "You feel it, too. I know you do, Elizabeth."

"I do." I swayed toward him. I wanted nothing more than to press against him again, to feel his mouth on mine, but I couldn't allow it. I'd already indulged myself way more than I should have. If I'd learned anything in my twenty-five years on the planet, it was that pleasure came with a price. I could get away with seeing Evan for a little while, but he would eventually realize I'd been lying to him. And he didn't deserve that, so I had to let him go now.

I swallowed the lump in my throat and forced myself to look him in the eye. I spoke quickly before my resolve weakened again. "I just can't think right now. Can we talk tomorrow?"

He looked like he didn't quite believe me, but he nodded. "All right."

We walked the rest of the way to his car, and he opened the door and handed me in, then shut the door gently behind me. He seemed to sense my anxiety, because he didn't speak on the short drive to the bookstore. He didn't break any traffic laws, but he didn't waste any time, either.

He pulled into a parking spot near the front of the building. Before he could offer to walk me to my car, I grabbed my bag from the floor and opened my door. "Thank you. I had a really nice time."

"Elizabeth, are you sure nothing is wrong?"

"Just tired." Inspiration struck. "The days are long with Brittney in charge."

His face clouded, and a pang of guilt shot through me. "I hope you'll reconsider letting me help. You're not alone, Elizabeth. Not anymore."

An ache shot through my chest. He was so good.

And I was going to break his heart.

"Thank you," I said. Then I closed the door and walked away, a single thought drumming through my head.

Liar. Liar. Liar.

12

J ackson's truck idled in front of the building. He jumped
when I opened the door and tossed my bag on the floor.
He'd obviously been expecting me to leave through the
front of the center.

"Hey," I said, reaching for my seat belt. "Sorry to be late."

"It's all right. You okay?"

"Yes, of course." I glanced at him as I tucked a loose curl
into my braid. "Just work, you know?"

He didn't reply, just put the truck in reverse and pulled out
of the spot.

We rode in silence until we reached the highway, when he
gave me a sideways look. "Listen, Liz," he began. He sent me
another look, his eyes moving from my face back to the road in
a nervous slide.

"What is it?"

"I just want you to know . . . I won't tell anyone where you
were."

My stomach dropped, and I swallowed a few times before
replying. "What do you mean?"

He cleared his throat. "I know you weren't at work, okay?" He glanced at my clothes.

I plucked at my shirt. "This? I always change before I leave the center. You know that."

He took his eyes off the road long enough to level a decidedly skeptical look in my direction. "Look, I know you went to dinner somewhere."

I let my shoulders slump. "How can you tell?" My outfit was a little unusual, but not so far out of the ordinary to make it obvious where I spent the past few hours.

"You smell like garlic. If I were a vampire, I'd be dead right now."

I drew a deep breath. "Jackson—"

"I said I won't tell anyone, and I won't," he told the road ahead. "I'm not going to ask any questions. The less I know, the better. But, Elizabeth, you can't put me in this kind of position again."

"I know. I am so sorry, Jackson." I bit my lip. He was right. It wasn't fair to drag him into my sins. I looked at him. "I'm really very sorry."

He tossed me his usual grin. "At least bring me some leftovers next time?"

"There won't be a next time."

The grin faded, replaced by a weathered maturity that had no business on a sixteen-year-old's face. "It's better that way," he said.

"I know."

The lights along the highway flashed past as we drove the last few miles home. Jackson put his hand, palm up, on the seat between us.

I placed mine on top. He said nothing about the tears tracking slowly down my face—just curled his fingers over mine.

THERE WEREN'T MANY LIGHTS ON IN RIVERVIEW HEIGHTS. THE Priesthood Council strictly enforced the community's curfew. Get caught, and you could expect to be hauled in front of the Council to explain why you were outside past dark.

There weren't many streetlights, either, which was why I jumped when a pair of bright headlights flickered to life as we drove past the town hall.

"It's Theron and Bragg," Jackson muttered. His knuckles turned white on top of the steering wheel.

"What are they doing?"

Jackson shook his head. "No idea. They weren't supposed to have patrol duty tonight."

The headlights followed us. I sat straighter in my seat as the truck bumped along the narrow road leading through town. We turned onto Dinah's road.

Theron and Bragg turned, too.

Jackson shot me a worried look. Dinah's sons hadn't earned a reputation for being fair . . . or kind.

"As soon as we park, I want you to go straight inside." Jackson spoke in a low, hushed voice, as if Theron and Bragg could hear us.

"What about you?"

"They're not going to hurt me," he said, the implication being that they might hurt *me*. I was grateful for Jackson's willingness to put himself between me and his half brothers, but he was wrong if he thought I would let him fend for himself. At twenty-two and twenty, Theron and Bragg were grown men. Jackson was smarter and faster, but he was no match for their strength.

He was also wrong to assume I'd be safe in the house. With Thomas, Dinah, and Jonah still in Utah, there was no one home. If anything, I was safer outside, where I could run to Patty's or scream for help.

"They're not going to hurt anyone," I said as Jackson pulled the truck to a stop in Dinah's driveway.

I got out and squared my shoulders, even though my knees were quivering. Jackson rounded the back of the truck and stopped.

Theron and Bragg slammed their doors, their bodies two large, dark silhouettes in their truck's headlights.

Bragg's boots crunched on the gravel as he approached. His features came into view as he neared, and a sneer twisted his mouth as he looked me up and down.

"Is this how you dress when my father is away?" Like all of Dinah's children, he had thick brown hair and brown eyes. Whereas Theron was tall and muscled, Bragg was smaller and more wiry than bulky.

He wasn't weak, though. I'd seen him swing a hammer on Thomas's work sites.

I hitched my bag up on my shoulder. "Thanks for the escort. We're okay, though. You should get back to your patrol."

On the other side of the truck, Theron snickered. "You've always been an uppity bitch, *Mother* Elizabeth." Unlike his brother, there was no question of Theron's strength. He stood well over six feet, with shoulders that could have taken out a doorframe.

He also had no problem throwing his weight around. Thomas had received several complaints about him harassing younger girls in the community. During the brief time we lived under the same roof, he'd found several excuses to show up in my bedroom when I was stepping out of the shower or undressing for bed.

Jackson's shoulders twitched, but I spoke before he could say anything. He had nothing to gain and a lot to lose by being a hero. Theron and Bragg were bullies.

I knew how to handle bullies.

I smiled at Theron. "I'll be sure to let Thomas know how you feel."

He narrowed his gaze. Unlike Bragg, whose IQ left much to be desired, Theron wasn't stupid. He knew exactly why his father had told him to move out. Thomas wouldn't be pleased to hear his oldest sons had harassed his youngest wife.

He crossed his arms. "You're out past curfew. Where were you?"

As a patrol officer, he had a right to ask. Riverview Heights didn't have its own police force. Technically, he was the law in the community, as scary as that was. Theron and Bragg, along with a few other men from the Righteous Brethren, had been deputized by the local sheriff's department, which meant they had police and arrest powers.

They also had a shotgun strapped to a gun rack on the inside of their truck.

Jackson spoke up from the other side of his truck's bumper. "Elizabeth worked late. We stopped for some dinner on the way home."

Theron's gaze flicked to him. "Is that right?" Without warning, he advanced on me, moving far faster than a man his size had a right to.

Jackson pivoted, but Theron marched past him, not stopping until he was inches from me.

I held my ground. A bead of sweat trickled down my spine.

Theron's nostrils flared, like a bloodhound taking in a scent. He stood inches away, forcing me to tilt my head back to meet his eyes.

And I had to meet his eyes. He was a predator through and through. Take your eyes off a predator, and you can count on being a victim.

In a blur of movement, he snagged a thick finger in the neck of my shirt and pulled the fabric away from my body.

I gasped and stumbled forward.

He peered down the front of my shirt. Without my garments, my bra and the swells of my breasts were visible, along with my bare stomach below.

I slapped at his shoulders. "Let me go, you ass!"

He gathered the white fabric in a meaty fist and tugged me up and against him. With his other hand, he sent a charging Jackson sprawling onto the grass next to the driveway.

Bragg laughed, then strode to Jackson and gave him a vicious kick in the ribs.

Jackson cried out.

A strangled scream caught in my throat.

Theron put his face next to mine. "How dare you threaten me," he said in a menacing voice. The hand holding my shirt clenched tighter, and I heard fabric rip. "You think you can parade around here, flaunting yourself like a whore, just because your Father's favorite?"

I jerked against his hold. "I'm no whore—"

"Oh, really?" He gave my breasts another long, lingering look.

My skin crawled. I jerked again. It was like trying to move a boulder with a toothpick.

Theron smiled. "Rumor has it Father isn't all that happy with you right now. Piss him off too much, and he'll have you reassigned." He put his mouth near my ear, his breath hot on my cheek. "Who knows, you might even end up in my bed. I'd take a great deal of pleasure in teaching you some respect." His tongue touched the curve of my ear. "The old man may not be able to knock you up, but I guarantee it wouldn't be a problem for me."

Nausea burned my throat. Saliva filled my mouth. Thomas would never give me to Theron.

Would he?

I jerked my head away from his mouth. "I would rather die."

Theron was unmarried. If the Council reassigned me to him, I'd be a first wife.

And I would have to marry him in the secular world as well as ours.

He slid a hand down my side to my butt. Then he squeezed, his fingers digging into my flesh. A whimper escaped my lips before I could stop it.

"I'm sure we can arrange that, too, sweetheart." Another squeeze. "But not before I get a few rides out of you first."

He released me, and I staggered back.

Bragg's gaze lowered to my chest, and he smirked.

With shaking hands, I pulled the halves of my ruined shirt together. I lowered my eyes. *It was better to go unnoticed.*

Theron chucked me under the chin. "That's better." He gripped my jaw, forcing my gaze to his. "You say anything to Father about this, and I'll make sure he knows you two little lovebirds went on a date tonight. We clear?"

I closed my eyes. It was probably stupid to let him out of my sight, but I didn't want him to see the hatred burning in my gaze. "Yes."

He gave my cheek a light slap. More of a pat, but it nudged my head to the side.

I stared at the ground.

Theron turned. "Come on," he said to Bragg. Their boots thudded against the ground. Doors slammed, and their truck's engine revved as they reversed down the driveway.

I ran to Jackson and fell to my knees beside him. "Oh m-my God. Are you all right?" My hands hovered in the air.

Jackson grunted. "Never better."

Relief coursed through my veins.

He started to sit, then clutched his side and fell back. "Bastard broke my ribs, I think."

"Let me look." I unbuttoned his shirt with quick fingers. A huge bruise was already blossoming over his rib cage. I pushed various spots on his chest, pausing when he sucked in breaths.

After a second, I sat back on my heels. "I don't think anything is broken. Just bruised."

"That's good, I guess."

He let me help him up, and I slung his arm around my shoulders as we shuffled to Patty's house.

"We made a lot of noise," I said, glancing at her window. "I can't believe no one came out."

"That's because they're all at Kelly's. Mom took the little kids over there for dinner."

I opened Patty's side door and helped him inside. We took it slow across the garage, then made our way up the steps and into the house.

I rushed to the kitchen table and pulled out a chair.

He sat with a grimace, then gave me a thumbs-up.

I stood back. "Let's move you to the living room. You'll be more comfortable on the sofa."

"No." Hunched over, he shook his head. "Once I lie down, I'm not getting back up. It's better to go to my room."

"Jackson, that's all the way upstairs. Your ribs could be broken!"

"You said they aren't. What kind of doctor are you, anyway?"

I put my hands on my hips. "I'm not any kind of doctor, and you know it. You need to see someone who is, if not tonight, then first thing in the morning."

"I'm fine."

"No, you're not."

He stood and straightened, as if to demonstrate how fit he was. "See? Totally fine."

"You're sweating."

He sighed. "I've had broken ribs before. I can tell the difference. I'll be all right in a few days." He looked down. "Go home, Liz, before someone comes home and sees you."

Guilt was like battery acid in my gut. First, I'd tricked him into helping me go on a date. Now, he was injured and hurting.

Also my fault.

"At least let me help you upstairs."

"I got it." He nodded his chin toward the door. "Go on home."

We stared at each other for a beat.

"Okay," I said. "But I'm checking on you in the morning."

"Fair enough."

I went to the door. Before I slipped through it, he called my name. I turned.

His eyes were shaded with pain, but his voice was steady. "Be smart, okay, Liz? Wherever you went tonight, just . . . be smart."

"I will. I'm putting a stop to it."

He closed his eyes, obviously relieved. "Good. That's . . . really good. I don't want anything to happen to you." He turned and limped toward the stairs.

I waited until he made it to the top. Then I let myself out and headed back to Dinah's. I closed the slider and leaned my forehead against the glass.

Theron's taunt replayed in my mind.

He'd called me Thomas's favorite.

I huffed a laugh. *Please.* In what universe?

Men in our faith weren't supposed to play favorites, but it seemed to happen anyway. My mother had always rolled her eyes at the power struggles among my stepfather's wives. She'd also warned that favorites never stayed that way.

"Men are fickle by nature," she'd say, then her eyes would get a sad, faraway look, and she'd add, "except for your father. From the moment he started courting me, Nathan Grant never even looked at another woman."

Even so, it hadn't kept them together. Their love hadn't been strong enough to stand against the prophet and the Righteous Brethren.

Evan's face floated into my mind. I pictured him sitting across from me at the table in the Italian restaurant, his eyes mischievous as he told me about the pranks he used to play on his brother. For a little while tonight, I'd felt like I belonged in his world. Our dinner had been like a fairy tale.

But it wasn't. In real life, the princess just stayed a housemaid. There were no glass slippers or magical pumpkins.

I flicked the door lock and went upstairs. Light from a three-quarter moon filtered in through the windows, drowning everything in silver.

In my bathroom, I started the shower and studied my reflection in the mirror while I waited for the water to heat up.

The woman gazing back at me looked anxious and haunted, with faint purple smudges under dark blue eyes.

It was the same look I'd seen my mother wear for six long years as time, illness, and worry had sapped her beauty and ravaged her health. She had never, not once, made me feel guilty for her situation, but as a woman with a child in the community, she'd had to choose between keeping me and following her heart.

Until tonight, I'd never quite felt the full weight of her decision.

I turned from the mirror, stripped off my clothes, and stepped in the shower. The water was too hot, but I left it. I needed to *feel*. Bracing my hands against the tiled wall, I stood under the spray and angled my head down so the water beat against my upper back.

In the five years since I married Thomas, I had never really been bothered by my inability to conceive. Dinah's snide little digs should have hurt.

They didn't. And now I knew why.

I didn't want a child with Thomas. A baby would tie me to

him—and the faith—forever. And my commitment to the faith was on shaky ground.

I stared at the water flowing in tiny rivers around my feet. When had the doubt crept in? I couldn't really pinpoint an exact lightning-bolt moment.

No, it had fallen away in bits, like chips of rock flying under an artist's chisel.

Over the past couple months, several things had made those chips more noticeable. Work had thrust me into the outside world, where I'd met Evan. The more time I spent with him, the more I realized the life I had with Thomas wasn't normal or happy. There was also Prophet Benson's visit, and Thomas's decision to marry off Daria.

Chip, chip, chip.

In my mind's eye, the years stretched before me, like miles passing on a lonely road in the middle of nowhere. Scenery flashed by, changing so little you didn't even notice it after a while, until eventually you grew numb to your surroundings and stopped looking for something interesting or different on the horizon.

Is that how my mother had felt? Is that how Dinah felt now? And how long would it take before Thomas tired of me and took a fifth wife? Or a sixth or seventh?

Growing up, I'd always heard how the faith was so good for families. With more than one mother in the house, children were never neglected or in want of affection. Men got all their needs met, too. If one wife was a bad cook, chances are another was skilled in the kitchen.

No one ever talked about the women's needs except to point out that it was only possible to have so many children when you had sister-wives to rely on. When she was well, my mother had often looked after my stepsiblings while their mothers ran errands or did housework.

She'd always considered herself very fortunate she hadn't

conceived again. "I don't need another reason for the others to hate me," she'd told me once, referring to her husband's wives. That had been in the beginning, before her illness had worn away most of her beauty.

In those first few years, my stepfather had summoned her to his bed several times a week. One of the other wives would knock softly on the door to the bedroom we shared, which was the signal Mother was supposed to go down the hall to the big bedroom at the top of the stairs.

No matter how many times I heard that knock, I always kept my back to the door. Feigning sleep meant I didn't have to meet my mother's eyes as she pulled on her robe and shuffled out of the room, her beautiful pale hair touched with silver in the moonlight.

In the shower, the water ran cold. I soaped my body, then did the same to my hair. My mother had been a woman of deep faith. But she had loved my father just as deeply.

I turned the water off and stood dripping and shivering in the darkened bathroom. What would she tell me to do now?

I wrapped a towel around my body and sat on the closed toilet seat. Would she be proud of me? A woman contemplating abandoning her marriage? Abandoning her faith?

It wasn't like I had anywhere to go.

Evan's voice flowed through my mind like a cool river. *You're not alone, Elizabeth. Not anymore.*

I lowered my head and squeezed my eyes shut. I couldn't tell him the truth about my life. He was from Connecticut, for crying out loud, the son of a renowned heart surgeon. He was educated and kind. He was romantic.

He was so many things I wanted but could never have.

Worse, confiding in him could put him in danger. The Priesthood Council had a long reach. Thomas had plenty of influence in Jefferson City. If he found out about Evan, who knew what he was capable of. He'd find a way to hurt Evan, if not physically, then maybe professionally.

I stood and went to the bedroom, where I stared down at the smooth quilt. My stomach twisted, and I turned away.

I brushed out my hair, then threw a nightgown over my head and grabbed my pillow from the bed. In the living room, I spread a blanket over the sofa and lay down.

So much had happened in the past twenty-four hours, I couldn't think anymore. Somehow, I had to distance myself from Evan while figuring out how to extricate myself from the faith.

In the darkness, I touched my lips, rubbing my fingertips over the spot where Evan's mouth had met mine. Something had happened between us tonight. The whole evening had been touched by magic.

A fairy tale.

And I was going to reach out and stifle it before it had a chance to become something solid and real.

13

The following morning, a different truck waited in the driveway to take me to work.

I froze, then memories flooded me.

Jackson's ribs. Right.

What excuse had he given his mother for missing work? I'd have to find a way to talk to him so we could get our stories straight.

My new driver didn't say a word when I climbed in the truck—just nodded and reversed down the driveway with businesslike precision. I looked out the window.

At work, I hurried into the locker room and right over to the laundry bin.

Empty.

My throat went dry. Someone from housekeeping must have already carted off the soiled scrubs to be laundered, unknowingly taking my garments with them. Allowing garments to fall into the hands of an outsider was a grievous sin. Fortunately, the Priesthood Council would never find out I'd thrown mine in a pile of dirty scrubs.

I changed and headed toward Brittney's office to get the

day's assignments. A thousand butterflies had taken up residence in my stomach. What if I bumped into Evan? He'd want to talk about last night, maybe even ask me out again.

The sight of Brittney was like a record needle scratch on my thoughts. She stood outside the medication supply closet, a clipboard in her hand and a frown on her face. She looked up as I approached. "Oh, hey, Elizabeth. Could you come over here?"

I hurried to her side. "Is anything wrong?" Panic streaked through me. Had she noticed the missing drug samples? I'd left them on Patty's kitchen counter that morning, along with a note for Leah.

"I don't think so," she said, looking down at her clipboard. "I'm just a little confused. You put Advair and Symbicort in two different spots. They're in the same drug family, so they really should go together."

I nearly sagged with relief. "No problem. I can move them around."

"That's fine." Brittney pulled a piece of paper from her clipboard and handed it to me. "We have another busy day on our hands, I'm afraid. I'll also need you to man the phones during lunch, since the pharm rep is still here."

"Okay." It would keep me away from Evan . . . and give me a chance to think.

The day passed quickly. I saw Evan just once, accompanied by the pharmaceutical sales rep, who appeared to be regaling him with stories about her latest trip to the Bahamas.

He caught my eye and smiled, a look of exasperation on his face.

I smiled back.

The rep leaned a slender hip clad in a pencil skirt against the white counter. Did she realize how much she waved her hands around when she talked? Long, manicured nails flashed like mini sabers every time she started a new sentence.

Evan looked at me again and winked. I ducked my head to hide my smile.

I carried the secret of our dinner in my heart like the treasure it was. I'd committed the whole evening to memory. Years from now, I'd be able to take out that memory and relive it. Maybe by then it wouldn't hurt so bad.

I was so occupied by the dilemma of breaking things off with him, I entered the locker room in a daze at the end of my shift.

So I didn't notice Brittney sitting at the break table.

"I know where you're from," she said.

I stopped. "You scared me." Then the force of her words hit me. A wrapped parcel sat on the table, its side stamped with a dry cleaner's logo.

She followed my gaze. "Nothing to say?" She touched the package. "See, I noticed these in the bin yesterday, after you left. I grew up just a few miles down the road from Riverview Heights." She leaned forward. "So I know *exactly* what you are."

"You had them dry-cleaned?" There was no use pretending I didn't know what was in the package.

She lifted a slim shoulder. "You threw them in the laundry. Didn't you want them cleaned?"

"You can't fire me." The library had all kinds of books about religious discrimination.

She laughed. "Who said anything about firing you?"

"If you're not going to fire me, what do you want?"

"Are you married?" She narrowed her gaze. "You must be. Or at least what you people consider marriage. Did your little date with Evan break some sacred rule?"

"Why are you doing this?" I was so tired of her shit.

Shit. I was going to say that one out loud as soon as possible. Maybe in the next few minutes.

Her smile vanished, and she stood. She put her palms flat

on either side of the wrapped garments. "Believe it or not, I care about Evan. I don't want to see him hurt."

"Neither do I."

She tilted her head. "Really? I find that difficult to believe."

"Evan and I are friends. I want it to be something more." I took a deep breath. "But it can't be."

"What about all your little lunch dates? All those longing looks at each other in the hallways?" She spat the last, and the hostility in her voice almost made me back up a step.

I gestured for her to give me my garments. "I don't owe you an explanation, but I'm going to talk to him. Soon."

She pulled the package close, a protective hand on the cleaning ticket. "What are you going to tell him?" She sounded like Dinah when she forced me to repeat a command so she knew I understood exactly what she wanted me to do.

I wanted to point out the ridiculousness of a grown woman using another woman's underwear as blackmail, but there was no point arguing with her. "You don't have anything to worry about. There can't be anything between us." I held her glittering green gaze. "If you really know as much about me as you think you do, you know why."

A few seconds passed, then she shoved the package. It slid across the table.

I caught it before it fell.

"Good," she said, then walked toward the opening. Just before she left the locker room, she stopped. "Tell him quickly," she said over her shoulder, "or I will."

I forgot about Jackson until I saw an unfamiliar work truck waiting for me outside the center.

The driver looked about my age, but a receding hairline would eventually make him look much older.

I got in and gave him a tentative smile. "Is Jackson feeling any better?"

The man shrugged and put the truck in gear.

Another conversationalist.

I sighed and looked out the window, fantasizing about what it would be like to have my own car.

I might even settle for a bicycle at this point. Just as long as I didn't have to share it.

I sat up straighter in the seat when we missed the turn to get on the highway. When the driver showed no sign of realizing his mistake, I hooked a thumb back toward the highway. "Hey, you missed the on-ramp."

He glanced at me. "Brother Hyde said to take you to the job site."

My stomach did a flip. Thomas was back? He wasn't supposed to arrive until later in the evening.

Theron told him.

There was no other explanation for his early return. My hand brushed the plastic armrest built into the door. For a wild moment, I contemplated jumping out the next time the truck stopped at an intersection.

I slumped back in my seat. It was a stupid idea. I'd probably break an ankle. And even if I managed to get out safely, where would I go? I still had the same twenty dollars Dinah had given me when I'd first started at the center. That might buy dinner, assuming Thomas didn't find me first.

Every once in a while, stories of a runaway filtered through the community. Usually, it was a young man, like Dinah's oldest son, Tom. He'd run fast and far. As far as I knew, no one from the faith had ever tracked him down. Others hadn't been so lucky.

I swallowed. Those were just stories, I told myself—whispered tales mothers told their children to keep them from seeking sin in the outside world.

We passed a few strip malls and a cluster of industrial-looking buildings before turning down a road that looked like it had been freshly poured. The concrete was so white and pristine it was like sand on a sunny beach.

Here, the buildings were all large, square monuments with small signs out front that proclaimed what each one manufactured. I spotted the work site ahead—a cluster of white trailers with *Hyde Construction* in red letters on the side. Thomas's blue work truck was parked in front of the largest one. Nearby, a giant yellow excavator crawled over a muddy field.

The driver parked, then turned to me. "We're here."

"Thanks," I said, not quite succeeding in concealing my sarcasm.

He stared, his face impassive.

I pulled my bag off the floor and left the truck without another word.

I'd taken two steps when the door of the largest trailer swung open and Thomas stepped out.

I froze. This was it. He was going to murder me.

Or, worse, reassign me to Theron.

But he smiled and jogged down the steps. "Elizabeth." He came to me and took my hands in his. "I've missed you." He looked over my shoulder and lifted a hand. "We're okay here, Joe. Thanks."

The driver started the truck and backed out.

Thomas looked at me, his blue eyes intense. "What's this, no greeting for your husband?"

"Um." I gave my head a little shake. "Hey. I m-mean, I missed you, too." I leaned forward, my mouth aimed at his cheek.

He made a tsking sound and pulled back. "Not here." His gaze scanned the trailers around us.

Right. Public. "I'm sorry. I forgot."

"We can take things inside. Come on." He tugged me toward the trailer's metal steps.

I followed him inside. The smell of coffee enveloped me. His white hard hat rested on a drafting table. A rickety looking card table and chairs held a box of donuts and a two liter of Mountain Dew.

So much for the Righteous Brethren's' no-caffeine rule.

Thomas leaned against the drafting table. "What's wrong?"

I pulled my gaze from the soda. "Nothing." I forced a smile. "I guess I'm just surprised to see you so early. And I wasn't expecting to come here."

He reached out and snagged the edge of my skirt, then used it to pull me between his thighs. "I missed you while I was in Utah. I guess I couldn't wait to see you."

"How did it go? Was Dinah okay?"

"Daria is happy, which helps." His tone was clipped. "Dinah is staying a couple weeks to help her settle in."

Two weeks without Dinah? It was my personal version of heaven.

Except it left Thomas free to make good on his fertility-clinic threat.

Fuck. I was fucked.

Thomas ran a hand down my braid, then moved his palm to my breast. He cupped it, as if testing the weight. Then he went for the buttons of my shirt.

"Wh-What are you doing?" I backed up.

He seized my hips and pulled me back. "What's it look like?"

"I . . . It's daytime."

He leaned back. "You think people only do this in the dark?" He tapped my nose like I was an endearing but not too bright child.

"No, of course not—"

"Then be quiet and enjoy it." He started on my buttons again.

I grabbed his wrists. "Thomas, stop."

He met my gaze, a frown between his eyes. "What is wrong with you?"

"It's not my night."

"I don't need to schedule a time to make love to you."

I pasted a smile on my face. "Of course not. I just . . ." I moved my hands to his shoulders, patted down the edges of his collar. "Can't we wait until we get home?"

A curious light entered his eyes. "Is there something going on at that job of yours?"

Panic bolted down my spine. My heart kicked into a hard, throbbing rhythm, the rush of blood in my ears so loud I shook my head. "No. There's nothing at my work."

His fingers tightened on my waist. "You've been distant with me. Ever since you started at that place."

Could he see the pulse in my neck? I licked my lips. "I-I'm sorry. I'll try to do better."

Silence stretched. He studied me, his face inscrutable. Then he patted my ass. "Start now."

I stared.

He drew in a breath, his face like a man who's used to suffering fools. "Take your clothes off, Elizabeth."

Take my . . . I stepped back, and he folded his arms.

Waiting.

This was the bargain. He was willing to let me keep working, as long as I stripped down and slept with him in his construction trailer. It didn't matter if my job was at the center.

No, Thomas's price applied to *any* job. Do this, his gaze said, or spend the rest of your days as Dinah's workhorse.

Was it prostitution if the john was your husband?

Well, sort of husband.

Like a robot, I unbuttoned my shirt and shrugged it off. My

skirt was next. Then my shoes. When I stood barefoot before him, in nothing but my garments, he pushed away from the table.

"Beautiful." He touched a nipple through the thin material. "Now the rest."

I pulled the utilitarian bra over my hand, then let the white briefs drop to the floor. The trailer was warm, but I shivered.

Thomas ran his gaze over my nude body before taking my wrist and tugging me to the drafting table. He backed me up, then pressed my shoulders until I perched on the edge. The wood creaked beneath me.

"I don't think—"

"Shush," he said. "Lie back."

I let him press me down. My shoulder blades hit the wood, and papers shifted under me.

He spread my thighs and stepped between them.

I focused on the ceiling tiles. Dark stains marred most of them.

Thomas slid his hands up my thighs, reaching my center. He worked a finger inside me and pumped it in and out, drawing moisture.

But it wasn't enough. No fire built. There were no tendrils of desire.

There was just the drafting table and the trailer, and the cold, demanding man between my legs.

Making me trade sex for a little bit of freedom.

"Loosen up," he said. "You're dry as a bone."

I curled my fingers around the edge of the table, gripping it tight.

After a minute, he sucked a finger into his mouth, then rubbed it over my sex, slipping it inside me.

I clenched my jaw.

He unzipped his pants, pulled himself out, and pushed inside.

My entranced burned. I squeezed my eyes shut.

He thrust once, twice, letting out a groan. Then he grasped my hips and pistoned in and out.

The table squeaked, shifting across the floor. Beneath me, the blueprints rustled.

Thomas buried his face in my neck, his lips hot on my skin. His soft grunts punctuated every thrust.

I counted them. *One, two, three, four.* He slowed, then started up again. *Five, six, seven . . .*

His breath hitched—the sign he was ready to finish. He thrusted one last time, then warmth flooded me.

He panted against my neck for a second, then pushed himself upright. Chest heaving, he tucked himself back into his pants. "I'll give you a few minutes to clean up."

The trailer door slammed before I even registered he was gone.

14

I lay on the table.

Except it wasn't me.

I was somewhere else—drifting up, somewhere far away from the spread-eagled woman below.

A car door slammed, and I was back in my body. I sat up, then wiggled down the table and stood. A paper detached itself from my butt and fluttered to the floor.

I dressed quickly, my hands on autopilot.

My braid had come loose, so I finger-combed my hair and put it in a low ponytail. I was straightening up the papers on the drafting table when a sharp knock rang out. A second later, Thomas stepped inside. "Ready?"

I nodded and started to walk past him. He stopped me with a hand on my arm. "I'm sorry I was a bit rough."

"It's fine." Everything was fine.

He leaned in and brushed a kiss on my forehead. "I missed you so badly," he murmured.

"I missed you, too."

He ushered me out of the trailer with a hand at the small of my back.

"Are you hungry?" he asked when we were backing away from the deserted work site.

"Not really." I concentrated on the scenery, the people in passing cars. Where were they going, I wondered?

Maybe they were on their way to a vacation. The closest I'd ever gotten to a vacation was the trip I'd taken from Illinois to Missouri when I married Thomas. But most people took vacations. Someone in one of those cars had to be going somewhere exotic and exciting, didn't they? More likely, they were just headed home from someplace ordinary, like work or the grocery store.

"Still full from dinner last night?" Thomas asked.

Slowly, so very slowly, I turned my head toward him. He *knew*. He'd known the whole time.

And he raped you for it, a voice said in my mind.

I shoved it aside.

"Theron called from the deputy's office last night," Thomas said, his big hands on the steering wheel. "He said you and Jackson didn't return home until well after nine. Where were you?" He said the last in the same easy tone, but I heard the underlying tension in the words, each word spoken with whip-like precision.

"I worked late, Thomas, that's all. We stopped for dinner on the way home."

"You should be careful about such things," he said as he merged onto the highway. "Even the appearance of impropriety is unacceptable for the wife of a member of the Priesthood Council."

I looked at him. "Jackson is your son. He's also sixteen."

He glanced at me. "I keep forgetting you were an only child. Teenage boys can't control themselves, especially around pretty women."

A lick of worry flared to life in my mind. I didn't have any biological siblings. But I had lived with more than a dozen stepbrothers. The same pattern had repeated over and over again in my stepfather's house. Once a boy reached fourteen or fifteen, he'd stop showing up for meals. That's how we'd know his time in the house was over. Most boys ended up in one of the rundown houses on the outskirts of the community, but others . . .

No one ever seemed to know where the others went. The one time I'd mentioned it to my mother, she'd turned white and begged me to never bring it up again.

Jackson and his older brother, Aaron, had already spent years on the work detail. The next boy in line, Kevin, was just fourteen, but Thomas had already put him on a few smaller jobs. Patty's sons were all just two years apart. If Thomas threw them all out at once, she'd be left with just little Ginny.

I dared another glance at him. What kind of man would toss his own children out like garbage, just so the older men in the community could have young wives?

If I had a son with Thomas, I'd have to hope he was one of the lucky few who were permitted to have a family. And if I had a daughter, I would be forced to raise her to step into a life exactly like mine.

I looked toward the horizon, at the freedom it represented.

If only I could think of a way to reach it.

15

I woke in the dark, gasping.

I was on the sofa again, and I sat up, squinting toward the stairs.

Thomas shouldn't be here now. It was Patty's night.

And we'd already had sex today. Or yesterday, I guessed.

It wasn't sex, the voice in my head reminded me.

I glanced at the old VCR. What time was it, anyway?

"It's two in the morning," Patty said from the stairs.

I jumped. "Good grief, Patty. You scared me to death." Had she watched me sleep? As my eyes adjusted, her face was a pale oval in the darkness. I stood and wrapped the blanket around my shoulders.

She stayed put, her feet on the top step. As if she wanted to separate herself as much as possible from my personal space. "You slept through dinner."

I tightened my hold on the blanket. "Sorry. I hope you guys left the dishes. I'll take care of them in the morning."

"Thomas wouldn't let us wake you up," she said, as if I hadn't spoken. "He said you need your rest, that your job wears you out."

"Patty, I—"

"As far as I can see, your only job is parading around here, acting the *slut*."

"What are you talking about?" Did she know about the construction trailer? Because if she wanted private time with Thomas, she could be my fucking guest.

"Don't act like you don't know!" She took a step into the room. "Jackson is my *son*. He is sixteen years old. Whatever game you're playing, you had no right to drag my child into it."

My knees loosened. Oh no. Oh no, oh no, oh no. I had to swallow before I could get words out. "What happened?"

Her breaths were heavy, like she'd just run a long distance. If looks could kill, I would have died on the spot. "Thomas ordered Jackson to move into one of the workhouses. I had to pack up his room this afternoon."

I sat down.

"Very convincing, Elizabeth. I can almost believe you didn't know anything about this."

"I didn't." I put my head in my hands.

There was a rustle of cloth, then the sound of footsteps retreating down the wooden stairs.

I lifted my head. "Patty."

The footsteps stopped. "What."

"I'll talk to Thomas. I will fix this."

Silence swelled. I waited for her to continue down the steps, but she spoke, her voice quiet. And sad.

"You can't fix this. None of us can fix this place."

16

F atigue dragged at me as I walked into work.

After Patty left, I never fell back asleep. How could I? Jackson was at a workhouse because of me.

Maybe I could talk to Thomas . . .

As I entered the locker room, I shook my head. After the trailer, there was no talking to him. He proved he couldn't be reasoned with. Or trusted.

I had to figure this out on my own.

I'd just tied the string of my scrub pants when Natalie walked in.

"Hey, Nat." I got a look at her face, and my smile died. "What's wrong?"

"Brittney and Dr. Adgate need to see you in the conference room." She didn't quite look at me.

"Now?"

She nodded. Still not making eye contact, she said, "I'm supposed to make sure you go straight there."

My heart rate picked up. A curious sense of detachment came over me as I followed her out of the locker room and down the hall to the conference room across from the nurses' station. I'd only been in there once, to clean it. Then, I'd only switched on a couple of lights—just enough to keep me from stumbling into something. This morning, the rectangular room was lit with a blaze of fluorescent lights. Evan sat at the head of the large conference table, Brittney immediately to his left.

Natalie waited for me to step inside, then followed me in and closed the door.

Evan spoke. "Please, have a seat, Elizabeth."

I sat. Why wasn't he looking at me?

Brittney didn't, either. She rifled through a stack of papers, the tip of her tongue between her lips.

Evan cleared his throat. "I'm going to get right down to business. Brittney has brought something to my attention." He grabbed a TV remote from the table and pointed it toward an open cabinet set in the wall. He punched a button, and a grainy, black-and-white image appeared on the television screen.

The image was me. This was surveillance footage. On the screen, I stood in front of the medication closet, then I looked up and down the hall and stuffed a few boxes in my scrubs pocket.

I clutched the side of the conference table. How could I have been so stupid? Brittney had told me there were security cameras all over the center.

Evan paused the video. The room was quiet as everyone stared at the blurry image of my frozen face.

Finally, Evan spoke. "Elizabeth, did you take medication from the med closet?"

His question was a formality. Probably something HR made him ask. We'd all just watched me help myself to prescription drugs. I looked at Natalie, who stared at her folded hands on top of the conference table, a little frown pulling her light brown eyebrows together.

My gaze moved to Brittney, who regarded me with an impassive expression. I'd expected her to gloat, but I guessed she didn't need to. I'd been the instrument of my own undoing. There was nothing for her to feel triumphant about.

I swallowed and forced myself to meet Evan's eyes. "Yes. I'll get my things."

"Not without an escort, you won't," Brittney said.

"Brittney." Evan's tone held a warning.

She flung a hand toward the screen. "We just watched her steal medication. Are you really going to break policy and let her leave?"

My heart pounded. What policy? Were they going to call the police? That couldn't happen. "Please," I said, "I'll pay for it. Or replace it, if I can."

Evan held up a hand. "That won't be necessary." He looked anguished. "Can you explain this video? What happened here? Are we missing something?"

He sounded so hopeful. Even now, after what he saw, he believed in me—or at least he wanted to. I shook my head, and a little light in his eyes died.

"I'm so sorry, Evan."

"Natalie will escort you to your locker," Brittney said. "Please clean it out and leave the building."

At her words, Natalie rose and opened the door. Unable to bear the look on Evan's face, I got up and followed her back to the locker room. The good thing about feeling so numb, I thought as we passed the nurses' station, was that I didn't even feel my heart breaking.

IT TOOK ME ABOUT TWO MINUTES TO CLEAR OUT MY LOCKER. Maybe somewhere in the back of my mind, I never really expected to stay, so it held a bare minimum of personal property—just a toothbrush, which I threw away, and a tube of lip gloss, which I stuffed in my purse.

When I was done, I left the door open and stepped back. Natalie had told me she needed to inventory its contents. She'd scribbled on a clipboard as I removed items. She stepped forward, took a quick glance inside, and then sat on one of the benches. "Why?" she asked. "Why, hon?"

My eyes burned. "I can't explain. At the time, I thought it was for a good reason. I justified it in my head." I gave a little shrug. "But it was stealing. There's never a good reason for that."

Natalie brushed at her eyes. Then she stood and pulled me into a hug. When she spoke, her voice vibrated against my shoulder. "I know you, and I know you wouldn't have done this unless you felt you had to. Lay low for a while and let this blow over. Give it a few months, then call me, okay? I've worked all over the Jeff. I can put in a good word for you somewhere."

I nodded, tears clogging my throat. Aside from Leah, she was the only female friend I'd ever had. I hadn't realized how much I needed that sort of companionship until now.

Natalie pulled back. "Please keep in touch, okay? This isn't the end."

"I will," I whispered.

"About Evan—"

"I can't right now." Maybe later, I could talk about him. But not right now.

She seemed to sense I was close to breaking apart, because she nodded and released me.

"Here." She grabbed my street clothes from the bench and held them out. "Go change before I show real human emotion and scare us all."

I SPENT THE REST OF MY SHIFT IN A McDONALD'S DOWN THE street from the center. My heart leapt each time the door swung open, and I slumped down in the hard plastic booth, but no one from work came in.

Fortunately, it was a newer McDonald's, and the owner had installed flat screen TVs around the dining room. I watched so many episodes of *Ice Road Truckers*, I never wanted to see a semi again.

At three thirty, I walked back to the center and waited until my ride showed up.

If the driver noticed I smelled like a chicken nugget, he didn't say anything. Once again, we rode home in complete silence, and once again he dropped me at Dinah's without saying a word.

I let myself in the house and watched the truck until it reached the end of the driveway and turned onto the main road.

I turned and headed upstairs. What was I going to tell Thomas? Maybe I could say the center downsized, and they no longer needed me.

I was so preoccupied with my thoughts, I didn't notice the figure sitting in the chair by my bed until I was halfway across my bedroom.

"Thomas!" I gasped, one hand splayed on my chest. "What are you doing in here?"

He sat by the window, in a wide swath of shadow cast by the late afternoon sun. He'd clearly been waiting for me.

"Where have you been?"

A frisson of alarm raced down my back.

"Work." I stepped into the bathroom before he could say anything else. Something was wrong. Did he know about me taking the asthma drugs for Simon? Maybe Brittney had called the house. The number I listed on my employment paperwork went to a phone in Dinah's office. Hands shaking, I turned on the cold tap and let the water run over my wrists.

"Is something bothering you?" he said from the doorway. He watched me fill up a paper cup and gulp water.

"I wasn't expecting you," I told his reflection in the mirror.

"Clearly."

I tossed the cup in the trash and moved to the shower. "I'm just going to rinse off."

A hard hand closed over my arm. "You're not doing anything."

"What are you doing?" My voice was high, panicked.

He pulled me into the bedroom and flung me toward the bed. I landed with a bounce and scrambled upright. Bile burned my throat.

Somehow, he knew about what had happened today. But why was he so angry? He didn't like my job. He should be happy I got fired.

I held still as my heart threatened to pound from my chest.

He stared at me for a moment, then walked to the chair, where he picked up a small package. It was one of those padded envelopes people use to send photos or small items through the mail. Without warning, he tossed it at me. I was unprepared, and it smacked my chin before plopping in my lap. The envelope had been slit open. The outside bore the address for Hyde Construction's corporate headquarters in Jefferson City, but it was addressed to Elizabeth Grant. My stomach dropped. The only place I used my maiden name was the center.

"Open it," he said.

I looked up, searching his face for some kind of clue as to what I'd find inside, but he merely stared at me, his blue eyes narrowed in anger.

"Open it. Now."

Gingerly, I reached in and withdrew a . . . bundle of cloth? I stared at the white fabric in my hand for a second before I realized what it was. Slowly, I lifted my gaze to his.

"That was delivered to my office today."

I lowered my head, my garments limp in my hand. They were the same ones I tossed in the laundry bin at work. The ones Brittney had returned to me wrapped in paper from the dry cleaner's.

Or had she? I closed my eyes. The package was still in my closet, unopened. I put it there after Thomas brought me home from his work trailer. Brittney must have put the real garments in the mail the same day she "returned" them to me in the locker room.

Thomas's voice interrupted my thoughts. "Who's Evan?" He walked toward me, unbuttoning his cuffs.

"I don't know."

Thomas rolled up his sleeves. "See, I know that's a lie, because the note in that envelope says you left your clothes at his house and he wanted to return them to you. I guess he couldn't do that at work, right? Better to keep these sorts of things secret. Wouldn't want anyone to know you're *screwing* around, would you?" His voice had risen as he spoke, and he struck me across the face with his open palm.

The blow knocked me sideways. Tears of shock and pain sprang to my eyes. I cradled my stinging cheek. My face felt ten times larger than normal. "Thomas, please—"

"Be silent!" He jerked me to my feet. Then his fist flew. I didn't have time to react. To duck. To do anything.

Pain exploded in my skull. The ground rushed up, and then I was sprawled on my stomach. A high-pitched whine filled my ears. The taste of pennies filled my mouth.

A ridiculous image of a knocked-out cartoon character with a circle of stars above its head sprang into my mind. The left side of my head was both numb and hot. I tried to sit up, but my body wouldn't obey my brain. Someone moaned.

It took me a second to realize the sound came from me.

Sounds infiltrated the ringing in my ears. A metal-on-metal

clinking, then a rustling of cloth. Without warning, lightning curled around my left hip and licked at my back. I screamed.

The lightning struck again. And again.

I got my arms underneath me and pushed up. Then I was on all fours and crawling away. My long skirt tangled under my legs.

"No, you don't." A rough hand gripped the back of my shirt and hauled me up, then tossed me facedown on the rumpled bed.

"I understand your reluctance now," Thomas said, his breaths coming in short puffs as he planted a knee in the middle of my back. "You've been pushing me away for weeks. Suddenly, a lot of things make sense."

He yanked up my skirt, and cool air hit my legs. I slapped my hands backwards, bumping against his knee.

There was a sharp whistle, then his belt struck my bare thighs. White-hot agony licked my skin.

I sucked in a breath, coughing.

Again, he brought the belt down. *Fire.*

Again. *Fire.*

Again. *Fire.*

The blows came so quickly, I couldn't count them. Leather snapped, and fire followed. In the distance, a strangled scream echoed each crack, the sound like an exclamation point on every snap.

Darkness gathered in the edges of my vision. Then something lifted me. Movement. I swayed like I was on a boat.

Nausea sloshed in my gut.

"Stop," I tried to say, but my voice came out a strangled whisper. The swaying continued.

Footsteps now. And bouncing. My head bobbed against something hard.

I was going to be sick. Dinah would be so mad if I puked on her floor.

The movement stopped.

Thomas's voice filled my head. "Then ye shall bring them both out unto the gate of that city, and ye shall stone them with stones that they die."

There was carpet under my cheek. The air was damp.

Basement. We were in the basement.

"The damsel, because she cried not, being in the city, and the man, because he hath humbled his neighbor's wife."

Someone knelt beside me. Thomas's voice hissed in my ear. "So thou shalt put away evil from among you."

Then he was gone, leaving me in darkness.

17

W hen I was a child, I used to lie in my parents' four-poster bed. I'd hold up my chubby toddler hand, sunlight from the window streaming around it, and my mother would touch each of my short, dimpled fingers with her own slim ones.

"This is earth," she'd say, wiggling my thumb and making me giggle. Her low, musical voice grew more serious as she folded down my pointer finger. "This is the telestial kingdom." Then the next finger. "Terrestrial kingdom."

I watched, mesmerized, as she drew a path down my ring finger, her voice hushed with reverence. "The celestial kingdom. That's where Heavenly Father lives."

"Will I live there, Mama?"

"Of course, because you will live a good life, and you follow the prophet."

Only good people were allowed in the heavenly kingdoms. I waggled my pinky. "Where do the bad people go?"

My mother tapped the smallest appendage. "Outer darkness, Lizzy-bell." She rose up on her elbow, her white-blond hair a cloud around her beautiful, beloved face. Cornflower-blue eyes smiled down at me. "You never need to worry about that."

I jerked awake. A black void surrounded me.

I lay facedown on the floor, my skirt bunched under me. I lifted my head.

Agony exploded across my back.

I put my head down.

Shit.

How badly had Thomas whipped me? I let out a whimper. Even that slight movement in my jaw made saliva rush into my mouth.

Hot tears trickled from my eye and rolled down my nose. He was going to reassign me.

If I was lucky.

The Bible verse he'd quoted was reserved for disgraced wives. Better to be dead than to be labeled a fallen woman. That's what the faith taught. Adultery was the lowest, most vile sin. It didn't matter that Evan and I had never been intimate with each other. It was enough that I lusted after him in my heart. In the eyes of the faith, I was ruined.

His face drifted into my mind. I would never see him again. Not now.

For a few minutes, I gave in to despair. My shoulders shook with great, heaving sobs. Salt from the tears trickling down my face stung my cheek. My shirt pulled against the skin on my back. Almost like it had been wet and then dried.

Eventually, I cried myself out, and my head cleared enough for me to think.

First, I had to get out of the basement. I couldn't lie on the floor, waiting for Thomas to return.

That meant getting up and making my way to the stairs. I didn't have any broken bones. A whipping couldn't do that.

Getting up was going to hurt, but I had to do it.

Maybe I should just jump up as fast as possible. Like ripping off a bandage.

Before I could try, the basement door opened and light bounced down the stairs, making a small puddle on the landing.

Anxiety swamped me. I tensed, waiting for the sound of Thomas's voice, but the footsteps on the stairs were light.

Seconds later, Leah was beside me.

"Elizabeth? Oh my God." She touched my arm. She smelled like baby powder and soap. I wanted to rest my head in her lap and sleep for the next two years.

Her voice trembled. "What happened? Where are you hurt? Can you walk?"

"I think so." Agony ripped through my jaw. I whimpered.

"Okay, don't talk." She stroked my hair off my forehead. "The lights aren't working down here. Let me go get a flashlight."

Protests leapt to my lips. She couldn't leave me, even just to grab a flashlight. But I stayed quiet as she rose and rushed back up the stairs.

A minute later, her voice, muffled and urgent, drifted down from the kitchen. She was talking to someone. The police? Somewhere in the back of my mind, I remembered we weren't supposed to do that. We couldn't risk outsiders getting involved in our business. Nearly everyone in the community had a grandfather or great-grandfather who had spent time in prison for practicing plural marriage. I tried to muster the energy to yell for her to stop, but I was so tired. If I could just close my eyes for a minute . . .

A hand shook my shoulder. Despite my back, I tried to scrabble away. I couldn't take another beating. I just couldn't. I threw up a hand to protect my head.

"Easy! Easy, Elizabeth," Leah said, her pale face illuminated by the flashlight, like she was telling a scary story around a campfire. "It's me."

"Where is Thomas?" I kept my voice low. As if saying it too loudly might conjure him from the air.

She hesitated. "He left for work two hours ago."

What? That meant I'd been in the basement all night. Anger and outrage built in my chest. He'd beaten me and thrown me in the basement like a piece of garbage, then slept in his own bed?

"He said you were sick," Leah continued. "That you thought you might be coming down with the flu. At breakfast this morning, he told us you wanted to rest and we should keep the kids away from the house. I came over anyway," she said, a defiant undertone in her voice. "When you weren't upstairs, I thought you might be down here doing laundry. He cut the power to the basement somehow. That's why it's so hot down here."

"He thinks I've been seeing someone from work. A doctor."

"Have you?"

"Yes."

She was quiet for a long minute. Leah had always been unfailingly devout. I waited for her to shove me away or tell me I deserved what Thomas had meted out. Instead, she said, "My father used to beat my mother. All the time." The words flowed from her in a rush. "For burning his dinner, or making the wrong dinner. For talking too loudly. Because she looked at him funny. Because he felt like it. She was an expert at covering up bruises. She could have worked as a makeup artist, she was that good. A few of my brothers don't even know about it, because they never saw the marks and he didn't hit their mothers. Just mine."

"Why?" I couldn't help asking. "Why just her?"

"I don't know," she whispered, pain in her voice. "I've asked myself that question since I was a kid. You'd think someone capable of that sort of thing would be totally out of control, you know? Like, he shouldn't have been able to hold down a job with that kind of temper. But it was the opposite. My dad was the most controlled, methodical person I've ever met." She stroked my hair. "He'd beat her, then take the rest of us to meeting the next morning like everything was totally normal. I tried talking to him about it once, a few years ago before he died. You want to know what's crazy? He acted like he had no idea what I was talking about. What's even crazier is I believe him. He rewrote history in his head, and eventually he couldn't remember anything different."

A male shout from the top of the stairs made me jump. I sucked in a terrified breath, but Leah patted my arm. "It's Jackson. I called him." She pulled away from me a little so should yell up to him.

Booted feet descended the stairs, then Jackson was squatting in front of us. "You're gonna be all right, Liz," he murmured. "Come on," he said to Leah, "let's get her upstairs."

"No," I said. "If he finds out you helped me . . ."

Leah made a shushing sound. "Elizabeth, you need help. Let us help you."

Jackson moved into the flashlight's halo. "What happened, Liz?" He had a healing black eye. It must have looked horrible when he first got it.

I reached up to touch it, but he captured my fingers and covered my hand with both of his. "It's nothing," he said quickly. "Liz, you have to tell us where you're hurt, so we can help you." He spoke each word with deliberate emphasis, as if he were explaining something really important.

I focused hard on his face, which had started to look blurry around the edges. "Belt," I said, my voice a croak. "He whipped me. All over." And there was my face, of course. That was self-explanatory.

"We need to get her to a hospital," Jackson said.

I lifted my head. The room spun, and I put it back down. "No hospital."

Leah spoke. "Elizabeth, you can't even walk. You need a doctor."

I drew in a big breath. They had to listen to me. "The first thing the hospital will want to know is who did this. They'll call the police, and the police will try to arrest Thomas. Is that what you want?

Doubt shaded her eyes.

I pressed her. "Think of your kids, Leah. If they take Thomas, they'll start looking into removing the kids next."

It was every woman's worst nightmare, or it least it was for the women in our faith. Riverview Heights had never had any trouble with outside law enforcement, but other communities had. Other groups with similar backgrounds and belief systems as ours had been decimated by raids. Men had been imprisoned. Children had been torn from their mothers' arms. I knew Leah was imagining that now.

Jackson watched her, then swung his gaze to me. "You still need help. I'm not leaving you here."

I didn't want either of them involved in my escape, but I couldn't do it on my own. I needed a doctor, but I couldn't go to a hospital. That left just one option. Voice trembling, I told them the name of Evan's condominium complex in Doverton.

"I don't know the address," I said.

Jackson pulled a phone from his pocket. "We'll find it."

He glanced over my head, and he and Leah seemed to silently agree on something. She pulled my right arm over her shoulders so my armpit fit snug against the back of her neck. Jackson did the same on my left. Together, they counted softly. "One, two, three—"

Searing agony blazed through my back. Blackness rushed up, and I let it take me.

SOMEWHERE, A LIGHT WAS FLICKERING ON AND OFF. I STRAINED, but all I could make out were undefined shadows and vague impressions of movement. Annoyed, I squinted, which is how I realized my eyes were shut, and the light was on the outside of my closed eyelids.

As soon as I opened them, everything came rushing back: Thomas, the belt, the basement. The pain. I was flat on my back in the back seat of a truck.

A welcome change from being stuck on my stomach in the basement.

Leah's anxious face appeared over the front passenger seat. "She's awake," she told the driver. Jackson. That's right, I remembered. She'd called him for help. To me, she said, "Almost there, Elizabeth. Just hang in there, okay?"

It took me a few tries, but I managed to ask, "How'd you find it?"

"GPS." Jackson spoke from the front. He held up an iPhone and waggled it in the air. "And a little internet stalking."

Evan's condo was in a gated community. The only ways in or out were through two guard stations positioned at the front and back of the complex. I couldn't see much from my position in the back, but an impressive-looking gate swung into view as Jackson rolled to a stop. Warm air and a few quiet traffic noises filtered in as he lowered his window.

"We're here to see a resident. Evan Adgate," he told the guard. A minute later, the gate shuddered, then swung open.

I fought down waves of nausea as Jackson drove down a long, winding drive leading to clusters of modern, brick colonials. The curvy path might have looked pretty, but it was doing a number on my already delicate stomach. Finally, the truck stopped, and Leah and Jackson both threw off their seat belts and popped open their doors.

Evan must have been waiting outside, because I heard him before the truck's engine had a chance to stop rumbling. "Elizabeth?" He sounded polite, but confused. The voice of a stranger. "What's going on? Oh, *Jesus*." The back door swung open, and his face filled my vision. He smelled clean, like he'd just gotten out of the shower, and he was dressed for work. Tears filled my eyes at the safe, familiar sight of him.

Within seconds, he was inside the truck, tugging the blanket off, his eyes and hands moving over me. "There's blood, sweetheart." He pulled my eyelids up one by one, his fingers gentle. "Where's it coming from?"

"Back. Legs." I grabbed his hand. "No hospital."

Eyes grim, he squeezed my hand, then released it so he could probe my jaw, his fingers firm and sure. "I don't think it's broken." He glanced back, to where Jackson and Leah hovered in the open doorway. "You," he barked at Jackson. "Start talking. Now."

In a halting voice, Jackson told him what happened. Leah must have filled him in on the rest on the drive over. Hearing it out loud was almost as bad as enduring it the first time. All I could do was lie there and listen, ashamed to the core.

Evan made light tapping motions on my stomach, and I knew he was checking for signs of swelling that might indicate internal damage. He glanced back at Jackson. "You said this Thomas is your father. What's he to Elizabeth?"

"My husband," I said before Jackson could answer, and Evan's hands stilled. Our eyes met. "He's also Leah's husband. She's my sister-wife. There are four of us."

Evan closed his eyes in a long blink, then he continued with his assessment as if nothing out of the ordinary had happened and I hadn't just dropped a bombshell worthy of any daytime soap opera. He gestured to Jackson, who scrambled in next to him. "I need to get a look at her back." He motioned for Jackson to slide his hands under my legs. "Gently," Evan snapped as they tried to turn me.

I'd forgotten how painful it was to move. As fire shot through my back, I couldn't muffle my scream. A deep trembling started in my muscles.

"All right, this is what's going to happen." Evan's voice was matter-of-fact. "There's a level-one trauma center about five miles from here—"

"No." I tried to sit up.

Evan held me down with a firm palm on my sternum. He leaned forward, his gray-blue eyes charged with some indefinable emotion. Despite the storm clouds there, his voice was calm and assured. In this setting, he was accustomed to giving orders and expecting to be obeyed. "Elizabeth, you have been beaten with a belt, possibly the metal buckle. There's blood on your shirt, which means he hit you hard enough to break the skin. If there's a fracture"—he took a deep breath, like he needed a moment to compose himself—"the longer you go without treatment, the greater the likelihood of swelling, which will put pressure on your spinal cord. You're risking paralysis with every passing moment. Do you want to be a paraplegic? Or worse?"

"N-No."

"Then we're going to the hospital. Now." This was said with a glance over his shoulder, and Jackson and Leah climbed back in the truck, their doors slamming one after the other.

"Thomas can't find out where I am," I told Evan. "The hospital will tell him." I had to make him understand.

"I know the chief of surgery," he said, his voice softer now. "And the attending physician in the ER. I'll take care of things. You don't have to worry."

Yes, I did. He knew my big secret now, but he didn't know the thousands of little secrets that went along with it. I wanted to tell him everything, but I didn't know where to begin. Mostly,

I just wanted him to know I was sorry. Then the truck moved, and I squeezed my eyes shut against the pain.

"I've got you," he murmured, smoothing my hair back from my forehead. He stayed in a crouch next to me. It couldn't have been a comfortable position, but he didn't move. The last thing I remembered was the feel of warm, strong fingers entwining with mine.

18

I walked across a field of wildflowers, my fingertips skimming the tops of the purple and red blooms. As if by magic, the tall grass parted before me, creating a perfect path. That wasn't supposed to happen, but I didn't think much of it. The day was too warm and beautiful for me to care about anything, even miracles or magic.

I scanned the horizon, and a smile curved my lips when I spotted the man standing at the top of the next hill. His back was to me, but I knew him. His dark blond hair looked lighter in the sun. His shoulders stretched the cotton of his shirt across his back. I moved toward him, eager to put my hands there, to see if the fabric was as warm as it looked. If the skin underneath was taut with muscle.

His head turned as I approached. "Elizabeth."

I called out to him, but it was as if my words were snatched by the wind.

"Elizabeth." His voice grew more insistent. "*Elizabeth.*"

My eyes flew open. The wildflowers were gone, replaced by sterile white . . . curtains?

"Elizabeth." Jackson sat by my bedside, his dark brown eyes

holes of worry in his pale face. His hair stood at odd angles, as if he'd run his fingers through it over and over again.

"Wow, you look terrible," I told him.

He put down the magazine he'd been holding and inched his chair as close as possible to the bed. His hand hovered over mine for a minute, as if he wasn't sure he should touch me.

I grabbed his hand before he could decide. "How long have I been here?"

"Since yesterday morning." He glanced at an industrial-looking clock on a far wall. "It's dinnertime now. How do you feel? Are you in pain? Do you feel like eating?" His babbling trailed off, and he stared at me, worry shadowing his normally cheerful face. I must have been in rough shape, to warrant that level of concern.

I looked down at our joined hands, at the IV in the back of mine. They must have given me pain medication, because I felt numb and a little nauseated. My head was clear, though, which was a nice change. A blood pressure cuff on my arm buzzed and inflated. This wasn't the ER. It was far too quiet for that. The curtain around the bed was open enough for me to see a heavy brown door behind Jackson. Another door in the corner was ajar, a tiny sink barely visible through the opening. I fumbled around in the bed and found the controls, then raised the bed up enough so I could peer over the side. Sure enough, a catheter bag hung from a plastic clip.

Glamorous.

"The nurse said you could probably tolerate broth or something. Or Jell-O. I highly recommend the red."

"Where is Leah? She needs to get back. If Thomas finds out—"

"She left yesterday, right after they said you were stable."

That eased my mind, but only for a second. "Your mom—"

"Will do nothing to put me in danger. She'll keep her mouth shut." He nodded, as if agreeing with his own assessment. "Leah's going to talk to her. Mom likes her. She'll go along with it."

I nibbled at my lip, weighing his words. Jackson was right. Patty might have her flaws, but she loved her children. She would agree to just about anything to make sure he was safe. She'd looked anguished the other night, when she told me Thomas banished Jackson to the edge of town.

I swallowed against a dry throat. "You can't go back." Thomas was no fool. And it was because of *me*. Jackson was the logical choice to have helped me escape Riverview Heights. I slumped against the pillows. "This is all my fault."

Anger sprang into his eyes. "This is *not* your fault. Believe me, the Priesthood Council has wanted me out for a while now. They would have found one way or another."

He was probably right, and the bitter resignation on his face broke my heart. What would he do now? He had a high school diploma. I'd seen to that. But he had little else in the way of marketable skills. Construction was most likely out. Thomas could make those doors slam shut in a heartbeat. I tried to think of something positive. "This isn't all bad, Jackson. You have a chance to start over. To get paid for the work you do. To meet a girl and have a family the right way, without the prophet assigning someone to you."

"Is that what you wanted with Evan?"

"Yes. No. I don't know." I offered him a weak smile. "I don't know what I was thinking. I certainly wasn't expecting this." I gestured to the hospital room around us. "I don't blame Evan if he hates me for pulling him into it."

"I can guarantee he doesn't hate you."

"Did he say he'd come back to the hospital?" He would have gone to work for the day, but I wanted to see him at least once before they released me. I needed to thank him for his help. To apologize for betraying his trust and getting him involved in my . . . what was happening with me, anyway? It wasn't really a crisis of faith, although I was definitely questioning my convictions. It was more than that, and enough to make me willing to risk abandoning the only life I'd ever known.

Jackson scoffed, as if I'd said something absurd. "He never left. I thought he was going to punch the ER doctor when we brought you in."

"What? Why?"

"The guy wasn't moving fast enough, I guess. You should have seen it, Liz. Evan walked him right up to a wall and said to treat you *now*. I've never seen people move so fast. They had you in a private room in like two seconds, and that ER doctor spent the rest of the time shooting these nervous little looks at Evan. I thought he was going to crap his pants. It was awesome."

Oh boy. I was relieved Jackson was safe and that Evan had obviously looked after him, but I wasn't sure this hero worship was a good thing. Jackson was still just sixteen years old, even if he'd been forced to mature much more quickly than a typical kid. He was coming off a physical assault and being kicked out of his home and his entire family. If anyone had ever needed a positive male role model, it was him, and he'd clearly latched on to the first one available.

I cleared my throat. "Um, where is Evan now?"

"He ran home for a bit. Said he needed to take a shower and get a change of clothes. He's picking you up something to wear, too. They, ah . . ." He lowered his eyes.

"What is it?"

He looked pained. "They had to soak your shirt off. It was stuck to your back. Dad—" He took a deep breath. "*Thomas* cut your skin open with the belt. You have some stuff called ster-il . . . steri—"

"Steri-Strips."

"Yeah, that's it." He swallowed. "Anyway, your clothes were ruined."

I smiled, but it must not have been too convincing, because his expression didn't change. "It's okay. I wasn't too fond of that outfit, anyway."

He gave me another agonized look. "Liz . . . There's something else. Your back is broken. Evan's surgeon friend looked you over and they stood in front of the X-rays for like a half hour. They think you'll heal fine on your own, which is a good thing, right?"

I squeezed his hand. "Yes," I whispered. "Don't cry."

He huffed a laugh. "Take your own advice." He wiped at the moisture on his cheeks, then snagged a tissue from a box near the bed and dabbed awkwardly under my eyes.

After a few minutes, he said, "What are you going to do?"

"I don't know. Get better?" I took a deep breath, surprised and grateful when it didn't hurt. "I'm not going back, though. Ever." The thought of setting foot anywhere near that basement made me feel like getting up and running out of the room.

"You can stay with me." He ducked his head, pink staining his cheeks. "A few of the other runaways from the Heights have a place," he mumbled.

I'd heard the rumors. It was an easy enough solution, although it would probably be at least a month before I could work again, assuming I could still find a job after everything that had happened at the center. If Brittney was spiteful enough to send my garments to Thomas, who knew how far she'd go to hurt my reputation in the medical community. All that was nothing, though, compared to the fear that gripped me when I thought about being forced back to Riverview Heights.

"I've never heard of a woman running away," I told him.

Jackson swallowed. "Me neither. What if they find you?"

A deep voice spoke from the doorway. "They won't."

Evan strode from the door and pulled the curtain aside. He stared down at me, his face grim. How much had he heard? After several tense beats, he put a comforting hand on Jackson's shoulder. "Why don't you run down to the cafeteria and get some dinner? I need to take a look at Elizabeth."

"Sure." Jackson rose, and Evan clapped him on the back with an easy familiarity that told me they had spent a lot of time together over the past day and a half. Jackson was clearly comfortable with him, which was more than I could say. Jackson touched my arm briefly before nodding at Evan and disappearing through the doorway.

Evan waited until Jackson's footsteps faded, then sat in the chair he'd just vacated. "How's your pain?" His gaze roamed over me with a professional detachment I recognized. No one seeing him now would mistake him for anything but a doctor, despite his jeans and University of Missouri T-shirt.

"Fine. I'm fine."

He nodded, then tapped the bed's controls. "It's best if you lie as flat as possible. The Dilaudid works both for and against you, in a way. It masks the pain, but it also encourages you to push yourself too far, since those pain signals never make it to your brain." He waited for the bed to lower. "Better?"

It *was* better, actually. Still, it was frustrating how something as simple as sitting upright and talking to Jackson had worn me out. I had a thousand different questions, and a thousand things I needed to say to him, but the mention of medication made one particular item rise to the surface.

"Evan, I have to tell you something." When he just watched me patiently, I cleared my throat. "I took the drug samples for a boy at home. Leah's son, actually. He—"

"She told me."

"Oh." I bit my lip, unsure what to say to that.

"She doesn't know that you took them without permission. She assumed you got them from me. She wanted to thank me, since she doesn't have any health insurance."

Neither did I. Few people in the faith did. The Righteous Brethren's doctor accepted cash and the occasional trade. I looked around at the spacious private hospital room. I'd never be able to pay the bill for my care in this place.

"I've been in constant communication with your doctor," Evan said. "There's no reason why you can't go home tonight, as long as you can tolerate stepping down your pain meds a bit. You're very lucky, Elizabeth."

"Oh, yes, I feel lucky."

His shoulders stiffened. "I didn't mean it that way." The chair made a sharp noise against the floor as he stood and walked away, flinging the curtains open as he went. I blinked against the early evening light that poured in through a big window I hadn't seen before. Evan stood in front of it, arms crossed, his head bowed as if in prayer. I wanted to call after him, but he seemed overcome by some strong emotion.

Besides, what could I possibly say? Sorry for lying to you? Sorry for leading you on and, oh, by the way, I'm married and my husband has three other wives? I wouldn't have blamed him if he'd dropped me at the hospital door and washed his hands of me.

But he hadn't.

He was still here, and I didn't know why. But now that he was, I was willing to do just about anything to keep him here. Terrified of saying the wrong thing, I kept silent, the beep of the heart monitor and some distant rumbling traffic noises the only sounds in the room.

He sighed, his big shoulders lifting and falling as if he bore the weight of the world. He scrubbed his hands over his face and turned, walking to a file holder on the wall, and plucked my chart from it.

He pulled out an X-ray film and flicked on the wall-mounted viewer. Then he tacked up an image of the spine. "You have two minor fractures." He tapped the black and white image. "Both in the lumbar spine, both in the spinous process." He glanced at me. "The bony parts that stick out from the vertebrae." He pointed to a shadowy spot lower on the film. "Dr. Garrett—the surgeon here, he's a friend—suspects another fracture in the vertebral body at L4, but it's tough to tell with so much inflammation. Garrett wants to give it a couple weeks and take another film."

I released a slow breath. It wasn't as bad as Jackson had made it sound. Fractures came in all shapes and sizes. The slight shadows Evan pointed out were barely noticeable.

He flicked off the viewer and walked to a cabinet set in the wall, where he pulled a pair of surgical gloves from a box. "Are you comfortable with me looking at your back and legs?" He turned toward me, pulling on the gloves with a practiced air. "If I need to change your dressings, I'd prefer to do it here rather than at home. I stock a decent medical kit at the condo, but you can't beat the hospital for supplies."

Home? Condo? The pain medication must have addled my wits. "What do you mean?" I raised the bed back up. I couldn't have a serious conversation flat on my back.

"You need a place to stay, not to mention medical care." He lifted his hands away from his body, either in supplication or to maintain a sterile environment—maybe a little of both. "I have two bedrooms."

It was unbelievably generous, and it confirmed what I already knew about his character. But staying with him? In his home?

"Elizabeth, you can't live in a trailer with Jackson and God knows how many other teenage boys," he said, sounding a little exasperated.

So he'd heard that part. I closed my eyes. When I opened them, he'd moved closer, so incredibly attractive and . . . *good* it hurt to look at him. I definitely didn't deserve this, or him. "I can't ask you to do that."

"You didn't ask. I offered. I'm not asking anything of you. And you've seen where I live. The outside, at least. It's safe.

Secure. Which is something you need after what that bas—"
He bit off the last word, his jaw tight. "I can't watch over you
while I'm at work, which means you're vulnerable here. Hospi-
tals are the first place they'll look, right?"

Fear shot through me. I looked toward the door, as if
Thomas and the rest of the Priesthood Council might barrel
through it at any moment.

Evan glanced at the heart monitor, which had picked up my
elevated heart rate. When he turned back to me, I took a deep
breath and nodded. "Okay."

"THE PAINT SMELL SHOULD GO AWAY IN A FEW DAYS," EVAN SAID
as he led me into his condo's small foyer. He tossed his keys on
a table next to the door, then slid a supporting hand under my
elbow and walked me forward.

After a brief, tearful exchange with Jackson, who promised
he would check in within the next day or two, I'd allowed Evan
to orchestrate my discharge from the hospital. Apparently,
being a doctor made that sort of thing a lot easier. I'd gone from
being hooked up to an IV and bedridden to the front seat of
Evan's car in the span of about twenty minutes.

"Wait," I whispered, bringing us to a halt where the tile of
the foyer met the carpet that stretched before us. I slid out of
my new flip-flops and nudged them to the side of the rug in
front of the door. They were black and a half size too big, since
he'd had to guess my size. The hospital had tossed my clothes,
which didn't bother me in the least. I would have gone home in
the hospital johnny before wearing anything from Riverview
Heights again.

The other items Evan had picked fit perfectly, though. The
black yoga pants were more formfitting than anything I'd ever
worn, but they were soft and comfortable.

He'd also brought an equally soft tank top and hooded sweatshirt that zipped up the front. I'd blushed when the nurses who helped me dress cut the tags off the bra and panties he'd picked out. They were far from racy, but the knowledge that he'd shopped for my underwear felt more intimate than the kiss we'd shared.

"Take your time," he said.

I gazed around the entryway. Plush, beige carpet started on the edge of his foyer and continued through a small but comfortable-looking living room. I also spied a kitchen through an archway.

"I think I'm good," I said.

He led me to a bedroom on the first floor.

I was sweating with the effort of holding myself upright, despite the back brace that kept my spine rigid. "I can't imagine what it feels like to have a true break," I said, taking shallow breaths through my mouth as he helped me ease onto the bed.

"Yours is nothing to sneeze at," he murmured. He undid the Velcro fasteners at my sides and slid the flexible brace out from under me. "How's that?"

I closed my eyes and gave a jerky little nod. "Better."

He glanced at his watch. "You're due for another Toradol. Do you think you can tolerate a little food? It can be hard on your stomach."

"Maybe."

He came back with saltine crackers, a ginger ale, and a pharmacy's worth of prescription bottles, which he lined up on the nightstand next to the bed. "Normally, I'm staunchly anti-eating crackers in bed, but I'll make an exception in this case." He handed me two pills and a tumbler of ginger ale.

I swallowed the pills and nibbled at the crackers as he unpacked the supplies the hospital had sent home. There was a compact-looking walker with fold-out legs, a shower chair, and a plastic toilet riser that fit over the toilet seat. This last item made my cheeks heat.

If Evan felt any embarrassment, he didn't show it. He toted everything but the walker into the en suite bathroom and busied himself setting it up. When he emerged, he stood in the doorway, looking me over with a clinical eye. "How do you feel? Toradol kicking in?"

Judging from the warm lassitude creeping up my legs, the answer was a definite yes. My eyelids drooped, and a little smile played around his mouth. I'd missed that lopsided grin more than I could say, and I closed my eyes to hide any telltale emotion there. He was helping me because he was a nice person. That was all. If I hadn't ruined the possibility of anything beyond friendship between us when I'd stolen medication from work, I'd definitely done it by lying to him about my life. Hiding a husband was a surefire way to ruin a relationship.

The bed sank beneath his weight. When I opened my eyes, he sat beside me, a thermometer in his hand. Gently, he moved my hair aside and turned my head so he could get to my ear. A few seconds later, there was a small beep and the rustle of his shirt as he pulled away. "No fever." He tossed the little plastic guard in a small trashcan I hadn't noticed before. "Sleep, now," he said in the calm, authoritative voice I'd grown accustomed to hearing over the past two days.

Just before I nodded off, I could have sworn I felt a pair of lips brush my forehead. "You're safe," a voice whispered.

19

The next two days passed in a haze of medication-induced sleep. I was dimly aware of Evan as a shadowy but comforting presence, checking the bandages on my back, coaxing me to eat the occasional piece of toast, and helping me back and forth to the bathroom. During these infrequent trips, I roused myself enough to insist he stand outside the bathroom. He complied without too much of a fight, although he won the battle to keep the door open.

By the third day, I opened my eyes to bright morning sunlight, my thoughts more lucid than they'd been since before I entered the hospital. For the first time, I really took stock of my surroundings. Evan had said he wasn't much of a decorator, but the bedroom was furnished in plain but tasteful fashion, with dark brown furniture. The bedspread was a dark gray, and the window, which must have faced the rear of the condo, was covered with a bright white honeycomb shade. Overall, it was a pleasing space, if a little impersonal. I chalked that up to it being a guest room.

Evan's tall frame appeared in the bedroom doorway. It took me a minute to realize what was different about him. He hadn't shaved, and his jaw was covered in a dark blond stubble that gave him the look of a pirate . . . or maybe a brooding underwear model. I jerked my gaze right back up to his face, where it belonged.

"You look better." He walked over and sat beside me, then grabbed a blood pressure cuff from the nightstand. He fastened it around my arm and plugged a stethoscope in his ears. I was silent as he took my blood pressure, trying not to show how his gentle but brief touches on my skin made little zings of pleasure zip through me. He pronounced my blood pressure "excellent" and smiled when my stomach rumbled loudly, his gray-blue eyes crinkling at the corners. "I take it you're ready to move on to something more substantial than toast and crackers. I'm not the greatest cook in the world, but I can manage a decent grilled cheese."

"Grilled cheese sounds perfect."

Twenty minutes later, I sat at the small round table in his kitchen, my mouth watering as he slid a golden-toasted sandwich dripping with cheese in front of me.

The kitchen was by far the best room in the house, with its gleaming hardwood floors, sleek stainless appliances, and polished gray countertops. Evan said they were concrete, which made me blink. Set against the dark-stained cabinets, they gave the kitchen a modern yet homey vibe. It was a kitchen made for someone who loved to cook.

Evan confessed he didn't get much use out of it.

"I'm a one-trick pony." He sat across from me with his own grilled cheese. "I learned how to make one thing really well, and this is it."

"Well, it's amazing," I said around a mouthful of melted cheese and warm ciabatta bread. I'd never tasted anything so good. Even the ice water he set in front of me was heaven. I polished off my sandwich, half a dozen apple slices, and a few baby carrots. Then I drained the water and seriously considered eating the ice at the bottom of my cup. If Evan felt wary about sitting across from a woman intent on devouring as much food as possible, he didn't show it. As I nibbled the last baby carrot, I noticed my nails were dirty. Suddenly, I felt grimy all over. My scalp itched, and the Steri-Strips on my back felt constricting and uncomfortable.

"What is it?" Evan asked, concern in his eyes.

My face heated. Why, oh why couldn't I manage to avoid looking like a beet any time I became the least bit embarrassed? At this point, Evan had probably seen every part of me. Still, there was a difference between someone looking at you when you're sick and looking at you when you're fully aware and capable of functioning on your own.

Eventually, my desperate need to feel clean again overrode my inconvenient modesty. "I would love a shower." I held my breath, prepared for him to say I was still too weak, or that my stitches couldn't get wet. But he pushed his plate away, stood, and walked around the table so he could help me stand.

"Do you think you can walk up the stairs? My shower is a lot bigger."

As much as I tried to tell myself there was nothing intimate or personal about using Evan's bathroom, it felt significant to venture into his private space. I was winded by the time we reached the top of the stairs, and I let my eyes gaze roam while I paused to recover.

The condo's upper floor was a glorified loft, with an open hallway that held a treadmill, a flat screen television, and a jumble of gaming consoles that would have made Jackson drool with envy. Open double doors led to Evan's bedroom, which was easily double the size of the one I'd been using.

And the bathroom. I gasped when we stepped over the threshold. "You weren't exaggerating about the size," I murmured, and he laughed.

"It's the reason I bought the place." He jerked his head

toward the shower, a huge glass box that dominated an entire wall. "Once I hit thirty, I couldn't bounce back from a race like I used to. I'd hobble around for days afterward. Twenty minutes in there, though, and I'm a new man."

He left me leaning against the sink while he turned on the water. Jets lined the tiled walls, and a giant square showerhead rained water from above. A huge stone bench was built into a recessed alcove. Steam swirled, filling up the bathroom, a fragrant mist that beckoned me toward the promise of cleanliness. An overpowering urge to rid myself of the last traces of Thomas and the basement made me want to throw off my clothes and stand under the spray.

I stood, docile, while Evan unstrapped the back brace, but I jumped when his hand accidentally brushed the underside of my breast. My stitches made it impossible to wear a bra, and I was suddenly aware of my nipples straining against the thin fabric of my tank top.

Something shifted between us. Where we had been doctor and patient before, now I was consciously aware of him as a man, and if the flush creeping up his neck was any indication, he was definitely aware of me as a woman.

"I think I've got it from here," I said, stepping away from him.

He clutched the back brace. "Um . . . okay." He tossed it on the bathroom counter, then bent and rummaged through the cabinet, producing a new toothbrush still in the package, which he set on the counter.

"Toothpaste is in the drawer," he said. He gave me one last, considering look. "Are you sure—"

"I'm fine. I'll call for help if I need it."

He nodded. "I'll be right outside."

EVAN'S SHOWER DELIVERED ON ITS PROMISE OF AMAZING SHOWERY goodness. I soaped every inch of my body, then rinsed and repeated the entire process. Careful of my still-tender back, I tipped my head back under the main showerhead and sighed as the water carried away days of sweat and oil. A shelf built into the tiled wall held an assortment of shampoos and conditioners, and I sniffed at each one before choosing something that smelled of herbs and mint.

I gazed with longing at the disposable razor next to a can of men's shaving cream, but ultimately decided Evan wouldn't be thrilled to learn I'd used it on my legs. I couldn't stop myself from swiping it under my arms, though. My body hair is blond and sparse, but I draw the line at hairy pits.

I stood under the spray until my skin wrinkled and my legs grew shaky. When my head swam, I turned off the taps and wrung out my hair with trembling hands. My head pounded, probably a result of standing in the steam after so many days in bed. Once I'd wrapped myself in one of the bath sheets Evan had draped over the top of the shower, I padded carefully to the sink, where I wiped a small circle of steam from the mirror. I didn't dwell on my reflection. I'd already seen the bruise on my jaw . . . and the hunted, wary look in my eyes. I didn't feel like facing myself just yet.

I slathered way more than the American Dental Association's recommended pea-sized amount of toothpaste on the toothbrush and reveled in the feeling of clean teeth for the first time in days. By the time I'd rinsed and wiped my mouth, my legs felt ready to give out.

Evan must have been hovering just outside the door, because he was next to me before I'd finished calling his name.

"You're white as a sheet," he muttered, taking my arm. He guided me into his bedroom and helped me sink into an over-size chair I hadn't noticed on the trip upstairs. It was a dark tan, with piping a shade lighter than the upholstery. All it lacked was a teetering stack of books and a comfortable throw blanket.

I balked as he stuffed pillows on my sides to support my back. "My hair. I'll soak the cushions."

"The last thing I'm worried about is the chair. Don't move," he said, as if I were going anywhere, enveloped as I was in the chair. It was like being hugged by furniture. He scooped my legs onto a matching ottoman and grabbed another towel from the bathroom. Then he set about rubbing my wet hair briskly with the terry cloth.

I clutched the bath sheet over my breasts. When he finished with my hair, he produced a brush from somewhere and began pulling the bristles through the damp strands with gentle strokes.

"Okay?" he asked, working at a tangle.

"Yes." My eyelids drooped. "I don't think anyone's brushed my hair since . . ."

"Since what?" His strokes grew more rhythmic as he removed the tangles.

I tried to make my voice light. "It was a stupid thing. Leah and I read in a magazine that honey lightens your hair, so we smeared a bunch of it on our heads once and sat in the sun for a few hours." I chuckled. "I think every fly in Riverview Heights descended on our heads. We must have looked like a couple of idiots, running toward the house with honey dripping all over the place. It took us hours to get it all out. My hair's much thicker than hers, so she helped me comb through it. I think I had honey in it for about a week, though."

He pulled the brush from my crown to the tips of my hair. "She was really worried about you. Back at the hospital."

The drowsy feeling vanished. "I'm worried about her."

"Jackson called yesterday. He said he spoke to his mother."

"Patty."

"Leah and her children are fine." There was a slight pause

in the rhythm of his strokes, then he added, "Your husband doesn't know she helped you."

I didn't know what to say to that. I wasn't quite ready to discuss Thomas, but I knew Evan had questions. How could he not? So I just nodded and whispered, "Thank you for telling me."

He gathered my hair at the base of my skull and divided it into three sections. My eyes widened as I felt him braid it with quick, practiced movements. He secured it with a hair band, then placed the thick rope over my shoulder. "I'd like to examine your back if you're up to it."

"O-Okay." Where on earth had he learned to braid hair?

He moved to the front of the chair and handed me another pillow. "Hold this against your front. Like this." He showed me how to tuck the pillow between my chest and the tops of my legs so I could lean over without arching my spine. When I was situated, he tugged the bath sheet to my waist, exposing my back. Even though I was expecting it, I jumped at the first touch of his fingers on my skin.

"Easy," he murmured, pressing a reassuring palm against my shoulder blade, as if he were gentling a horse. He waited for me to grow accustomed to him, then ran his fingers over my back, stopping here and there to examine the healing lacerations. His fingers were warm, like beams of sunlight against my chilly skin.

When he didn't say anything, curiosity got the better of me. "How is it?" I'd seen my jaw often enough during bathroom trips over the past two days to know it couldn't be pretty. The swelling in my face had gone down, but the bruise on my cheekbone had gone from dark purple to an ugly, mottled green.

He didn't answer.

"Evan?" I turned my head. "Is something wrong?" Maybe I shouldn't have taken such a long shower, after all. The stitches were made to withstand water, but you weren't supposed to soak them.

He removed his hands, then gripped the squared-off back of the chair and dropped his head. He let out a heavy, shuddering breath.

"Evan?"

His reply was muffled. "You ask me if something's wrong." Another deep breath. "Of course something is wrong." He laughed, but it was a harsh, ugly sound. "Your back is a mess. It's a giant bruise, from your shoulders to your ass, and you ask me if something is wrong. There are whip marks—" He pushed away from the chair, away from me, grabbed the hairbrush off the bed, and flung it across the room. It smacked against the wall and dropped to the floor with a thud.

My shoulders tensed. "I'm sorry."

He whirled, his gray eyes wide with something that looked like indignation. "Don't ever apologize for that son of a bitch. He beat you hard enough to fracture your spine." He held out shaking hands. "I swore an oath, Elizabeth. An oath to do *no harm*. I promised to heal, but so help me, God, if I see that sick fuck, I will end him. Do you understand what I'm saying? I will *end* him. I don't care if he's your husband."

I hugged the pillow tighter to my middle. The last time I'd been alone in a room with an angry man, I'd left with a swollen jaw and whip marks all over my back. My heart knew Evan posed no threat to me, but the primitive part of my brain—the part that had kept my ancient ancestors alive when they were being stalked by predators in the wild—screamed at me to make myself as small as possible, to hide from the dangerous male with the power to hurt my broken body.

The instant he saw me shrink away from him, he crossed to the chair and knelt. The fury that had gripped him drained away like air released from a balloon, and his shoulders slumped. "Sweetheart, I'm sorry." His voice was raw. "I'm sorry,

Elizabeth. I'm sorry." It fell from his lips like a litany. Like a prayer.

"No." I couldn't bear the sight of him humbling himself like this. "It's my fault." Hot tears trickled down my face. "My fault. It *is*," I insisted when he started to protest. I gulped against the hot tightness squeezing my throat. "I led you on. I had no right to get involved with you. You had no way of knowing where I'm from or the kind of crap I'm involved in. At first, I think I just needed a friend, but then it was more. You paid attention to me, to the things I had to say." I gazed at his face, at the square jaw covered in golden stubble, at his straight, proud nose and gray, piercing eyes. Eyes that were so often crinkled in amusement but looked at me now with pain and regret. "I should have told you. But I was afraid of scaring you away."

I fell silent, too miserable and heartsick to say more.

We stared at each other for a long moment. Then he reached out and took the hand I'd clenched in the pillows he'd piled around me. He held it loosely in his own, as if he wanted me to know I could withdraw at any time. "I don't scare easily."

I dropped my gaze to our joined hands.

He rubbed his thumb across my knuckles, then he drew himself up and sat on the edge of the ottoman. "Let's begin again. You said you needed a friend. I assume that still holds true."

He hadn't phrased it as a question, but I nodded.

"Then let's be friends. Only this time, no secrets. Can you do that?"

Sitting there, it hit me that this was the first time in my life I could actually say yes and not be lying. I didn't have to keep secrets anymore. Didn't have to worry about accidentally using the wrong last name or removing my wedding ring when I ventured into public. Evan knew everything already.

"Friends," I said.

He raised our hands and kissed my knuckles. "Friends."

By Monday morning, I was surprised at how good I felt. When Evan asked where I would be the most comfortable while he went to work, I automatically said the big chair in his bedroom. Like a benevolent fairy godmother, he granted my wish, setting me up with a big stack of books and a soft throw blanket so big I could have used it as a ship's sail.

"Promise me you won't try going up and down the stairs with that thing. It's three times your size."

I moved my feet so he could sit on the ottoman, trying not to drool as I looked him over. The man could have made a career out of modeling surgical scrubs for medical supply catalogs. He wore a tight-fitting, dark-blue, three-quarter length shirt under his scrub top, which made the light sprinkling of blond hair on his arms stand out against his tanned skin. I felt like a Victorian lady, getting hot and bothered by a forbidden glimpse of forearm.

"Have you decided what you're going to tell work?" I asked to distract myself. He hadn't been to the center in almost a week. True to our pact about being honest with each other, I'd told him how Thomas had found out about our dinner date— information he could have only gotten from Brittney.

Evan had fumed all weekend. But I convinced him that confronting Brittney was a bad idea. I wasn't going back to the center anyway, and it was better if no one knew where I was. The fact that she knew where Evan lived worried me almost as much as the thought of Thomas tracking me down.

He seemed to read my thoughts. "Are you nervous about being here alone? No one gets in without express permission from a resident. The security guards are a little overzealous about it, actually. My mother complains every time she visits."

"Of course not. Like you said, it's gated." A pang of guilt shot through me. Here I was, breaking our honesty-only policy three days in. But I knew he wouldn't leave if he thought I was afraid.

He looked like he wanted to argue, but he leaned over and realigned the prescription bottles on the table next to me. "Two Motrin every six hours." He held up two fingers. "With food. There's bagels and cream cheese in the fridge. If the Motrin isn't cutting it, you can take a Percocet."

"Yes, Doctor."

He grinned. "Am I being overbearing?"

"Maybe just a little."

"I can't help it. I have a captive patient."

I caught my breath at the sight of that grin. He was so unconsciously charming, so effortlessly handsome, I wanted to reach out and cup my hand around his jaw, to absorb some of his essence any way I could. He'd shaved the scruff, and I found that I missed it.

"You're not overbearing," I said. "You're good at what you do. I can never repay you."

The grin faded, replaced by a softer, subtler expression. "I don't want you to thank me, sweetheart. I just want you to get better."

There was a shrill beep, followed by the deep timber of a hornet buzzing. He sighed, then pulled his pager off his waistband and looked at the number. "Work," he muttered. "They can't even wait until I'm in the building." He tucked the pager in his pocket and stood, frowning down at me.

"I'll be fine." I patted my stack of books, all titles he'd brought home from the library in Doverton. He'd shown me how to run a search of the library's catalog on his laptop. I'd promptly made a list of all the books Thomas had forbidden me to read.

"I know you will. But call me if you feel sick or in pain. It's no problem for me to run home." He bent and kissed the top of my head. Then he walked to his dresser, grabbed a weathered-looking messenger bad from his dresser, and left.

I spent the rest of the day alternating between reading and thinking about that kiss. Evan had said we were friends, so it had been friendly, right? A kiss on the head was more brotherly than anything. Of course he'd meant it as a protective gesture. I was silly to read into it.

Still . . . I replayed our interactions in my mind, hunting for signs he intended for us to pick up where we had left off. For the most part, his behavior toward me had been that of a doctor tending his patient. Although, lately I hadn't exactly been in a state conducive to romance.

When I'd woken in the hospital, I had assumed he was angry I had deceived him. The more time that passed, however, the less I believed that. For some reason, he'd chosen to forgive me.

And the spark that had pulled us together was still there. At least, it was for me. If anything, I was more attracted to him than ever before, as though by finally breaking from my life with Thomas, I felt free to acknowledge my feelings.

But what if Evan didn't feel the same? Maybe he was exactly what he seemed—a really nice man who felt obligated to look after a coworker who'd been hurt and had nowhere to go.

The sound of the doorbell pulled me abruptly from my thoughts. Without thinking, I tried to stand up like I normally would, and the sudden movement wrenched my back. My book tumbled to the carpet, catching my big toe on the way down. Squinting against the pain, I caught at the chair's armrest to steady myself, my eyes darting to the window, then the door, like a trapped animal searching for the quickest way out of danger.

The doorbell rang again, the clear, high note singing through the condo. I glanced at the phone Evan had left on the table next to the pill bottles. He said he could be home in ten minutes. The longer I stood there, the more ridiculous I felt. Even if Thomas knew where I was, he wouldn't just walk up to Evan's door and ring the bell. If I'd learned anything during my years with him, it was that Thomas rarely did anything unless he was in complete control of the situation. Confronting Evan on his own turf didn't seem like something he would do. And the security guard hadn't called. Thomas couldn't get in without permission.

When the doorbell rang a third time, I untangled myself from the blanket. *I'm an adult*, I told myself, and ordinary adults answered the door instead of cowering under a blanket upstairs.

"I'm coming," I muttered as the doorbell rang again. I negotiated each stair with deliberate concentration. I clutched the railing with one hand and used the other to hold the waistband of my scrub pants. With only one outfit to my name, I'd been rotating between the yoga pants and a pair of men's scrubs Evan had found in the back of his closet. The pants were too long and threatened to trip me up with each step. Annoyance buffeted at the anxiety that had threatened to choke me just moments before. I seized the feeling.

Better to be irritated than terrified.

The doorbell chimed again.

Who could possibly want to speak to Evan this badly? Maybe a door-to-door salesman, although I doubted the condo association allowed solicitors. There were some religious groups that walked around neighborhoods, knocking on doors. A lot of outsiders confused the Righteous Brethren with the mainstream Mormon Church, even though we weren't affiliated in any way. In fact, the Latter-day Saints largely shunned us, although they were more tolerant of us than other groups who had splintered from the church.

The thought of confronting two teenage boys in white shirts and black name tags bent on discussing the fundamentals of my own religion on Evan's doorstep was so absurd, I forgot to be afraid.

When I peeked through the narrow window beside the door, however, there were no missionaries. No Girl Scouts selling cookies, either. Just a tiny elderly woman holding an equally tiny dog.

I opened the door.

The woman flashed a broad smile, revealing an impressive set of veneers. "Hello!" She leaned around me. "Is Dr. Adgate here? His car's gone, but you never know with that boy. Comes and goes all the time. I've never seen a more active person, always running and such. I'm Mrs. Warren, but you can call me Trudy. This is Napoleon." Her gaze took in my scrub pants. "You must be a coworker. Are you a doctor, too, honey?"

All this was said in a stream-of-consciousness flow that would have left anyone else winded. But she just stood there, smiling a brilliant white smile, tickling her dog under the chin. She wore one of those matching velour tracksuits in a bright purple that complemented a startling violet pair of eyes.

I blinked a couple times, trying to decide which part of her speech to address first. Finally, I settled on what seemed to be the most important thing. "Um, no, I'm afraid Dr. Adgate isn't home. He's working today."

She frowned, black eyebrows pulling together over a pert nose that had seen more than one cosmetic procedure. "Well, that just won't do. He's supposed to check my pressure." She brightened. "But you're here. *You* can do it." Then, without warning, she bent down and released the dog, who trotted into the foyer and down the hall toward the kitchen.

20

Two hours later, I was certain I knew just about all there was to know about Mrs. Trudy Warren, who was eighty-three and thrice widowed. She'd lived in the unit adjoining Evan's since her last husband died six years ago. She had a daughter who'd retired from the Air Force and a son who lived in South Carolina.

"He keeps pestering me to move down there, but I know he'd stick me in one of those awful assisted-living communities. Besides, my boyfriend's here." She poked a finger in her hair, which was dyed black and teased into a fluffy pouf only little old ladies seemed able to achieve.

The water I'd been about to swallow went down the wrong way, and I let out a sputtering cough, my eyes streaming from the effort of holding myself rigid to protect my back. We sat at the table in Evan's kitchen. Napoleon rested in Trudy's lap, blinking drowsily as she scratched behind his ears.

"Oh my, are you all right, dear?"

I waved a hand to show I was okay. "Yes," I gasped between coughs, "just took too big of a drink."

She waited for me to recover, then sighed and said, "It's so nice to see Dr. Adgate dating again. How long have you two known each other?"

Unsure how much I should tell her, I rose and carried her mug to the fancy coffee machine. "Um, about three months."

"He's a fine boy. Always willing to put my old mind at ease. Reminds me of my dear, sainted Edward. My third husband. Not much in the sack, that one, but he had a good head on his shoulders."

I bit my lip and flipped the top down on the coffee maker. At a loss for words, I tried to steer the conversation into safer territory. "How long were you married?" I asked, carrying the steaming mug back to the table. I suspected her vision wasn't all that great, because she hadn't seemed to notice the faint bruise still shadowing my jaw or the stiffness in my gait. Having spent time in her company, something told me she would have remarked on it.

She smiled a dreamy smile that for a second transformed her face into the beauty she must have been in her youth. "Forty-five years. He's my Ronald's father. Now, my second husband, Antonio, he was something. A Sicilian, you know, from the old country. Oh, those first years were rocky." She laughed, a pleasant tinkling sound filled with memory. "Would you believe it, we divorced, then remarried about a year later."

I raised my eyebrows. "Sounds passionate."

"It was, it was." Her eyes gleamed. "We used to fight like cats and dogs. I once threw my grandmother's antique china at his head. Made a huge mess. I found pieces for days. That was par for the course with Antonio. I'd scream at him. He'd yell the house down in broken English. But the makeup sex made it all worth it."

I was prepared this time, so I didn't even flinch. Napoleon and I made eye contact. I wondered what sort of stories that dog had heard.

"But," she said with a little lift of her shoulders, "that's all you got with Antonio." She tapped her forehead with a manicured nail. "All balls and brawn, and not much upstairs. The fool got himself killed in a bar fight in St. Louis. Can you imagine? Well, that was enough adventure for me. I settled down with a steady man. Still, even Ed and I had our challenges. Marriage is not for the faint of heart, my dear."

"So I've heard," I murmured. For a minute, I considered telling her I was married to a man with three other wives. Somehow, I didn't think anything could shock Trudy Warren, and I was interested in what she might make of my situation. But common sense overrode my impulsiveness. She was Evan's neighbor, after all, and apparently held him in high esteem.

She turned her coffee mug in little quarter circles, her mouth screwed up like she'd eaten something bitter. "As for my first husband, well, he was a sonovabitch if ever there was one. That man never met a problem he didn't think he could solve with his fists."

Goose bumps rose on my arms.

"He used to slap me until my ears rang. Did you know, I only have partial hearing in this ear?" She tugged on a dangling gold clip-on.

I swallowed. "Why did you marry him?"

She shrugged. "He knocked me up. Ooh, Mama was fit to be tied. She threw my clothes in a suitcase and put it right on the front porch. Told me I'd made my bed and now I had to lie in it. I stayed three years, and it was three years too long."

My heart rate picked up. "What made you decide to leave?"

"My daughter. I packed that same suitcase and bummed a ride to Mama's. You could hitchhike in those days without worrying about some psychopath murdering you. I stood on the porch with two black eyes and my little daughter and told Mama I'd sit outside until she let me in."

"Did she?"

Trudy waved a beringed hand. "She left me out there long

enough to make her point. Mama was a tough woman, but she'd lived through a lot. When she was a girl, they used to replace the soles of their shoes with cardboard when they wore through. She didn't suffer fools, you know, and I admit I was a bit of a fool as a girl."

"What happened to your husband? Did he try to force you back?" I held my breath.

She stroked down Napoleon's back. "He might well have tried, but there wasn't a man in Perry County who would go toe to toe with my mother. He died in Korea. In the war, you know."

I exhaled. "I'm sorry."

"Don't be. I certainly wasn't. Anyway, you won't see me walking down the aisle again. I'm content to play the field." She slapped the table, and I jumped. "Now, let's take my blood pressure."

I tried to explain that I wasn't a doctor or a nurse or anything of the sort, but she wasn't having it. She waved a dismissive hand and said, "You're dressed like a doctor. That's good enough for me."

As I pumped the cuff bulb, it occurred to me that I was actually well qualified to take her vitals. It's what I should have been doing at the center all those weeks. Brittney had put a considerable dent in my self-esteem, making me believe I was fit for little more than dusting and emptying trash cans.

"One-twenty over seventy-five," I said with a smile. I pulled the cuff from her arm. "Very good."

She touched my arm. "You're a doll, Elizabeth. And such a beauty!" She winked at me. "I can see why Dr. Adgate snatched you up."

I LEFT THAT PART OF THE STORY OUT WHEN I TOLD EVAN ABOUT her visit later that night. He groaned and dropped his head in his hands at the mention of her name, then laughed when I shared what she'd said about her husbands.

"I should have warned you about Trudy," he said, a reluctant grin on his face. We were in the living room, where he'd collapsed in a chair positioned next to where I sat propped on the sofa, my feet on an artsy tufted ottoman. I wore the nonskid socks they'd given me in the hospital. They had two little smiley faces and the words *Doverton Health System* printed on the bottom.

"I enjoyed talking to her. It was nice to do something medical again. I haven't taken care of a patient since I graduated from MA school."

Evan's face clouded. "Because of Brittney."

"How did it go today?" I was afraid to ask, but I had to know.

He sighed. "She doesn't back down, I'll give her that. Tried her damnedest to find out where I'd been. I mean, you left and then I was gone for a few days. Of course she's suspicious."

"But you didn't say anything?" My scalp prickled with nerves.

"Of course not."

"Good. That's good." I released the breath I hadn't realized I was holding.

He dropped his head back on the cushion and watched me through hooded eyes. "I wanted to, though. After what she did to you."

"I don't think she realized what the consequences would be."

"You're giving her far too much credit. What she did was crazy. She has no business being around patients. She's gone as soon as you think it's safe."

I didn't revel in the idea of Brittney losing her job, but I had to agree with him. Brittney's behavior rivaled anything Dinah had ever done. She'd had her reasons, however unfounded. Brittney's actions bordered on criminal.

Evan rose and sat beside me, a respectable space between our bodies. "Elizabeth, I understand if you don't want to talk about what happened. I won't ever pressure you to. But I have to know—" He broke off, as if searching for the right words.

"It's okay," I said, even as panic rose in my chest. There were so many things he probably wanted to know. If I were in his place, I'm sure I would have felt a mixture of fascination and revulsion. Just because I'd grown up in the faith didn't mean I was blind to how outsiders saw us. I'd been raised to believe in the absolute truth of my religion. Other people were poor, misguided souls to be pitied. After all, hadn't Christ been persecuted by all but his closest followers? I'd heard the prophet say that since I was old enough to attend meetings. But one bad experience after another had slowly opened my eyes to reality, and what I saw wasn't good.

I could only imagine what it looked like to Evan.

"Do you really think your husband will track you down? Hunt for you?"

I looked down at my hands. "I don't know. I think . . ." I shook my head.

"What is it?" Evan's voice was gentle.

"I don't think he cares about me. Me personally, you understand. I know that sounds crazy to an outsider, but marriages are almost always arranged in the community, and I didn't know him very well when I married him. We're not even legally married. Ours is—was—a spiritual marriage. His first wife is his legal wife. Anyway, he wasn't exactly happy with me before he found out about . . . everything." I took a deep breath and met Evan's gaze. "But Thomas cares deeply about what other people think of him. It's rumored he might be the next prophet. A runaway wife will make him look weak. He might force me back just to make a point."

"And what would he do, once he got you back?"

"Reassign me. Marry me to someone else. As punishment."

Evan stared at me, his face inscrutable. When he spoke, it was in a dull, emotionless voice. "He would pass you off to another man. Like a desk or some other piece of furniture he doesn't need anymore."

Well, when he put it that way, it didn't sound very flattering. I tried to make him understand. "It's part of our faith, Evan."

"Are you kidding me? That's not a religion—it's abuse. It's a cult." He got up and strode to one of the windows that flanked the living room mantel.

His anger made my heart pound. Even as I recognized my sudden anxiety as a by-product of what Thomas had done to me, I barely controlled the urge to cower in the corner of the sofa. I focused hard on the fireplace. It was the oddest thing. Where there should have been logs, there were just half a dozen tall candles of various heights. Those pillar things. Dinah had some she took out around the holidays. Absently, I wondered if Evan ever lit them. Probably not. There was no chimney. Not even a flue that I'd seen.

He turned from the window. He pushed a hand through his hair, then dropped it to his side. "I shouldn't have said that. I'm sorry. It's just hard to hear these things."

"That part of my life is over. I'd already decided to leave."

"You're safe here. You know that, right? This is the real world. He can't get to you here."

I started to tell him he was wrong, but maybe I was overestimating Thomas's influence. Sure, he knew people in high places around Jefferson City, but he was just one man.

Evan walked over and crouched in front of me, just like he had up in his bedroom a couple days before. "You're not powerless, or friendless. You have me." He smiled. "And Trudy."

I returned his smile. "According to her, I have a bright future as a doctor."

He laughed. "As beautiful as you look in scrubs, I think

you're overdue for some new clothes. Think you can manage a trip to the store?"

I'D SEEN TARGET FROM A DISTANCE PLENTY OF TIMES, BUT THIS was the first time I'd ever been in one. Before we left the car, Evan turned to me, a serious expression on his face. "Fair warning, this place has a reputation for being the retail equivalent of catnip for women."

"You realize that's disturbingly misogynistic, right? What would Natalie say?"

"She'd say we're wasting time better spent inside, hunting for incredible bargains."

Three hours later, my back hurt so badly I could barely hobble to the car, but it didn't matter. I was the proud new owner of a pair of skinny jeans, a regular pair of jeans (apparently, everything I'd read was wrong, and black denim was socially acceptable after all), a selection of tops, and the skimpiest underwear I'd ever owned. Evan had stood quietly on the edge of the lingerie section while I discovered the wide world of intimate apparel.

"Everything is so tiny! Can you believe this?" I held up a pair of bikini briefs. Target really was the wonderland he'd described, and it was overload to my culture-starved senses. It was like seeing a celebrity in real life. I was now touching and holding things I had only seen on television. Everything was both familiar and completely novel.

Evan had been studiously reading the back of a shampoo bottle he'd plucked out of our cart. "Hmm? Oh. Yeah."

Cheeks flaming, I'd stuffed them in the cart. And when he wasn't looking, I'd added a matching bra and thong set. It had taken me a minute to figure out where the string was supposed to go, and my eyes had nearly bugged out of my head when things finally clicked into place. I'd probably never wear it, but if the bikini briefs made Evan's eyes narrow that way, I wanted to see what happened when he laid eyes on a thong.

Not that things between us showed any sign of moving beyond the easy friendship we'd established. I gave him a sideways look as he backed out of our parking spot. Aside from the brotherly peck he'd given me before leaving for work, he hadn't touched me in any way except to check the Steri-Strips on my back and, later, help me into the car.

I found myself looking for excuses to touch him. A quick tap on his hand. An innocent brush against his thigh.

"Are you hungry?" he asked. "I doubt you're up for sitting down somewhere, but you're probably sick to death of grilled cheese." He slid me a cocky look. "No matter how astonishingly good they are."

I laughed. "You have a rare talent for melting cheese on bread."

He took us to a local burger place straight out of a 1950s movie. Instead of the ordinary drive-thru window, teenagers on roller skates swept up to the line of cars parked under an aluminum canopy.

"How did you find this place?" I asked while we waited for our food.

"Someone at work told me about it." He shot me a smile. "Word got around about how much I like to eat. Locals always know the best places."

"You found the Italian restaurant on your own, though."

He scratched at his cheek, laughing a little self-consciously. "Yeah. When I was a kid, Brian and I would spend the summers with our dad. One of those custody plan things. Mom hated it because she knew Dad didn't pay any attention to us. It's not that he didn't want to see us. He was just busy. His job is demanding, and it was even more so then. I think he forgot to eat half the time. Anyway, he'd leave Brian and me thirty dollars and tell us to get whatever we wanted for dinner. It was a different time then. We'd jump on our bikes and ride all over New Haven. I think it became a sort of game for us, trying to find weird and unusual places." He chuckled. "I remember this one time, Brian got so sick from this Indian food we tried. You've never seen a kid pedal a bike so fast. I thought he was going to stop on the sidewalk and jump into the bushes."

I laughed with him, imagining the scene he'd painted.

He shrugged, his smile lingering. "I guess I'm still that adventurous little kid on a bike. All through college and med school, I felt like I was a nomad, even though I knew I could always go home to Mom's house. When I made an effort to mingle with the locals, it felt like I was part of something instead of just passing through. Like I had a family."

We stared at each other, his words hanging in the air between us.

A shrill voice made us both jump. "Two burgers with the works, onion rings, fries, and two Cokes?" A young girl in a pair of short-shorts and a tank top stood outside Evan's open window, her hands filled with paper bags, an impatient look on her made-up face.

Evan balanced on one butt cheek so he could remove his wallet. "Um, yeah. Here you go. Keep the change."

One perfectly sculpted eyebrow lifted, and the impatience was gone. She looked Evan over, her eyes appreciative. "Thanks," she said with a wink and skated off into the building.

Evan stuffed the bags between us and shot me a look. "Good God, I pity parents these days. Girls did *not* look like that when I was a kid." He started the car and backed out.

I gazed at the succession of fast food restaurants and small strip malls as we drove through Doverton's commercial center. In Riverview Heights, a girl that age would most likely be married by now. Childhood in the Righteous Brethren was incredibly short. Suddenly, I couldn't help thinking about Thomas's youngest children. Leah's girls. Patty's little Ginny.

And Simon. What would Leah do now that I wasn't around to intervene with Thomas? I had no idea what was happening at home. Jackson could get information through his mother, but we had agreed it was best for us to avoid contacting each other, at least for a couple of weeks.

"What is it?" Evan asked.

I turned away from the window. "Just thinking about home." Except I couldn't call it that anymore. Not that Riverview Heights had ever been my home. Like Evan, I'd always felt like I was just passing through. Like I was waiting for something to happen.

Evan glanced at me, his face lit up by the headlights of a passing car. "Are you worried about them? Your, ah . . ."

"Sister-wives? Yes, although I'm sure Leah is the only one who's worried about me."

He cleared his throat. "You didn't like the other two?"

I grimaced. "Patty never really cared for me, but she wasn't really openly hostile. Dinah disliked me on the spot."

"And you lived with all of them? All together in one house?" There was shock in his voice, but also curiosity.

I took a deep breath. "We had two houses," I said softly. "Dinah and I lived in one, Patty and Leah in the other. Since Dinah is the first wife, she's sort of in charge of everything."

"In charge of everything," he said, his tone flat.

"Schedules, chores." *Assigning nights with Thomas.* I took a deep breath. "Nothing got past her, that's for sure. Thomas might think he's the ruler in that house, but the wives know it's really Dinah." I shrugged. "It's not an unusual situation in the faith. If the first wife doesn't like you, you learn to tread very carefully around her."

We'd reached the security gate, and Evan rolled down his window to punch in his code. He was silent until we pulled to a stop in front of the condo. He stared at the building for a moment, his hands still on the wheel, then he turned to me. His voice low, he asked, "Your back. What he did. Was this the first time?"

I'd known he would ask at some point. I swallowed. "Never like this."

Evan swore, a harsh whisper that sounded like a gunshot in the quiet car. "What were the other times like?"

I looked away, unable to meet his eyes. My voice sounded hoarse when I spoke. "He sometimes used a switch. It's a springy branch—"

"I know what a switch is. I've just never seen someone beat another human being with one."

I found myself in the odd position of defending Thomas. "You don't understand. The other times were different. More controlled . . ." I groped for an explanation. "This is a matter of faith for us. The Bible says that to spare the rod is to hate a child, that the husband is the head of the wife and to be obeyed. It's up to the husband to mete out discipline." Even as I said it, I realized how foreign it would sound to someone raised in the mainstream world. "He never really hurt me before this. The other times, I mean. It was more embarrassing than anything else."

"Do you think you deserved it? The other times?"

I opened my mouth, an automatic *yes* on my lips, but then I thought about it. *Had* I deserved it? Aside from this last time, Thomas's punishments had never truly hurt me. The physical discomforts were nothing to the humiliation I'd felt.

Thomas called it pride. "You're too proud, Elizabeth," he'd say when I dared to voice my opinion about being switched. "You need to humble yourself." The faith called it "husbandly correction," and it was supposed to purify the soul, to bring a woman closer to God.

But there was something wrong with me, because all I ever felt was shame and a burning anger.

When I hesitated, Evan said quietly, "You didn't deserve it, Elizabeth. You didn't."

My chest grew tight. "I don't want to talk about it anymore." He didn't understand. How could he, when I didn't really understand it myself? "We should eat." I gestured to the bags of food between us. A grease spot had formed on the side of the bag closest to me, and the smell of hamburgers wafted around us. As if on cue, my stomach rumbled.

"All right." Evan nodded to himself as if he'd reached an important decision. He jumped out of the car and was at my side, helping me out, before I could blink.

Curiosity drifted through me . . . followed by the realization that I wasn't alarmed. Or scared.

Because Evan would never hurt me.

He drew me close, his body not quite touching mine. His hands steadied my waist as he waited for me to adjust to standing. For a moment, he held me there, his head tilted forward, his forehead brushing mine. "Do something for me, would you?" he murmured.

"Yes," I whispered.

When he spoke, his breath stirred the fine hairs around my face. "Think about what I said. No one deserves the life you had. I'm not judging your faith. I'm just asking you to keep an open mind. We don't have to talk about it, but just promise me you'll think about it. Be open to something different, to new experiences." He leaned away, his eyes searching mine. "Will you do that? Will you try?"

He wasn't asking me to do anything difficult or unpleasant. And it was what I wanted, wasn't it? I wanted to taste the outside world. To measure reality against the cartoon version I'd been warned against my whole life.

I'd been prepared to do it alone—something that seemed

ridiculous to me now. I thought working at the center had been enough to acquaint me with how people lived outside Riverview Heights. How wrong I'd been. This whole time, I'd merely been visiting the real world, dipping in and out of it like someone touring a movie set.

Now I was in it for real, and it was terrifying. I'd been overwhelmed by Target, for crying out loud. With Evan's help, though, maybe I could make it work. Maybe I could keep my faith without being Thomas's wife. Because that door was closed. Even if Evan kicked me out tomorrow, I knew I would never go back.

Evan waited, patient for my answer.

"Yes," I told him. "I'll try."

21

E van took me at my word. It was as if by agreeing to try new things, I'd given him a license to expose me to as much mainstream culture as possible. He started with books, which I devoured as my back continued to heal. He moved to movies once he found out how little television I'd been allowed to watch.

"Not even a Disney movie?" he said, horror plain on his face.

I thought about it. "Just the really old ones, like *Mary Poppins* and *Pollyanna*. None of the cartoons, though."

"No *Pocahontas*?"

"Her outfit was too skimpy."

"Ariel?"

"Also the outfit."

Evan put his hand over his eyes and peeked at me through his fingers. "*Beauty and the Beast*?" he asked hopefully.

"Nope."

"There is nothing wrong with Belle's clothing." The expression on his face was so outraged, I burst out laughing.

He drew himself up. "We are watching every princess movie in rapid succession. Starting now."

"This really means that much to you, doesn't it?"

He smile was so bashful, my heart turned over. "Don't tell my brother, but I had a crush on Pocahontas for a solid two years."

As my back slowly healed, he started coaxing me out of the condo. We had dinner at all of his favorite places, from a hole-in-the-wall Mexican cantina that served steaming-hot fajitas, to a swanky place in Jefferson City that had more silverware than I knew what to do with.

"There are no prices on this menu," I said with a frown. "Does yours have any? Maybe mine's a misprint." I turned it over to look at the back.

A quick look of surprise crossed Evan's face, but he covered it so quickly I couldn't be sure. He cleared his throat. "Ah, no. There aren't supposed to be any."

That was stupid. "How are you supposed to know the prices?"

Evan leaned forward, a small smile playing around his mouth. "The people who eat here aren't usually worried about the prices, sweetheart."

I sat back in my chair. "Oh."

He raised his eyebrows. "Oh," he said, clearly amused.

"I don't think it's very nice to make fun of me." I looked around at the other diners. Was my outfit okay? Evan had assured me my black jeans and thin white shirt (he called it a "boat neck") were just fine, but I was suddenly hyperaware of the people around us. The men were all well groomed, the cut of their clothes clearly expensive. A few of the women were dressed casually, but the majority wore tight little dresses that hugged their bodies, leaving little to the imagination. I felt like a frumpy, sweaty teenager next to their beauty and sophistication.

For the first time, I was uncomfortably aware of the financial divide between Evan and me. Just two years out from completing his residency, he said he didn't earn a huge salary, but I was willing to bet his definition of huge varied considerably from mine.

Then there was his family background. He didn't often speak about his father, but he'd dropped hints here and there. His dad was known and respected around the world. His mother sat on the boards of several charities. Only rich people could afford to just give money away. Evan's family was well off by any standard. What would his parents think if they knew he'd taken in a runaway from a polygamous community?

"You always do that when you're nervous," he said softly.

I froze. "What?"

"Play with your braid."

I flung the offending hair over my shoulder. "I'm not nervous."

His eyes gleamed. "You shouldn't be, you know." He turned his head and let his gaze wander over the room before settling it back on me. "When you walked in here, every man in the room watched you. They're trying not to look now, but they can't help themselves."

I glanced around. What was he talking about? No one was looking at me. Although, maybe that guy in the corner shot a few looks my way.

Then again, he might just be trying to signal his waiter.

"They're not judging your clothes, sweetheart," Evan said. "They're trying to figure out what I am to you and if they might have a chance with you." This last was said almost apologetically.

I gazed at him. "I don't believe that."

He shrugged, the movement pulling his thin black T-shirt tighter across his chest. He'd paired it with charcoal dress pants that hugged his legs. "I didn't say it was rational. Men rarely are.

We see a beautiful woman, blood rushes south, and we start thinking she might actually speak to us." His eyes flicked to my hands, which were fussing with the tail of my braid.

I dropped it, my cheeks flooding with warmth. *He called me beautiful.* Did that mean he couldn't keep his eyes off me, either? I looked down, flustered. Was this flirting, what he was doing? I had no idea how to respond. Aside from examining my back and that quick, platonic kiss he'd dropped on my head, he never touched me. If anything, he'd put more physical distance between us. He was never unkind. He was always asking me how I felt and whether I needed anything. But I couldn't help thinking he belonged with a woman like the ones sitting around us—women with arched eyebrows and glossy hair.

My braid lay heavy on my shoulder, the bound strands ranging from dark gold to palest platinum. "I'd like to cut it," I said suddenly.

If he was confused by this unlikely turn in our conversation, he didn't show it. He just winked and said, "May I make a small suggestion? Don't try cutting it yourself. I admit I don't know much about women's hair, but considering that you once smeared honey all over your head, I'd say we need to keep you far away from scissors."

THE NEXT AFTERNOON, HE TOOK ME TO A LARGE HAIR SALON IN the heart of Jefferson City. It was a beehive of activity, the sounds of blow-dryers and women's chatter drifting up the stark white walls. They were a beautiful contrast to the black wood floors. I touched the tip of my new loafers to the polished surface, pitying the poor soul tasked with keeping them clean.

"So, what were you thinking of?" the stylist behind me asked. She'd let out a little crow of delight when she'd unbraided my hair and now stood running her fingers through the wavy strands that spilled over the black cape she'd draped over my shoulders.

I bit my lip, my resolve from the night before fading in the harsh light of reality. "I don't know. I've never cut it before."

"Mm-hmm." She nodded. "It's virgin hair, for sure. Gorgeous." She raked the hair away from my face and hefted the bulk in one hand. "Heavy, though, huh? I bet it gives you headaches."

It did, but cutting it had never been an option. I'd had a handful of trims over the years, but nothing more than that. Thomas had liked it loose whenever we were alone together.

I met the stylist's eyes in the mirror. "Cut it."

"You sure?" Doubt shaded her voice. "Why don't we start with a few inches and go from there? Change is good, but there's nothing wrong with baby steps." She turned the chair away from the mirror.

Half an hour later, I gasped in astonishment when she swiveled me back.

She grinned. "Like it?"

"I love it," I breathed, barely recognizing myself. She'd shortened it to just above my elbows, with shorter layers around my face. She'd also talked me into adding what she called "highlights," which involved sticking pieces of foil, of all things, in between carefully separated layers, then slathering small sections of hair with dye. The result was a subtle lightening of my overall color that picked up the platinum streaks and brightened my entire face. "It's so curly," I said, touching the waves.

The stylist tilted her head. "Most of my clients would pay through the nose for curls like this. You can wear it curly with the right product, but you can also pull off a blowout if you have time in the morning. Here, I'll show you." She'd spritzed my whole head with water for the cut, and now she took out a blow-dryer and a giant round brush. After a few minutes, my hair fell in a soft curtain around my face.

I was so mesmerized by my hair, I nodded absently when she asked me if I wanted a complimentary makeup touch-up. "You have great cheek bones," she murmured as she stroked what looked like a miniature paintbrush over my face. I watched, fascinated, as she dabbed color here and there. She used her ring finger to smear a shimmery tan color over my eyelids, which should have made me look like a raccoon but ended up turning my dark blue eyes a deep sapphire.

Evan blinked when I walked toward him, the magazine he'd been reading lying limp in his lap. He stood slowly, and it slid to the floor with a plop.

"What do you think?" I ran a nervous hand over my hair. "I know it's a big change. I didn't even ask for the makeup. Is it too much? Too dark? I'll probably take it all off . . ." My voice faltered as he continued to stare.

He doesn't like it.

He came forward. His hand lifted, and I thought he'd touch my cheek, but it just hovered in the air for a minute before falling slowly to his side again.

And I wasn't disappointed. I wasn't.

"It's beautiful," he said finally. "*You're* beautiful."

Happiness zipped through me, and I couldn't control my smile.

He settled me in the car while he paid the bill, then surprised me by placing a large paper bag in my lap when he returned.

"What's this?" I peeked inside and was rewarded with a whiff of botanicals. Curious, I withdrew a tiny purple box with a scrolling font on the side. There were several other boxes of various shapes and sizes at the bottom of the bag. He must have purchased all the makeup the stylist had used on me. "Evan." I chewed my lip. "This must have cost a fortune."

He winked. "It's a birthday present."

"My birthday's in January."

"An early birthday present."

I sighed. "I appreciate it. I'm grateful for everything you've done for me. But I can't depend on your charity forever."

It was his turn to sigh. "It's not charity, Elizabeth."

"Yes, it is. I need to get a job."

He shook his head. "Out of the question. Your back isn't fully healed."

His quick rejection grated. "Why don't you let me be the judge of that?"

"Oh? And when did you earn your medical degree? I've told you before, you don't owe me anything. But you owe it to yourself not to be stupid."

My shoulders stiffened. "I'm not stupid." I should have been used to the slur, considering how often Dinah had said it. But it sounded like blasphemy coming out of Evan's mouth.

"You are if you let your pride get in the way of your physical recovery."

I looked out the window so he wouldn't see how much his words bothered me. He meant well, but he didn't understand how vulnerable I felt. I might have more freedom now than I'd had in Riverview Heights, but I was still at the mercy of a man. If anything, I was more dependent on Evan than I'd ever been on Thomas. My injuries and my unfamiliarity with the secular world kept me tethered to Evan, whether I liked it or not.

Worry gnawed at me. What if he was just as tethered to me? Maybe he didn't even realize it. It's not like he could just ask me to leave. He'd been interested in me when we were just coworkers, but would that relationship have gone anywhere on its own, without external forces shoving me into his life? His home?

I looked at him. "I want to be independent. I can't thank you enough for helping me, but I need to pay you back. I need to be able to take care of myself."

We'd reached the security gate, and he swiped his card with a slashing motion and stuffed it back in his visor. "I have no problem with you getting a job. *Eventually*. But right now I have to say no."

Shock made me speechless. But only for a second. "I don't need your permission to get a job, Evan."

He parked and faced me. "That's not what I meant, and you know it."

"Do I? How do I know that?" I put a shaking hand on the door latch.

His eyes tracked the movement, and his mouth hardened. "What, you think you need to run from me? Is that it?"

"If I wanted to leave right now, would you allow me to go? Or would you try to stop me?"

"Why are you goading me like this? You're starting a fight for no reason."

"Would you try to stop me?" My voice rose. Accusation hung in the air, like a dark cloud between us. "Just answer the question."

He swore and lifted both hands, his palms out in a mocking parody of surrender. "Of course not. I'm a *doctor*, Elizabeth, not some megalomaniac nut job who uses religion as an excuse to have sex with a harem of teenage girls."

The scathing, hateful words made my breath catch in my throat. I fumbled with the handle, my hands clumsy.

"Elizabeth!" Evan reached for me, but the door opened and I slipped from his grasp. Ignoring the twinges in my back, I hurried up the condo's steps. It was pretty ineffective as far as escape routes went, but I had nowhere else to go. The car door slammed behind me, followed by the sound of Evan's slower steps. He waited silently behind me as I stood facing the door.

"I don't have a key," I told the door.

Wordlessly, he reached around me and unlocked it, pushing it open with a little shove. "Slow down," he barked when I almost tripped going across the threshold.

Having a large, angry man at my back was doing nothing good for my heart rate, but Dinah's rules were too deeply ingrained, and I paused in the foyer to toe off my shoes. I turned toward the hallway leading to the spare bedroom.

"Elizabeth." Evan's voice was low. And tired.

I stopped, shoulders tight, and turned. "I'm not going anywhere. I have nowhere to go."

He remained by the door. He even slouched a bit, as if he knew I found him physically intimidating and was intentionally making himself smaller. Which was laughable. Evan was not a small man. His hand could have fit around most of my head. My brain knew he'd never hurt me, but the rest of my body urged me to get as far away as possible.

"We need to talk," he said.

"All right. Just not now, okay?" I turned on my heel and fled to the spare bedroom, aware I was literally running from my problems.

THE NEXT FEW DAYS PASSED IN A SORT OF UNSPOKEN TRUCE. EVAN and I were polite and courteous to each other, but we restricted our conversations to mundane topics. He got up early and left for work without disturbing me. And when he came home, we ate dinner in front of the television, each lost in our own thoughts. Or avoiding them.

With summer making the days longer, he took to going on long runs in the evenings. He said it helped clear his head after a long day of dealing with patients and coworkers. He meant

Brittney, but he didn't say her name or allude to any mishaps involving her.

It was lonely in the condo without him. I missed his teasing comments, and the way he was always doing little things to make me comfortable. I even missed him fussing over my injuries.

But all the bruises were gone now. I wasn't his patient anymore.

A few days after our argument, he surprised me by returning early. "I have something to show you," he said from the doorway of the kitchen, where I was busy slicing vegetables for a stew. I'd started preparing dinners in the evening, pleased to be doing something useful for a change.

"Or, rather, *someone.*" He stepped aside.

"Jackson!" The knife I'd been using to slice carrots clattered to the cutting board, and I rounded the island and threw myself at him.

"Watch your back," Evan said, his voice sharp.

Jackson's arms came around me, his hold loose, like he didn't know if it was okay to hug me. When he drew back, his expression was startled. "Liz . . . what? You look *hot.*" His gaze skidded down my body, then bounced to Evan before settling on my face, his eyes wide. Two spots of color appeared high on his cheeks. "Sorry," he mumbled.

Evan stepped beside him and put a hand on his shoulder. "It's the yoga pants," he said in a commiserating tone. "I'm thinking about composing a sonnet to them."

I shot him a look on my way to the fridge, but he was ushering Jackson to the dining room table. I grabbed a couple sodas and joined them.

"Nice place, Evan," Jackson said. He continued sneaking startled glances at me. Had I really changed that much? The morning after Evan and I had argued, I'd found the bag of makeup tucked in a corner of my bathroom. It couldn't be returned, so I figured there was no point in wasting it. I was nowhere near as skilled as the woman at the salon, but I liked the way the eyeliner made my eyes smoky and more defined. My hair had changed, too, of course. Free of the bulk, I'd taken to wearing it down or pulled back with a narrow headband, like it was now.

Jackson cracked open his soda and took a swig, smiling a little at the can. He raised an eyebrow. "What's next, coffee?"

I glanced at Evan. "We're not supposed to drink caffeine." Soda wasn't really my thing, but I'd taken a childish pleasure in drinking it, along with the occasional cup of coffee.

Jackson snorted. "I know for a fact every Hyde Construction trailer has a coffee maker in it."

"How are you?" I asked him. He wore his same worn jeans and an old T-shirt that had seen better days. He looked clean and well fed, though, if in desperate need of a haircut. "Have you heard anything from ho—Riverview Heights?" I nearly bit my tongue to stop from saying *home*.

He sat back with a sigh and used both hands to brush his shaggy brown hair out of his eyes. "Theron and Bragg paid me a visit." His mouth twisted. "Roughed me up a bit, but nothing serious. There are too many witnesses in the trailer park for them to really do anything."

My heart pounded. Like most teenagers, he dismissed danger too easily.

He toyed with his soda can. "Everyone knows it was me who helped you. It wasn't exactly hard to figure out." He shot me an apologetic look. "They excommunicated us both."

"I'm sorry," I murmured, guilt like a heavy stone in my gut.

He waved it off. "That part's not important. They came to deliver a message. They told me Thomas stood up in meeting and declared you an apostate." He glanced at Evan, who sat in frowning silence. "He called for blood atonement."

I shrank in my chair.

Evan looked between us. "What does that mean? Elizabeth?" When I just shook my head, he focused on Jackson. "Tell me what that means. Is it a Mormon thing?"

Jackson reached across the table and put his hand over my cold one. "It's part of our faith, yes, but something rarely used anymore. Some sins are considered unforgivable." He lowered his voice. "Like fornication. Adultery. Especially from a woman. The only way to atone is to spill the offender's blood on the ground."

"It's a death sentence," I said.

"Only in name," Jackson said quickly. "It's been like fifty years since anyone actually died."

I had my doubts about that, but I stayed quiet.

Jackson squeezed my hand before sitting back. "Really, it just means she can't come home again," he told Evan. "The Righteous Brethren own that land and all the buildings on it. They're pretty serious about shooting trespassers. If you give them an excuse . . ."

"I wouldn't set foot there if you paid me," I said. "Thomas did this because I hurt his pride. It's just a way to save face."

We talked for another half hour before Jackson rose, promising to call with any news. He planned to move into his own apartment soon, which would make it easier for him to visit without worrying about being tailed by Theron or anyone else. He'd found work with a crew of roofers—another group of "lost boys" from Riverview Heights. My heart hurt thinking about him trying to make his way on his own, cut off from his family.

Evan saw him out, then walked slowly back to the kitchen and sat in the chair across from me. "Are you okay?"

I curled my hands around my half-empty soda can. "Just worried about Jackson. I don't think they would hurt him, but . . ." I stopped. I couldn't bear to speculate about what might happen.

Evan rubbed his hand over his mouth. He still wore his long, loose running shorts, but he'd pulled on a lightweight long-sleeved shirt with a Yale logo over his bare chest when Jackson showed up. He'd told me his track-and-field prowess had faded his sophomore year of college, when he'd hit a late growth spurt and put on twenty pounds of muscle. He'd gone to Yale for his medical degree as a way of offering an olive branch to his father. His Ivy League education was just one more divider between us. I thought of the junior college certificate I'd been so proud of and winced.

"Hey, Jackson will be all right," Evan said, misunderstanding the source of my anxiety. "He's a smart kid, and a heck of a lot more mature than I was at sixteen."

"He didn't have a choice. Riverview Heights makes you grow up fast."

Evan studied me. "What he said . . . about the blood atonement. How serious is it?"

I opened my mouth to lie but all that came out was a dry sob. Evan was around the table in seconds, pulling me up and into his arms.

"Shhh, what's all this?" he said softly. "I've got you."

I pressed my cheek against the hard muscles of his chest, inhaling the scents of clean sweat mixed with the laundry detergent he used. It felt so good to be held. Thomas had never just held me, not in five years of marriage. He'd touched me only as part of sex. There was nothing sexual about the way Evan held me now, but his arms felt so good, I wanted to press my body harder against his. The power behind the urge was so overwhelming, I pulled away, startled by how much it affected me.

He released me at once but pressed me gently back into my chair before hooking another with his foot and dragging it over. He sat and threaded his fingers through mine. "Why don't you tell me exactly what this means, this blood atonement? Is Jackson wrong? Is it more than a symbolic gesture?"

I used my free hand to brush the tears off my face. "I grew up in Illinois, where the Priesthood Council is headquartered. My grandfather sat on the Council in his day, and my father was expected to follow in his footsteps." I fell silent. I'd never told this story to anyone, and the few people who knew it had done their best to conceal the truth.

"But he didn't?"

"No. He met my mother. They fell in love." I smiled, picturing them together. My memories of that time were hazy, but I remembered bits and pieces of happiness, and a house filled with laughter and music. "My mom used to sing all the time. She had a beautiful voice. She got sick the winter I turned six. The Council had already started pressuring my dad to take another wife. A man needs at least three wives to enter the highest level of heaven." I shot a hesitant look at Evan, expecting to see shock or censure, but he just watched me, his gray eyes solemn. "The Council threatened him, but my father didn't want anyone else. It was just my mom for him. Then she got sick, and he had to spend a lot of time looking after her."

Evan opened my hand and smoothed his fingers down my palm in long, soothing strokes. "That must have been a relief for your mother, not to have another woman come between them."

"That's just it, though. She loved him, but she was very religious. She had an unwavering faith in the Principle. He insisted on monogamy, even though she begged him to take another wife. And the irony is, it probably would have kept them together. Dad started missing work to stay home to help her. Another wife could have kept things in order, helped my mom, whatever."

Evan frowned. "You said 'could have kept them together.' Is

that why they divorced? Because she wanted him to have more wives?"

I shook my head. "I used to think that, but now I know better. He knew it would have destroyed her, but she would have gone along with it because that's what she was brought up to believe. He knew she wouldn't have been able to share him, so he protected her from having to try it. The prophet called him before the whole community and publicly commanded him to take another wife. He proclaimed my dad an apostate when he refused to have anyone but my mother. My dad tried to persuade my mom to leave the faith with him, but she wouldn't go. She loved him, I know she did, but she really believed she was saving all of our souls—his, hers, mine—by staying behind. They excommunicated him. The prophet declared blood atonement, and my dad had to leave. I never saw him again. He died just a couple years after the divorce. Thomas told me."

Evan twined his fingers in mine again. "Could he have been mistaken? Or maybe he lied?"

"I wish that were true, but no. It was in the paper. A work accident in Arizona."

I told him everything, how my mother had been reassigned to my stepfather to prove she wasn't some sort of irresistible enchantress who made men abandon their faith. I described the long, lonely years in my stepfather's house. How we'd struggled to get enough to eat. I rushed through everything in a low, emotionless voice, telling him how I'd learned not to get caught alone with my stepbrothers . . . and then, eventually, my stepfather. I went through my mother's final illness, recalling how her sister-wives had divided her few possessions within hours of her passing.

"So, you see, marrying Thomas was like a dream come true. It could have been much worse."

"How old you were you?"

"Nineteen. Thomas was forty-seven."

He stood and walked to the island, pushing a hand through his thick hair, before turning to face me. "Does it happen often? Girls that young sleeping with older men?"

Was that what was bothering him? It hadn't occurred to me before, but now I realized he might feel strange about the idea of me being with Thomas. I felt torn between shame and indignation. To me, my relationship with Thomas had taken place within the bonds of marriage, but maybe Evan didn't see it that way. As an outsider, the whole arrangement probably seemed sordid and exploitative. I chose my words carefully. "The Priesthood Council usually won't assign a girl until she's out of her teens. Outsiders frown on it, and the Righteous Brethren don't want to risk losing chances to do business with them." I thought of Daria. "There are always exceptions, though. You weren't wrong . . . what you said the other night."

"Elizabeth, I—"

"No, it's okay." I held up a hand. "I'm not mad at you for saying it. I've been questioning things for a long time. I just . . ."

"What is it?"

I reached for my braid, only to remember it was no longer there, then sighed and decided to just lay everything out in the open. "I don't want you to think of me that way, like I'm one of *them*. Like I'm part of some harem or . . . cult."

Evan rubbed the back of his neck. "It was a stupid thing to say." He put his palms on the counter. "And I don't think that. Not about you."

"But things are different between us," I blurted.

He looked at me sharply. "Different how?"

"I don't know, just . . . different from before. Something changed when you found out where I'm from. You don't seem to like me as much," I finished miserably.

He pushed away from the counter. "Whoa, whoa, whoa.

Where are you getting that idea?" He gave a small huff of laughter. "I can assure you, I like you just fine."

I stared at him, bewildered. His smile seemed genuine, even a little self-deprecating, as if he were enjoying a private joke. My cheeks heated, but I plunged ahead. "You haven't kissed me since that first night, after dinner. You don't even like to touch me if you can help it." I wanted to sink into the floor as soon as the words left my mouth. This man had taken me in, even after I'd lied to him. He'd nursed me back to health, fed me, clothed me. And now I was complaining that he hadn't tried to seduce me.

The smile dropped from his face, replaced by an expression I didn't recognize. He stepped away from the island, his eyes locked on mine. He moved toward the table, but instead of sitting down, he walked right around it, and stopped at my side. My heart sped up as he took my hand and raised me gently from my seat. With a single finger under my chin, he pulled me close. The heat of his body reached me through the thin material of my shirt. I stared up at him, helpless under whatever spell he'd cast. His storm-cloud eyes burned a dark silver.

"I want to show you something," he murmured, his eyes on my mouth. The pad of his finger under my chin urged me that much closer to him, until our hips touched. His other hand curved around my hip and pressed my pelvis against his—against the unmistakable hardness there.

I gasped.

"Yeah." He raised an eyebrow. "You feel that, don't you?" His lips dusted my forehead, my eyelids, the bridge of my nose. He put his mouth next to my ear. "Now tell me I don't like you."

I swallowed.

His voice dropped lower than I'd ever heard it. "I like you very, very much."

It was a second before I could talk. "I don't embarrass you?"

He sighed, and I mentally kicked myself for spoiling the moment.

When he pulled back, the confusion on his face was unmistakably genuine. "Now, where did you get that impression? Have I given you any reason to think that?" He didn't wait for me to answer. "Hell, Elizabeth, I want to show you off. I want to show you the world. *Aladdin* style."

I gave a small shake of my head. "What?"

He waved an impatient hand. "Disney movie. We'll add it to the list." He brushed my hair away from my face. "But you've just been through a rough experience. You're being forced to adjust to a lot of changes all at once. I don't even know if you totally realize just how much trauma you're dealing with. I'm okay taking it slow. I don't expect you to jump into bed with me."

My voice was a thread of sound. "But that's something you want?"

He moved his hands to my upper arms, his body no longer touching mine. "Of course I do, but I don't think you're ready for that. Sex shouldn't be about taking. It's about giving. You haven't said this outright, but I suspect you've known nothing but taking." His chest lifted in a sigh. "I thought about what you said . . . what we argued about the other night, and you're right. I have no right to dictate what you do. It was a wake-up call for me. I think I've been enjoying my role of knight in shining armor a little too much."

"Evan—"

"No, it's true. You're a strong woman, Elizabeth. Never doubt that. Few people, man or woman, could have endured what you have and come out of it unscathed. But I saw you after what he —" His fingers tightened on my arms, and for a minute his expression was pure menace. I *felt* him master himself as they loosened one by one.

He took a deep breath. "I saw you afterward. To me, you still seem vulnerable. I want to protect you, but I can't smother you. I feel like sex would just complicate things right now. Your self-worth shouldn't be wrapped up in whether you can please a man. I'm happy just being with you. I don't need more."

Thank goodness there were no mirrors near the kitchen, because I was certain my face was fire-engine red.

He gave my arms a gentle squeeze before releasing me and walking to the fridge. "You hungry?" he said over his shoulder. "I didn't finish my run, but I'm starving. I was thinking Chinese for dinner." He pulled out a water bottle and cracked it open.

"Uh, sure, that sounds good." I turned and gathered the soda cans from the table.

"It's a date. I'm going to run up for a quick shower. Give me ten minutes."

I watched him go, then sank back into my chair and pressed one of the half-full cans against my cheek. Discussing sex in such a candid way was entirely new for me. Which was kind of ironic, considering I'd spent five years openly scheduling sex with my husband with three other women.

But somewhere underneath my embarrassment were the faintest stirrings of rebellion. He'd acknowledged he didn't have the right to make decisions for me . . . then he'd immediately decided I wasn't ready for intimacy. The fact that he was probably right did nothing to alleviate my unease. Shouldn't I have some say in deciding when I was ready for something so important?

I sipped my soda and grimaced when the lukewarm liquid hit my mouth. After months of trying to avoid sex, I was now in the position of trying to . . . what? Talk a man into seducing me? Cajole him? I had no idea how to convince Evan that starting a sexual relationship wouldn't be a mistake. If I were really honest with myself, it might be. At least right now.

But I was tired of being *told* how I was supposed to feel.

My eyes drifted to the ceiling as I heard him walking

around his bedroom, opening drawers. Somehow, I had to let him know that he couldn't just smooth a path for me for the rest of my life. I needed to learn how to overcome obstacles. I needed to make decisions of my own, even if it meant making mistakes. Even if it meant failing.

Because if I let Evan orchestrate my life, I was no better off than I'd been in Riverview Heights.

22

"You look frustrated, dear."

I turned from the kitchen counter, where I was stuffing the blood pressure cuff back in its storage bag. "What was that, Trudy?"

Evan's neighbor frowned at me from where she sat at the dining room table, a dozing Napoleon on her lap. Today, she wore high-waisted jeans and a shirt that said *I may be old, but I saw all the best bands*. She shot me a sharp look. "You heard me. I'm the deaf one here, remember?"

I just shook my head, accustomed to her bluntness by now. I carried her pill organizer and a glass of water to the table. "It's Thursday, so you need to take your iron pill and your Lipitor."

"The white pill and the red pill," she said, snapping open the lid marked *Thursday* and withdrawing the medication I'd divvied up for her over the weekend. Her vision wasn't terrible, but she had a difficult time reading her pill bottles, and she took so many prescriptions, even one mix-up could cause serious problems. Evan said she'd accidentally doubled up on her beta blocker before. Luckily, he'd checked on her that day. After a quick trip to the ER, he'd started checking her pill sorter at the start of each week—a job she had decided now belonged to me.

She accepted the water I handed her, then swallowed a pill with a grimace. "I'll never get used to that one. Tastes like dog food. Don't ask me how I know that."

I sat and warmed my hands around my coffee mug. "You should have seen the painkillers I took for my back," I said without thinking.

Trudy looked at me with interest. "Painkillers? A young thing like you? What happened to your back?"

"I pulled something," I said quickly. "It's better now."

She nodded. "I bet it doesn't hurt having a doctor for a boyfriend."

I sat up a little straighter. "He's not my boyfriend. Not really."

"Well you're living together. I'd say that makes him more than a friend. You don't have to worry about judgment from me, dear. Nothing wrong with trying the soup before you order the entree, I always say."

I'd certainly never heard it put that way before. It was a relief to know she wasn't offended by the idea of Evan and me living together. Still, my upbringing compelled me to set the record straight. "We're not together. That way. Evan and me."

Trudy looked outraged. "Well, why not? I tell you, if I were twenty years younger, I'd snap that young man right up."

I didn't tell her it would take a few more decades to make that scenario possible. Knowing Trudy, she just might have pulled it off.

She scooped up Napoleon and set him gently on the floor. Free of the little dog, she leaned both elbows on the table and gave me an expectant look. "So? Spill it."

Uh-oh. I knew that look. I'd seen it on Natalie plenty of times. She and Trudy both had a nose for gossip, and Trudy had obviously scented a juicy tale in the air. I arranged my face in what I hoped was a nonchalant expression. "What do you mean?"

Her lovely violet eyes grew sharper, taking years off her face. "Now, now, Elizabeth, you can't hide something like this from Gertrude Warren. You've got man troubles. I'm old and bored, and I demand you tell me about them right this instant." She tapped an imperious fingernail on the tabletop.

Napoleon circled around on the rug in front of the refrigerator a few times, his head nearly touching his tail, before plopping down with a contented sigh. The dog had a knack for knowing when the cooling fan was about to kick on and usually found a way to bask in the warm air from the vent.

Trudy cleared her throat, pulling my attention back to her.

What was the harm? She wasn't going to tell anyone my secrets. And who would care if she did? The nice thing about coming from a closed community was having complete anonymity in the real world. Outside of the center, no one knew Elizabeth Grant existed.

"Evan and I aren't . . . We haven't . . ."

"Had sex."

Ugh. Why had I opened this can of worms? "I was married before and it ended badly. Evan thinks I'm too . . . That I'm not ready . . ."

"He thinks you're not ready for a sexual relationship," Trudy said, a knowing gleam in her eye.

"That about sums it up." Hearing it out loud made it seem worse.

She put her chin on her hand. "But you are ready."

She'd phrased it as a statement, but I answered her anyway. "I think so. I want to know how it can be when—" I swallowed. "When there's love. But Evan's never said he loves me."

Trudy smiled softly. "Oh, honey, you have nothing to worry about there. That man is so hot for you I'm surprised he doesn't trip over his own tongue." She smirked. "Or something else."

"But that's not the same as loving someone," I said.

"Do you love him?"

"Oh, yes," I said automatically.

"Then why not tell him?"

I opened my mouth, then shut it again. "Well, I . . . wasn't brought up that way. We didn't talk about stuff like that."

Trudy scoffed. "What do you mean, 'stuff like that'? Love is all there is, dear."

Unexpectedly, tears sprang to my eyes, and I looked down, willing myself to get control.

Trudy reached across the table and covered my hand with hers. She had the knobby, painful-looking knuckles of someone with rheumatoid arthritis, but her skin was surprisingly soft and her nails were just as elegantly manicured as always.

"You said you were married before. How long, dear?"

"Five years."

She tilted her head to the side. "And you left him?"

"Yes," I whispered.

She made a little sound—surprise mixed with sympathy. "Was it that bad? With your husband?"

I gave a jerky nod, not trusting myself to speak.

Before I could stop her, she rose and plucked my mug from my hands, then shuffled into the kitchen and refilled it. While her back was turned, I used my shirtsleeve to wipe the tears off my face, grateful I hadn't applied any of my new makeup that morning.

She returned with the whole coffee pot, which she plunked down in the middle of the table. "I have a feeling we're going to need this," she said as she settled back across from me.

In the kitchen, Napoleon twitched and let out a soft bark.

"Dreaming," Trudy said, rolling her eyes with a smile. Then she sobered. "I was sixteen when I married my first husband. Back then, nobody talked about abuse or domestic violence. If your husband beat up on you, people just said you got a bad man. Like getting home from the grocery store and finding a broken egg in the carton. You were just expected to deal with it. Preferably, in private. Of course, I knew nothing back then. I thought I was a woman grown, but I was just pretending, acting out what I'd seen my mother and her friends do as housewives."

She trailed off, her eyes thoughtful and distant. It was in this silence that I said, "I was nineteen when I married Thomas. We'd known each other a day when we married, and he had —*has*—three other wives."

Trudy's eyes widened, but she showed no other sign of surprise, so I plowed on. I told her everything, from the way the Righteous Brethren had broken up my family, to the night Thomas had beaten me and thrown me in the basement. By the time I got to the part about how I'd come to stay with Evan, we'd finished the entire pot of coffee and several of the short-bread cookies I'd made the day before. My bladder was uncomfortably full, but it felt so good to unburden myself, I stayed rooted to my seat in the quiet kitchen.

"The thing is," I said, "it wasn't always bad with Thomas. Most of the time, he was good to me. He liked . . . being with me, I think." I sighed, too exhausted to be embarrassed about discussing my sex life.

Trudy had listened without interruption, her eyes kind and open. "Do you think he loved you?"

I mulled it over. Had he loved me? He'd rarely said it, and I certainly hadn't experienced the kind of mad passion Trudy had described feeling for her second husband, or the quiet, steady love she'd felt for her third. "I'm not really sure. We didn't spend much time together—at least not alone. I don't think it's possible to know anyone that well in a place like Riverview Heights. I've spent more time with Evan in the past month than I did with Thomas in five years."

A scuffling sound near the refrigerator made both of us turn our heads. Done with his nap, Napoleon lumbered to all fours and trotted back to his mistress, who scooped him up and held out a small piece of cookie, which he promptly swallowed whole. "Napoleon!" Trudy scolded, then softened the rebuke by dropping a kiss on his head. She cradled the dog in her arms and studied me. "Have you told Dr. Adgate how you feel?"

I thought back to my conversation with Evan the night before. "I tried. But he has this way of just *deciding* things."

Trudy nodded knowingly. "After three husbands and all these years, I think I've learned a thing or two about men. When you tell one about a problem, their instinct is to fix it. I once complained to Ed about the garage being too cluttered. He waited until I went out with a few girlfriends and cleaned out the whole thing, top to bottom."

I frowned. "That doesn't sound bad."

"No, except the fool man didn't sort through anything. Just packed up boxes and took every last bit down to the donation center. I had to buy back my own winter coat and my mother's spoon collection."

I laughed. I couldn't help it.

Trudy smiled. "If you want a man to do something, don't be vague or shy about it, dear. Give him very clear instructions."

"Do you really think that will work with Evan?"

She gave me a look. "I've never met a man yet who'd turn down a romp in the sheets."

23

"**Y**ou *what*?" I sat bolt upright in the chair in Evan's bedroom. The sudden movement made my back throb with a dull ache. At least the sharp pinching had stopped as of a few days ago. I felt almost normal except for when I tried to move too quickly. Like now.

Evan tossed his pager and keys on the dresser, then dug in his scrub pants and withdrew a small roll of medical tape, which he regarded with an air of bemused confusion before shrugging and putting it on the dresser, too. He faced me. "It's just for a couple weeks. I want you to see where I grew up."

"Evan, I am not prepared to spend two weeks with your mother. I've never even met her."

He folded his arms. "You'll meet her next Friday." He raised a forestalling hand when I would have protested. "I don't feel comfortable leaving you here alone all day, not with this blood atonement thing hanging over our heads. From what you've told me, Thomas isn't stupid. I'm sure he's already figured out where you are. I'm easy enough to find on the center's website. From there, it doesn't exactly take a bloodhound to follow the trail to this place. I've got the vacation time, and you said you've always wanted to see the ocean."

I sat back, still trying to wrap my head around his announcement. He spoke fondly of his mother, but really? Staying in her house for two weeks? With Evan? Where would we sleep? What would she think about him bringing a woman home? Oh God, what did she know about me? I pinched the bridge of my nose as my head began to throb. "Couldn't you have asked me first?"

He sighed and started to sit on the bed, then stopped and looked down at himself with a grimace. "I want to talk about this, but I really have to get out of these scrubs. Just give me a minute." He disappeared into his bathroom, and I heard the toilet flush, then running water. When he returned a few minutes later, his hair was damp and he'd changed into a pair of gray sweatpants and a plain white T-shirt that hugged his chest and biceps.

He sank onto the bed, his bare feet stretched out in front of him. "Listen, just give her a chance. My mom's easy to talk to. She's a clinical psychologist, you know."

A horrifying thought occurred to me. "Did you plan this trip because you think I need a shrink? Like I'm mentally damaged?"

"What? No! Elizabeth, I don't think you're mentally damaged. A victim of systematic brainwashing and verbal and physical abuse? Yeah, that I believe. It doesn't take a medical degree to see that. Hell, anyone with eyes could see it."

"I'm not brainwashed."

He ran a hand through his hair. "Fine. Isolated, then. You've gone from living on a compound run by a theocracy to living in a gated community with one other person as your sole source of human contact."

"That's not true. I talk to Trudy all the time."

Evan raised a dark blond eyebrow. "Trudy thinks the Illuminati killed Elvis. *And* JFK."

I huffed. "She doesn't really think that. She just entertains herself by theorizing about it."

He leaned forward and grabbed my hand. "Hey. I'm sorry for springing this on you. If you want me to cancel, I will. I just thought it would be nice to get away for a while." He turned our joined hands and feathered his thumb over the pulse at my wrist. "Also, I want her to meet you. I've never introduced a woman to my mother."

I caught my breath. "Never?"

He shook his head slowly.

Well, that was something. I bit my lip. "How much have you told her? About . . ."

"I gave her an abbreviated version," he said, immediately understanding what I feared the most. "*Very* abbreviated. She knows about Thomas, about your marriage. I told her you left because the situation was abusive. I didn't go into detail. That's your call. You can tell her as little or as much as you like."

"What if I don't want to tell her anything? Is she expecting me to do counseling sessions or something?"

"No. She's expecting to meet the woman I'm in love with."

All the air left my lungs in a little whoosh of sound. It felt like someone had punched me in the gut. I had to try a couple times before I could speak. "What did you say?" I whispered.

He smiled the lopsided grin I'd fallen in love with the first time I met him. "I said I love you. I thought you knew by now."

"I d-didn't." I swallowed. "I didn't know."

He reached out and smoothed the hair from my face, then cupped my cheek in one of his big hands. "Well. You do now."

"I love you, too, Evan. I do."

For the first time since I'd known him, I initiated a kiss. He seemed surprised when I leaned forward and pressed my lips against his. Then his body came alive. He rose, and in a single fluid movement, scooped me up from the chair and settled himself in it with me on his lap—all without breaking the contact of our kiss.

I turned on his lap so I was facing him, my legs on either side of his. He brought his hands up and braced them against my back, making my lips curve against his.

He pulled back, his eyes sparkling. "What's funny?"

"You. You're such a doctor."

"Is that a compliment?" he asked, his tone hopeful.

"It is." I touched my fingers to his lips. "You care about other people. You help them. It's part of who you are. It's one of the reasons I love you."

He grabbed my hand and kissed my fingertips one by one, making me smile. "Just one reason? What are the others?"

I thought about it. "I love how you're not afraid to explore things. How you're determined to find something interesting, even in the most boring places. I love your smile. And your hair. I love your shoulders." I trailed my fingers down his biceps. "I love what you look like when you walk," I added shyly.

"Ahh," he said quietly. "Now, that's something we have in common." He let his head drop back against the cushion and regarded me through half-lidded eyes. "Because I could watch you walk all day."

"Really?"

"Mm-hmm. You have the longest, most gorgeous legs." He smiled lazily and played with the ends of my hair. "And the prettiest blond hair." He tucked the strands behind my ear. "And these deep blue eyes that remind me of summer on the Sound."

I tilted my head. "Sound?"

"Long Island Sound. We went every summer when I was a kid. I'll take you there."

His words were making heat pool in the center of my body. I shifted on his lap, and he groaned. He closed his eyes, and a little frown appeared between his brows. "Elizabeth, if you do that again, I don't know if I'm going to be able to control myself."

"Would that be such a bad thing?" I asked lightly.

"I'm not going to take advantage of you."

I put a tentative hand on his chest, Trudy's advice running through my mind. His skin was warm through the thin cotton of his shirt. How could I tell him what I wanted? Should I just say it? I had no idea how to do this. My sexual experiences were limited to Thomas, and he had always been the one to initiate intimacy. There was no need for seduction when your husband scheduled the times you slept together.

"It's not taking advantage of me if I want you to do it," I said finally, shocked at my own boldness.

Evan pulled my hand away from his chest. "Sweetheart, I don't think you know what you want. You shouldn't be expected to. Anyone in your position would feel confused. You're vulnerable, and you've had to rely on me for everything. I don't want you to feel obligated to repay me. In *any* way," he added, his meaning clear.

I moved off his lap and stood silently beside the chair, wishing I could sink into the floor and just keep going. I was going to have to do this the hard way. Fine. "I don't feel like I owe you." I pushed my hair back from my face and squared my shoulders. *Don't be vague or shy*, Trudy's voice spoke in my head.

I grabbed the hem of my shirt and pulled it over my head.

He parted his lips.

Before I lost my nerve, I thumbed open the button fly of my jeans and skimmed them down my legs, then stepped out of them and kicked them aside. Clad in the skimpiest underwear I owned, I put my hands on my hips.

The movement drew his gaze to my chest, and a little thrill of satisfaction shot through me.

I lifted my chin. "But *you* owe *me*."

He rubbed a hand over his mouth, his eyes struggling to stay north of my chin. "Ah . . . what? I mean, how? How do I owe you?"

"You said I needed to be open, to be willing to try new experiences. And I *am*, Evan. I've done everything you've asked, even when it's out of my comfort zone. But you refuse to let me get closer to you." I gulped a breath. "You keep pushing me away, and it hurts! You accuse me of being brainwashed—"

"I changed it to isolated."

I slashed the air with my hand, cutting him off. "You said brainwashed first!"

He closed his mouth with an audible snap.

"You asked how you owe me." My voice trembled with a combination of anger and nerves. "You owe me the chance to decide for myself what I want. All my life I've been told what to believe, what to think"—I gestured to the clothes on the floor—"even what to wear. I love you, Evan. And you say you love me, but you're keeping us apart because you're too damn *noble* to make love to me!" I flung my arms out to the sides. "That's what I want! I want you to make love to me!"

A second passed, the space of a heartbeat, then he was out of his chair and over the ottoman, his big body against mine.

He tangled his hand in my hair, pulled my head back, and buried his face in the space between my neck and shoulder, his mouth hot on my skin. His other hand gripped my butt. I gasped, then let my eyes drift shut.

He stayed that way for a moment, his big hand kneading my ass, his lips caressing my skin.

Thomas never— I cut off the thought. Thomas had no place in my mind anymore. None at all.

Without warning, Evan bent and swung me into his arms. I clutched at his shoulders as he walked us to the bed. He dropped me on the springy mattress, forcing a soft grunt from my lungs.

He fisted the back of his shirt and pulled it over his head, then shucked his sweat pants, revealing a tight, muscular chest and defined abs. My gaze drifted downward, to the black boxer briefs barely covering the obvious sign of his desire.

His voice brought my head back up. "Do you still want this?" he asked, his voice lower than I'd ever heard it. "Now is the time to say yes or no." He flicked a glance down my body before piercing me with a burnt-silver stare. "Because once I start I don't intend to stop."

I sucked in a breath. He looked like he wanted to devour me whole. His hands were loose at his sides, but his body was a mass of tightly coiled power, every muscle cut and limned in golden-tanned skin. This was Evan as I'd never seen him before. It was as if he'd shed the sophisticated, genteel wrapping he wore for society to reveal the raw core that powered him. He looked rougher—no longer the educated man of science and reason. This was the man I loved stripped down to his most basic parts.

The man I love.

His hands clenched and unclenched at his sides, and his breath sawed in and out of his chest. He was holding himself in check, waiting as patiently as possible, for me to decide. And I knew without question that he would stand there as long as it took.

I rose up on my knees and reached for him.

He met me halfway, his mouth on mine before I could say a word. We clung to each other in the middle of the bed, his strong arms holding us upright. His tongue pressed against my lips, and I opened my mouth to let him in, then whimpered when he cupped between my legs with a firm hand.

He stilled instantly. "Okay?" he said against my mouth.

In response, I pressed my body more fully against his. "More than okay."

He pulled back, his gray eyes tender in his hard face. With a deft flick of his fingers, he undid the front clasp of my bra and pushed the straps off my shoulders, his hands brushing slowly down my arms. My breasts sprang free, and he ran reverent fingers over them, lightly brushing my nipples before cupping a breast in each palm.

"Ah, now these are beauties, Elizabeth." He slid one hand up and gripped my chin while the other continued to caress my chest, his fingers gentle on my nipples. "You're beautiful," he whispered before guiding my mouth to his and kissing me again, his tongue moving against mine, his lips soft but firm.

Heat spread low in my belly, as if the sun burned inside me. Or maybe Evan was the sun, blazing around me, raising fire with every touch.

My sex throbbed. My nipples grew taut. I thrust my chest against his hand.

He laughed low in his throat. Breaking off our kiss, he lowered his head and took one hard nipple into his mouth.

I cupped either side of his head. My heart pounded as he sucked, circling my nipple with his tongue, teasing at it with his teeth. Every pull of his mouth sent a pulse of desire straight to my sex.

With a final flick of his tongue, he moved his mouth to the other breast and gave it the same treatment. The nipple he'd abandoned stabbed out from my chest, the tip a lush, dark red from his attentions. Cool air teased at the wet, shiny peak—a contrast to the hot, demanding mouth pulling and sucking at the other one.

He released my breast with a popping sound, then leaned back, his gaze hot and possessive. "I need more of you."

Heaven help me, he could have as much as he wanted. I drew in a shuddering breath. "Make love to me. Please."

The possessiveness flared again. With gentle hands, he lowered me to the bed and covered my body with his, his weight pressing me into the soft mattress. He let me feel the hard length of him for a moment before propping himself up on his elbows, his long legs tangled with mine.

"Still okay?" he asked softly, and I nodded, daring to splay my fingers over his chest. He was smooth everywhere but his legs, which were covered in a light dusting of golden hair.

As if he'd read my mind, he smiled. "Blonds have more fun. And less body hair."

My laugh turned to a groan when he lowered his mouth to mine. He kissed me until I was breathless and panting, his hands roving over my body. He was everywhere—my breasts, my thighs—his touches light but confident. He smoothed his hands over the scrap of silk between my legs and let out a soft growl. "I've wanted to see this on you ever since the day you bought it."

So he *had* noticed the thong. Apparently, Evan wasn't as gentlemanly as he let on. "Do you like it?" I asked, even though the answer was obvious.

He seemed to ponder it, his face grave and considering, before saying, "I can't tell. I need to examine it more closely." When I giggled, he gave my collarbone a playful nip. Then his expression turned serious again. "In fact, I think I need to take a look all over. For medical reasons, of course."

"All over?" I said with mock solemnity.

"Mmmm. A full-body exam."

I swallowed. "Well, whatever you think is best, Doctor."

In answer, he stretched out a long arm and flicked off the bedside lamp, turning the bedroom a soft gray. He moved his body down mine, trailing kisses down my chest and stomach. My breath fluttered as he hovered over my hips, his dark golden hair illuminated by light streaming from a small night-light in the bathroom. He lifted his gaze to mine.

"Is this okay, sweetheart?"

I knew what he was asking. I hadn't told him about the construction trailer, but I didn't need to. The mix of tenderness and concern in his eyes told me he'd already guessed the worst thing I'd endured in my marriage.

I nodded. "Yes. Because it's you. I'm always okay with you."

He hooked his thumbs in the strings on either side of my thong, then pulled it slowly down my legs. Just as slowly, and never breaking eye contact, he removed his boxer briefs. My eyes had adjusted to the dim light, and I saw him clearly as he rose above me, his thighs spread on either side of mine. His gaze lingered over my breasts as he gripped himself, casually stroking up and down.

Oh, boy. He was . . . well proportioned. "Evan," I said, my voice pitched a little higher than usual, "I don't think—"

He put a finger over my lips, the ghost of a smile playing around his mouth. "Relax, sweetheart. It's nothing you can't handle."

I had my doubts, but all coherent thought fled when he pushed my legs apart and lowered his head between my thighs. Protests sprang to my lips and died as he kissed along my inner thigh, his breath hot against my core. My head fell back of its own accord, and my mouth opened on a silent cry.

He licked up my center, teasing at my folds with his tongue. Then he dipped inside my opening, working me over and over again with his mouth. Light smacking sounds filled the air as he stroked his tongue up and down, up and down. He lapped at my entrance, drawing hot moisture from my sex. I gripped the sheets on either side of my hips.

Never, never, never went the chant in my head. Never had anyone touched me like this.

Loved me like this.

Tension coiled like a spring inside me, each bend ratcheted tighter and tighter. Fire licked at me.

Evan licked at me.

He took my clit into his mouth and sucked. Hard.

Game over.

I sobbed my release, my body flying apart. Light burst behind my eyelids, and the world condensed to a single point, then exploded outward. I raked my fingers through his hair and gripped his shoulders, holding his face against my sex. Thighs trembling around his head, I clung to him like a raft in the ocean, no choice but to ride out the sensation screaming through me, the pleasure so intense it bordered on sweet pain.

I floated back down to earth slowly, and I became aware of Evan holding me, murmuring soft endearments as he stroked my damp hair back from my face. He smiled down at me, a lock of hair spilling over his forehead, making him look heartbreakingly young. His thumb brushed a tear from the corner of my eye, and he leaned down to kiss the tip of my nose, then my eyelids.

"I never knew," I said, wonder in my voice.

He put his mouth next to my ear. "Beautiful girl," he said with a smile in his voice, "I'm just getting started."

He kissed me, transferring my essence to my lips. Then he reached between our bodies and, gripping himself, teased the head of his shaft around my opening, filling the air with thick, wet sounds as he stirred himself in my juices. He circled my entrance, bumping against my clit. My inner muscles clenched, desperate for him.

A low groan escaped me. "Please," I begged.

He slid inside me in a slow, easy glide that sent little aftershocks shivering through my limbs.

When he was halfway inside, he pulled back out, the hard length of him sliding against my still-throbbing clit. Tiny sparks shot through me, and I arched off the bed.

He rose above me, his weight on his arms, his body a hard,

gray silhouette against the purple-tinged evening light leaking in through the edges of the window shades.

He pushed his hips forward, seating himself to the hilt. A beat passed, and he moved against me in shallow pumps. After a second, he went deeper, the rhythm like a slow, lazy current. He exhaled—a breathy sigh that ended on a low groan.

He groaned again when I slid my legs up his flanks and wrapped them around his back. Then I began to move with him, and he sucked in a sharp breath before dropping his head to my shoulder.

"You have no idea how good you feel," he murmured, his voice low and rough. "That's it, sweetheart. Open up for me."

He reached back and hiked my leg higher on his hip, his palm hot on my thigh. He shifted his hips, and his shaft nudged my clit. Again and again. A few more nudges and I was off again, the tight coil bursting apart.

Wave after wave of pleasure slammed through me, until I lost track of where one ended and the next one began.

Evan's whole body tensed. With one final, powerful thrust of his hips, he seated himself deep within me, his head thrown back as he shouted his release.

He'd settled his full weight on me, but I didn't mind. I wrapped my arms around his neck, savoring the feel of hard muscle encased in smooth skin. He'd collapsed with his head pressed into the pillow near my ear, his chest expanding as if he'd just run a sprint. Eventually, as awareness returned, he seemed to realize he was crushing me, and quickly rolled to the side. A long strand of my hair clung to the stubble shadowing his jaw, and he smiled and pulled it away, smoothing his palm down my cheek in the process. Head propped on his hand, he said, "I've loved you since the minute you choked on your sandwich in the lunchroom."

"What?" I asked, startled into laughter by this unexpected admission.

"You were so adorable," he said, and I heard the fondness of the memory in his voice. "I knew you were nervous and embarrassed. But you were willing to laugh at yourself. I was surprised you gave me the time of day."

I must have looked skeptical, because he said, "I was. You were so beautiful, I figured I didn't have a chance. But you were also sweet and down to earth. And funny. And smart."

I was grateful for the darkened room, which kept him from seeing me blushing. "I'm none of those things. Especially next to you."

"Please," he scoffed lightly. "Do you need me to start listing all the famous millionaires who never finished college?" he asked, correctly guessing that my lack of education was the sore spot between us. At least for me. He insisted it didn't matter to him.

"They're famous because they did something important. I'm a medical assistant who got fired for stealing medication."

"You had a good reason. And please don't let me hear you claim you've never done anything important. You escaped a lifetime of religious indoctrination and an abusive marriage."

I touched his cheek. "I couldn't have done it without you."

He turned his cheek into my hand, the whiskers rasping against my skin. "Are you okay?" His voice was tender. "Was it . . . ?"

"I'm totally fine." I twined my arms around his neck and lifted my head so I could kiss him. "It was perfect."

24

I woke slowly to the sound of birds singing to each other outside. A smile curved my lips as I remembered curling up next to Evan, my hand on his chest, the feel of his breath stirring the fine hairs near my temple.

I put my arms over my head and stretched, yawning until my jaw cracked. Vaguely, I remembered him leaning over the bed and planting a soft kiss on my forehead before he left for work that morning. I rolled to the side and pressed my face into his pillow, savoring the scent of him—a mix of shampoo, the detergent he used, and some indefinable smell that was uniquely his.

Out of habit more than necessity, I levered my body up sideways like I'd been taught in the hospital, putting all my weight on my hand as I pushed myself into a sitting position on the edge of the bed. I grinned. After last night, there was no question of my back being fully healed. Evan certainly hadn't held back.

I padded into the bathroom and looked myself over in the mirror. My hair fell in tousled disarray over my shoulders, and my features looked . . . softer somehow. Which was silly, not to mention impossible. One night of great sex couldn't change a person's face.

But it hadn't just been great sex, I thought, smoothing down the old Yale T-shirt I'd stolen from Evan's dresser. He'd told me he loved me, then he'd proceeded to show me with his body. And the things he'd done with his mouth . . .

I looked away from my reflection as my cheeks heated. Evan Adgate was a gentleman, but he'd been quite the opposite in bed. Rough and masterful, he'd taken what he wanted. It had shocked me, but I'd loved every second of it.

And I'd never once thought about Thomas. I forced my eyes back to the mirror. Somewhere in the back of my mind, I'd been worried that those brutal moments in the trailer would always be there, ready to rear up and ruin anything good I tried to have with Evan. Thanks to the skill of Evan's friend at the hospital, the wounds on my back had left no scars.

No, the only marks I bore from Thomas were on the inside, on my mind and soul. The care and companionship Evan had given me had gone a long way toward erasing those. I straightened my shoulders.

"You can never touch me again," I said to the mirror.

I spent the morning trying to decide what to pack for the trip to Connecticut. What was the weather like this time of year? Did people who lived near the water wear certain types of clothing? I pictured the grizzled fisherman in a hat and raincoat on the box of fish sticks Dinah used to buy. That was about as much exposure as I had to the East Coast. Mostly, I just didn't want to embarrass Evan. I was still adjusting to having the freedom to wear whatever I wanted whenever I wanted. When you spend the first twenty-five years of your life in ankle-length skirts and button-downs, even the smallest options are overwhelming. I wandered upstairs, where Evan had laid out two rolling suitcases on the floor in front of his bed.

Maybe I'd get him to take me shopping on our trip, I

thought brightly. I'd quickly overcome my shopping anxiety and now indulged every opportunity to wander up and down the store aisles, looking for something cute and useful for the condo, or some knickknack Trudy would love. Evan didn't mind. If anything, he seemed to enjoy playing the role of long-suffering boyfriend who sighed and handed over the credit card.

Whoa. *Boyfriend?* I straightened from the suitcase I was crouched next to. When had I started thinking of him that way? I sat back on my heels. In a way, things between us had evolved slowly.

In other ways, though, we'd been thrown together by external forces, rapidly progressing through all the normal relationship stages. If Thomas had never found out about Evan, I'd probably still be living in a loft apartment above Dinah's living room, carefully tracking my menstrual cycles and doing whatever chores she assigned. Or I'd be pregnant with Thomas's fifteenth child.

I suppressed a shiver and smoothed my damp palms down the short legs of my denim cutoffs. Evan had persuaded me to buy them, saying it was a "crime against humanity" to keep my legs hidden from the world. I smiled at the memory. He certainly checked all the usual boxes when it came to the ideal boyfriend—at least the ones I'd been reading about in the glossy women's magazines I'd bought to learn about makeup application and hairstyles. They were filled with odd quizzes, like *Find your best sex position!* and *What are your must-haves in a man?*

Evan fulfilled every requirement I had. He was smart and funny, and he had a great job that he loved. Most importantly, he treated me with a care and gentleness that took my breath away. And I knew without asking that he wouldn't give a crap if my legs were a little stubbly.

And if we weren't normal, so what? I folded several pairs of boxer briefs into little squares and tucked them in a corner of the suitcase. What I had with Evan was better than what I'd had before. It wasn't even a comparison. I'd been *given* to Thomas, a near stranger at the time and a man old enough to be my father. It was only now, being away from that environment, that I saw how unhealthy our arrangement had been. I wasn't going to call it a marriage—not anymore. Because I'd never been Thomas's wife. More like a servant who occasionally warmed his bed.

My stomach rumbled, and I realized I'd worked through lunch. Now that I wasn't taking pain medication, I wasn't forced to eat on a regular schedule and sometimes lost track of time. I squinted at the clock on the dresser across the room. It was too late for lunch, and if I ate now I'd ruin my appetite for dinner. Evan loved my cooking, which made it fun to surprise him with new dishes. I was currently experimenting with Asian fusion.

I flipped the lid closed on the suitcase and headed toward the kitchen. I was halfway down the stairs when a knock sounded on the door. Which was odd, because Trudy wasn't supposed to stop by. She'd said she was having lunch with a couple ladies from her book club. She'd been pestering me to join for weeks. I smiled on my way to the door, prepared to make excuses for why I couldn't go.

"Trudy, I'm so busy with packing," I said as I swung open the door. "There's no way I—" The next words stuck in my throat as I came face-to-face with Thomas.

"You look well, Elizabeth," he said, staring down at me with a stern expression. He was wearing his wire-rimmed glasses, which always made him look older. Even as I thought it, he pulled them off and tucked them in his shirt pocket. He gestured toward the foyer. "May I come in?"

I almost stepped back out of habit, the tiny synapses of my brain automatically responding to the authority in his voice.

Then I came to my senses and started to close the door in his face.

He shoved it, shouldering his way in with ease. The heavy metal door swung close to my bare toes, and I stumbled back.

"Thank you." His tone was polite, as if I'd just invited him in for tea.

"Thomas, I want you to leave." I kept my hand on the knob, deliberately holding the door open. I risked taking my eyes off him for a second so I could glance toward the parking lot. There was no sign of his truck. More importantly, there was no sign of Theron or any of the usual thugs he kept around.

He gazed around the foyer. "Not much, is it? I expected more, especially for a doctor." He leveled a look at me. "Although, he's still young, isn't he?"

"I want you to leave. Now, or I'm calling the police."

"There's no need for dramatics." He gave me a patient smile. "I simply want to talk to you. Nothing more." He spread his arms, the movement revealing a glimpse of a shoulder holster. Of course he was armed. He always carried when he left Riverview Heights. Most of the men did—a holdover, perhaps, from a time when they had to be constantly vigilant about the authorities tracking them down and forcing them to either abandon their families or face jail time. Traditions died hard in communities like ours. Jackson's voice flitted through my head. *He called for blood atonement, Elizabeth.*

I folded my arms. "I don't think we have anything to say to each other," I said, pleased when my voice didn't shake. My heart pounded hard against my ribs. If he wanted to shoot me right now, there was no way I could stop him. I was as much at his mercy at this moment as I'd ever been back in Riverview Heights.

He stepped forward. I moved back, but he walked past me and closed the door, locking it. With a sinking heart, I realized he'd positioned himself to block my only way out of the condo.

He turned and stuffed his hands in his pockets, as if demonstrating how harmless he was. "You may not have anything to say to me," he said calmly—then a glint of humor entered his eyes—"although, knowing you as I do, I doubt that. But I have a few things I'd like to say to you."

When I just stared at him in stony silence, he said, "Come now, Elizabeth, I'm your husband. Don't I have the right to talk to my wife?"

"How did you get here? How did you get past the security guard?"

He raised an eyebrow. "Your boss from the health center. Well, former boss, I suppose, considering they fired you. Brittney, is it?"

I didn't reply, since he wasn't really asking. He had the upper hand, and he knew it. I had almost zero options, but I didn't have to indulge his little question-and-answer game.

He leaned against the door, his tailored suit pants and white button-down as crisply starched as always. I wondered who was doing the laundry now that I was gone. Not Dinah. She'd probably pressed Leah's girls into taking over my chores. My heart squeezed with guilt at the idea of them spending days in the basement, sweating over an ironing board. In a few short years, they would be handed off to a husband so they could do the exact same thing for another man.

"I'll take that as a yes," Thomas said. "Anyway, Brittney was concerned about you. She thought you might have taken it hard, being let go, so she stopped by the office in town to check on you. She was shocked to hear you'd run off with your doctor friend. Luckily, she knows the code to the gate outside."

It took every ounce of willpower I possessed to keep my face blank. I'd known Brittney didn't like me, that she resented my relationship with Evan.

But I'd never believed her capable of something like this. She couldn't know what Thomas had done to me, but giving an access code to a man who suspected his wife of cheating on him was a new low, even for her. As a health care worker, she knew full well that abused women were at the greatest risk of being murdered by their abuser in the days and weeks following their decision to leave. She also knew I came from a patriarchal society. It didn't take a genius to guess that I didn't want my ex-husband to know where I was.

He pushed away from the door, and I jumped. "Is that what you came to say?" I demanded, nerves making my chest ache. Absently, I wondered if it was possible to die of fear, because my heart was skipping beats and my knees threatened to give out.

He drifted close, and I ducked my head, expecting a blow. But he only put a hand on my shoulder and turned me toward the kitchen.

"I see a table through there. Why don't we sit down." He nudged me down the hall, and the hairs on the back of my neck lifted in apprehension as I was forced to turn my back on him.

In the kitchen, he pulled out a chair and gestured for me to sit. "You changed your hair. I like it."

I didn't much care what he liked or didn't like. "The weight gave me headaches."

"And your clothes?" His eyes flicked to my lace-edged blue tank top as he seated himself across from me. "Was dressing modestly giving you headaches?"

I folded my hands on the table. "Actually, recovering from the spinal fractures and bruised jaw you gave me caused the most headaches. But I'm better now."

He leaned back in his chair. "I admit I was a bit heavy-handed, but you earned that punishment. I assume you're sleeping with the doctor? You know, Prophet Benson warned me against taking you as a wife. 'Bad blood will out,' he said, and apparently he was right."

"Then you should be happy to be rid of me." Frustration

bubbled up, making me reckless. "Why can't you just leave me alone? We were never married anyway, so it's not like you have to divorce me—"

"We are sealed before Heavenly Father." An ominous look darkened his face. "I don't need a piece of paper from a court of man to legitimize my marriage."

"Thomas—"

"I favored you above all the others," he said, startling me into silence. "Dinah has been determined to make my life miserable since the day she laid eyes on you, but I ignored her complaining because I wanted you to be part of our family. I tried not to play favorites, but my affection for you was obvious."

My lips parted. It sure as hell hadn't been obvious to me. Had I really been that blind? Or did Thomas just suck as a husband? It was impossible to say without knowing how he treated his other wives when they were alone, and that was information I didn't care to have.

"I want you to leave," I said again. Maybe the third time would be the charm.

"Not without you." He stabbed an imperious finger on the tabletop. "You're going home, where you belong, and you're going to repent your sins and serve me as a chaste, obedient wife. It's your choice, Elizabeth. Cooperate or suffer the consequences."

"You mean more beatings?" I threw back at him, anger at his arrogance overriding my fear. "Blood atonement? What happens if I don't cooperate, Thomas? What then? You kill me?"

His cold blue eyes bored into mine. "If it becomes necessary. It was in your father's case."

I felt the blood drain from my face.

"Although," he added, "he died because he refused to stay

away. You'll die if you decide to be stupid and try to leave again."

Before I could say anything, the doorbell rang. Our eyes locked. His mouth tightened as the bell rang twice more . . . then again, the sound echoing down the hallway.

"Elizabeth?" Trudy's voice called from outside. "I know you're in there!"

"It's the neighbor," I told Thomas. "She's an old woman. Harmless. Half senile," I added, trying to make her seem less of a threat.

The doorbell sounded again, followed by impatient knocking.

I looked toward the hallway, willing her to go away.

"Go answer it," Thomas said. He slipped a hand inside his suit jacket and withdrew a sleek black pistol. It was an ugly, alien-looking thing. He stood and jerked his chin toward the door. "Now."

It was like being in a dream. Everything moved slowly. I felt detached from my body, as I had in the trailer.

I rose from my chair and walked down the short hallway toward the door, Thomas a menacing shadow at my back. My skin felt like it was stretched too tight over my bones, and there was a low buzzing sound in my head. I had to consciously think about reaching out my hand and grasping the doorknob.

"Nice and slow," Thomas said from the corner. He'd be hidden behind the door when I opened it, but he'd still have a clear shot at me. As if to prove it, he clicked the safety off the gun and used it to gesture toward the door. "Don't do anything stupid."

My gaze snagged on the pistol, but I forced my eyes to his. "Don't hurt her. Please."

"Just get rid of her."

Sweat trickled down my back as I unlocked the door and pulled it open a few inches. Trudy stood on the step, her rhinestone-studded jogging suit winking in the late afternoon sun. She wore what she called her "going out" makeup, which consisted mostly of bright pink blush and false eyelashes so long they made shadows on her face.

"I have a bone to pick with you, Elizabeth," she said without preamble. "Bert—that nice young many up at the security gate —said Dr. Adgate told him you're going on vacation in two weeks. We always notify the association when we leave for any extended period of time, you know, so that's how he knew about it. Anyway, I said that can't possibly be true because my Elizabeth would never make plans like that without telling me." She put her hands on her hips and cocked her head to one side.

"Trudy, I can't talk right now." It was like I had to haul each word up from the depths of my lungs and physically push it out.

"Well, why not?"

"I'm just not feeling that well. I might be coming down with something. I wouldn't want you to catch it. I'll call you later." I moved to close the door.

Her eyes narrowed, and the mildly annoyed expression she'd worn when I first opened the door dropped away, replaced with what looked like a mix of confusion and concern. "At least let me come in and make you some tea or something." She stepped forward.

"No! I mean, no, that's all right." I forced a smile. "I'm just going to lie down. I'll be better after a nap." I gave her a little wave. "Go home, Trudy," I said, still smiling, but I put deliberate emphasis on each word. "I'll talk to you later." I closed the door in her face.

Thomas reached over and flipped the lock, then grabbed my arm and propelled me back down the hallway. "Get something to write with," he said when we reached the kitchen. He didn't bother to hide the gun now.

My hands shook as I grabbed a pen and a pad of paper from a drawer next to the refrigerator. I turned toward him, and he gestured curtly at the table. I sat, my back rigid.

"Now. Here's what you're going to write to the doctor." He loomed behind me, looking over my shoulder to make sure I wrote down exactly what he said. I took my time, hoping some brilliant escape plan would come to me if I just thought long enough.

When he was finished, I put the pen down and stared at the note. "Thomas," I said carefully, "this isn't going to work. He's never going to believe I went back with you willingly."

In response, he jerked my chair back, gripped my arm, and hauled me to my feet. He turned me toward him. "I don't care if he believes it," he said, pushing his face into mine. "The only thing that matters is that the police believe it. And, trust me, they'll believe just about anything for the right price."

I wanted to spit in his face, this man who had used my body and helped destroy my family. The gun poked my ribs, a hard reminder of what he was capable of.

As long as we were outside Riverview Heights, it was just Thomas I had to worry about. Once I set foot on the Righteous Brethren's land, there would be dozens of Priesthood Council minions ready and willing to do his bidding.

Which meant I needed to keep him talking. Keep him in the condo as long as possible.

I lowered my gaze, inwardly horrified at how easy it was to fall back into the cowed, submissive posture I'd adopted whenever he'd shown the slightest displeasure in the past.

He recognized it, too, because he released my arm with a satisfied air. "I knew you'd see it my way, Elizabeth. Let's go."

I stepped back. "I'll go with you, but I need my purse." When he would have argued, I added, "At least let me get my driver's license. The police will think it's strange if I leave it behind."

He studied me for a minute. "Where is it?"

"Just upstairs. I'll get it." I turned, but he clamped down on my arm again.

"You're not going anywhere alone." He nudged the gun against my ribs, making me wince. "Move."

I led him upstairs, fear warring with a reluctance to let him anywhere near Evan's room—the place where Evan and I had finally cemented our relationship in the most basic way possible.

When I hesitated at the top of the stairs, Thomas gave me a little shove forward, and I stumbled onto the second floor landing. He'd put the gun away, but he seemed more dangerous now. Tiny beads of sweat on his forehead stood out under the hallway light as he glanced around.

I stood to the side, my heart pounding.

He stopped at the threshold of Evan's room, his gaze roaming over the open suitcases on the floor. He looked back at me, a sneer stretching his mouth. "So the old woman was right. Planning a romantic getaway with the doctor?"

I didn't reply, and I didn't risk meeting his eyes for fear that he would easily read the hatred I felt for him. How had I ever imagined myself in love with this man?

"Get your purse. And put something else on while you're at it. You look like a slut."

With a clenched jaw, I knelt in front of the nearest suitcase and pulled out a pale aqua top with long sleeves. It was large enough to fit over my tank top, which meant I didn't have to strip down to my bra in front of him. That wasn't an option with my jean shorts, though. I no longer owned any skirts—at least not the kind I'd worn in Riverview Heights—so I grabbed a pair of jeans and stood.

"Hurry up. And turn around so I can see your hands."

I turned slowly, and my breath caught in my throat. Evan

stood just behind Thomas, a finger over his lips. The look on his face sent a chill down my spine.

"I said hurry u—" Thomas's words cut off abruptly as Evan lunged forward, wrapping both hands around his neck, his thumbs digging into the flesh above Thomas's collarbones.

"He's got a gun!" I shouted, but Thomas was too busy trying to pry Evan's hands off his neck to reach for it. He clawed at Evan's fingers, a gurgling sound coming from his throat. After a few seconds, his eyelids fluttered and he slumped to the side.

I clapped my hands over my mouth.

Evan lowered him none too gently to the ground, then bent and pulled the gun from its holster. He clicked off the safety and trained it on Thomas as if he foiled abduction attempts every day.

I sagged, my heart still thundering in my chest.

Evan stepped over Thomas and gathered me against his side one-handed, his eyes scanning me with a clinical look I recognized. "Did he hurt you?"

"I'm fine." I buried my face against his chest. "He killed my father," I said hoarsely.

Evan tensed, then his other arm came around me, surrounding me with his solid, comforting strength.

We stayed like that for a moment, then I pulled back so I could see the clock. Although it seemed like it had been hours since Thomas showed up, he'd only been in the house for forty-five minutes, which meant it was still way too early for Evan to be home from work. "How did you—"

"Trudy called me," he said, guessing the direction of my thoughts. He kissed the top of my head, then exhaled heavily into my hair. "She said you were acting odd, like there was someone in the house with you. I've never driven so fast in my life."

Before I could ask more questions, a booming voice yelled,

"Police! Don't move!" A second later, two police officers appeared in the doorway, guns drawn.

Evan and I both raised our hands, and Evan stepped away from me, Thomas's gun pointed toward the floor. He talked fast. "That's him, Officers, and this is his gun. I'm a medical doctor. I gave his carotids a good squeeze. He should be fine in another minute or two."

As if on cue, Thomas stirred, a soft groan escaping his mouth.

One officer collected the gun from Evan while the other bent to check Thomas's pulse. Apparently satisfied he wasn't going to die anytime soon, he nudged Thomas onto his stomach and snapped a pair of handcuffs on him. "He ain't going anywhere," the officer told me with a wink. "Now, let's get a statement from you two."

"Trudy, I'm so grateful for what you did," I said for the twentieth time.

Evan's neighbor waved me off, but her eyes sparkled. She'd spent the past few hours holding court in Evan's kitchen, a bored-looking Napoleon on her lap, as curious neighbors filtered in and out, exclaiming over Evan's dramatic rescue and praising Trudy for her quick thinking. A few had even brought casseroles and plates of cookies, then promptly invited themselves to sit down and hear the whole sordid tale from the people who'd been involved.

Crime was unheard of in the gated, upscale community, and Evan's neighbors didn't quite know what to make of it. Many seemed to view it with unabashed curiosity, as if it had taken place on reality television.

I guess that made us extremely minor celebrities—a role Evan and I hoped died quickly, but one that Trudy was clearly reveling in. The story had gotten a little more embellished each time she told it. If she kept going, we'd eventually end up with a version that had Thomas crashing through a window and spiriting me away on a helicopter.

The first thing Evan did after the police hauled Thomas away was to go to the security office and stop the property manager from firing poor Bert, the security guard. "He shouldn't lose his job because I was too stupid to not change my pass code," he'd said before he left, ushering out a few lingering neighbors as he went and sending me a look of amused exasperation over the head of a soccer mom who promised to bring over a lasagna the next evening.

Trudy scratched under Napoleon's ear. "Are you sure you're all right, dear?" Now that everyone had left, she regarded me with a look of genuine concern.

"I think so," I said, picking through a plate of cookies. Seeing Thomas again had been a therapy of sorts. After he'd beaten me, he'd grown into a caricature of himself in my mind. I'd been living in fear of him finding me.

Now that he had, and I'd faced him down, so to speak, the worst that could happen had happened.

And I was still standing. No matter what came of this, I knew he would never get near me again. I abandoned the cookies and looked at Trudy. "Except, I can't help thinking I should feel *something*. I should be relieved or satisfied that Thomas got what he deserved. But, really, I don't know what to feel, or if I feel anything at all."

Napoleon chose that moment to lift his head from Trudy's lap and bark halfheartedly toward the small pantry tucked in a corner of the kitchen. Still jumpy from the events of the day, I sucked in a sharp breath.

"It's the air conditioning clicking on," Trudy said. "A burglar could waltz right in, and this dog would roll over for a belly rub. Flush a toilet or turn up the furnace, though, and he lets you know about it." The stubby brown tail thumped against her knee, and she lifted him in her arms and rubbed noses with him. "You're such a brave Napoleon," she crooned, "warning Mommy about the mean old air conditioner."

"How did you know? About Thomas, I mean. How did you know he was inside?"

Trudy settled the dog back on her lap and was silent for a minute. She traced a finger over an embroidered leaf on the cloth napkin by her coffee mug. "It was the look on your face," she said finally. "In your eyes, mostly. I haven't seen that look in over fifty years, but it's one I've never forgotten." Her mouth tightened, and old pain flitted across her features. "The last time I saw it was in a mirror."

"I'm so sorry, Trudy." I reached across the table and covered her hand with my own.

"I used to read these self-help books, you know. They were all the rage in the eighties, probably before you were born. Any time they touched on abuse, they always warned that victims struggled with finding healthy relationships— that love was nearly impossible to find when you've been a battered wife. I thought something was wrong with me, because I'd found Antonio, and then my beloved Edward. They were both good men. Neither one would have harmed a hair on my head. But the books all said that shouldn't have been possible, at least not without a lot of work on my part. And I thought, why should *I* have to work? I'd done nothing wrong. There wasn't anything wrong with *me*."

She pursed her lips. "I decided those books were hooey. Being a victim of abuse doesn't mean you're broken in some way. It can happen to *anyone*. You don't have to be on your guard with every man just because one man betrayed your trust."

I dashed at the tear that had rolled down my cheek because

she was no longer talking about Thomas. She was talking about Evan.

She smiled. "You don't have to feel a certain emotion to be normal. And what's normal, anyway? Trust someone who's lived eighty years, honey, there's not a normal person on the planet. You are *not* broken, Elizabeth. I think you proved that today."

"But I couldn't have stopped him if you hadn't come to the door," I whispered. "If Evan hadn't shown up . . ."

She snorted. "He had a gun! Most people would have been a blubbering mess on the floor. You were smart and quick on your feet."

"And you protected your friend," Evan said from the kitchen doorway, making me whirl around.

He held out his arms, and I stood and rushed into them. "How'd it go?" I said against his chest.

"Bert isn't leaving us anytime soon," he said, stroking my hair.

"Well, I certainly hope not," Trudy said indignantly. "He's got the best butt on the entire security team."

Evan's chest shook under my ear. "I'm sure he'd be flattered to know you think so. Will you stay for dinner?"

"Thank you, Doctor, but no." She brushed past us, a dozing Napoleon in her arms. "I have to catch up on *The Bachelor*." She gave me a quick hug, reached up and patted Evan's cheek, and was gone in a blink, like some fairy godmother.

"Like what?" Evan asked. He was looking down at me with a bemused expression, and I realized I'd said the last part out loud.

"Nothing." I wrapped my arms around his waist and smiled up at him. "I was just thinking that some people in this world are magical."

"Well," he murmured, tightening his arms around me, "you certainly are."

EPILOGUE

"Close your eyes. Are you peeking?"

I laughed and held up a three-fingered salute, which was surprisingly hard to do with Evan's hands blocking my vision. "No peeking, scout's honor."

He pulled me back against his chest, then spoke next to my ear so I'd hear him over the sound of the nearby ocean. "Okay, then. Open them, beautiful girl."

He removed his hand, and I blinked in the bright sunlight sparkling off the Long Island Sound. As my vision adjusted, a small but beautiful cottage came into focus. I stared at it, confused for a moment, before my breath caught in my throat.

The windows were a little different, and it had a wraparound porch, but it was the same cottage I remembered from the sketch I'd seen in the art gallery window with Evan over a year ago.

I turned in his arms. "How did you . . . ?"

He grinned down at me. "I noticed you looking at that sketch. I actually went back a few days later and bought it."

I reached up and cupped his cheek, his golden stubble

rough on my palm. "It's beautiful." I twisted so I could look at it again. "I wonder who lives there."

He rested his chin on the top of my head. "You do."

I whipped around so fast, my forehead smacked into his nose.

He slapped a hand to his face and doubled over.

"Oh my God, Evan, I am *so* sorry! Are you okay?" I tried to pry his hand away from his face, but he was hunched over, his shoulders shaking. "Is it bad? Did I break it?"

He stood up and dropped his hand, a goofy grin on his face. He'd been *laughing*.

I smacked his shoulder. "Ooh, you *faker*! I thought I broke your nose!"

"Surprisingly, your head isn't hard enough, sweetheart." He rubbed the bridge of his nose. "Besides, I think it healed stronger after Brian broke it in middle school."

I'd met Brian and his wife, Julia, six months earlier, when we spent a week in South Carolina. Evan had quit his job at the center a few weeks after the incident with Thomas, and he'd been content to "be a beach bum," as he called it, for a couple months while he looked for a new position. He didn't have to wait long. Within a week, he'd received offers from several physician practices in both Missouri and Connecticut.

After about two seconds of debate, we looked at each other and said "Connecticut" at the same time. I knew Evan longed to be home, and I was anxious to put the past behind me as much as possible.

I looked back at the pristine seaside cottage. "How did you find this place?" It looked like a dollhouse from this distance, right down to the window boxes overflowing with flowers.

"Mom has a friend who's a real estate agent. I showed her the sketch. Texted a picture of it to her, actually. She was happy to help."

I faced him. "When did you do all this? *How* did you do all this, especially without me knowing?"

"I closed on it a few days before the wedding, while you and Julia were sampling cake flavors." His smile was smug. "She and Mom were in on the whole thing. Everyone was."

So *that's* why they'd insisted on going to lunch after the cake tasting. I'd tried to talk them out of it, having consumed enough buttercream frosting to last a lifetime, but they'd been so persistent. Now I knew why.

Evan had proposed to me on the beach near his childhood home, on a long stretch of pure white sand. "Be my wife, Elizabeth Grant," he'd said, tears standing in his eyes. "Make me the happiest man in the world."

Our wedding had been small, just close friends and family, including Trudy, who had nearly burst with excitement when I asked her to walk me down the aisle. She'd moved into a condo near her son in South Carolina, which meant she was close enough to visit us often. She already had plans to take a singles cruise up the coast later in the fall.

Natalie had flown in for the wedding, too, managing to get a week off from her new job as the charge nurse in urgent care. She'd been thrilled to take over from Brittney, who had resigned once Evan told the police about her involvement in my near abduction. Rumor had it she'd moved out of the state, but no one had heard from her.

As for Thomas, plenty of people were hearing about him. The county prosecutor had called to thank me for helping her finally pin something on him. She explained she'd been trying for years to get enough evidence to charge the leadership of the Righteous Brethren with a crime, but she'd never been able to secure a warrant to access the compound. Once she got inside, she and her investigators had uncovered evidence of welfare fraud, insurance fraud, and countless other crimes, mostly financial. Thomas and Prophet Benson had also been charged with murdering my father, and the police were looking into their possible involvement in half a dozen missing persons cases over the past twenty years. In their quest to gain power, they'd been thorough about removing anyone who stood in their way.

"What's wrong, sweetheart?" Evan asked, pulling me back to the present. He wove his fingers into the loose french braid I'd worn to keep the wind from whipping my hair into knots. "You look sad. Is it the house? I know I should have asked you about such a big purchase, but I wanted it to be a surprise. It's your wedding present."

"The house is wonderful. It's the best present I've ever gotten. It's just . . ."

"You're worried about them."

I nodded, relieved that he understood. The prosecutor had been wonderful about sparing the innocent families of Riverview Heights the pain and uncertainty of a raid. Still, Thomas's arrest meant Dinah and the others were forever out of favor with the remaining members of the Priesthood Council. "Leah doesn't deserve this. Neither do her kids. Neither does Jackson."

"Jackson will be just fine," Evan said. He took my hand and tugged me toward the little path leading away from the beach toward the house. "The welding program at Riverlands is excellent, and it has a job placement rate of over ninety percent."

He sounded like a brochure. In fact, that's *exactly* what the brochure said. I knew because all three of us had sat down around Evan's kitchen table and pored over a bunch of them to help Jackson decide what sort of program he wanted to enroll in.

The brochures tended to make everything sound exciting, but the school's administrators were honest about their job placement rates. Jackson was attending the same community college where I'd done my medical assistant training. Evan and

I were footing the bill for his school, but he insisted he would pay us back when he started working. I was just happy he was making a life for himself outside Riverview Heights.

As for Leah, she promised to visit as soon as she'd settled in at her mother's house in Utah. The Righteous Brethren's community there was a bit more isolated than the others, but the majority of the people who lived there were close relatives.

Evan stopped and looked down at me. A little smile played around his mouth.

"What is it?" I raised an eyebrow. "Any other surprises up your sleeve, Doctor?"

"Just thinking how lucky I am." He leaned down and kissed me. "To have you," he murmured against my lips.

"I'm the lucky one," I whispered.

He tugged at my hand. "Come on, Mrs. Adgate. Let's go see the inside."

I let him guide me up the winding path, my lips curving in a secret smile. When he wasn't looking, I brushed a hand over my stomach.

He wasn't the only one with a surprise up his sleeve.

～

ABOUT THE AUTHOR

Amy Pennza is a USA Today Bestselling Author of steamy paranormal and contemporary romance. After stints as a lawyer and a soldier, she discovered her dream job is writing about stubborn alphas and smart heroines. She lives in the Great Lakes region with her husband and five children.

Keep up with new releases by visiting amypennza.com

Want exclusive goodies like free books and fun giveaways? Sign up for Amy's newsletter at
www.amypennza.com/subscribe

ALSO BY AMY PENNZA

Check out all my books by clicking here.

If you like your paranormal romance steamy, read the scorching-hot stories of The Dragon Lairds Series:

Kiss of Smoke

Dark Fire Kiss

Kiss of a Dragon King

Want more menage? Get Lucas, Carter, and Isabel's story:

His Wolf to Take

And if you love wolf shifters, don't miss my ultra-steamy Lux Catena Series. Each book can be read as a standalone.

What a Wolf Desires

What a Wolf Dares

What a Wolf Demands

What a Wolf's Heart Decides

Lux Catena Series Shifter Romance Box Set

Printed in Great Britain
by Amazon